He followed all the rules...
until one man showed him a dozen ways to break them.

An Improper Holiday
By K.A. Mitchell

As second son to an earl, Ian Stanton has always done the proper thing. Obeyed his elders, studied diligently, and dutifully accepted the commission his father purchased for him in the Fifty-Second Infantry Division. The one glaring, shameful, marvelous exception: Nicholas Chatham, heir to the Marquess of Carleigh.

Before Ian took his position in His Majesty's army, he and Nicky consummated two years of physical and emotional discovery. Their inexperience created painful consequences that led Ian to the conviction that their unnatural desires were never meant to be indulged.

Five years later, wounded in body and plagued by memories of what happened between them, Ian is sent to carry out his older brother's plans for a political alliance with Nicky's father. Their sister Charlotte is the bargaining piece.

Nicky never believed that what he and Ian felt for each other was wrong and he has a plan to make things right. Getting Ian to Carleigh is but the first step. Now Nicky has only twelve nights to convince Ian that happiness is not the price of honor and duty, but its reward.

Warning: Just thinking about reading this book in 1814 could get you hanged, so the men in this book who enjoy m/m interaction of an intimately penetrative nature are in a hell of a lot of trouble.

A quirky holiday romance about Faith, Hope, and...er...glow-in-the-dark condoms!

The Dickens with Love

By Josh Lanyon

Three years ago, a scandal cost antiquarian "book hunter" James Winter everything that mattered to him: his job, his lover and his self-respect. But now the rich and unscrupulous Mr. Stephanopoulos has a proposition. A previously unpublished Christmas book by Charles Dickens has turned up in the hands of an English chemistry professor by the name of Sedgwick Crisparkle. Mr. S. wants that book at any price, and he needs James to get it for him. There's just one catch. James can't tell the nutty professor who the buyer is.

Actually, two catches. The nutty Professor Crisparkle turns out to be totally gorgeous—and on the prowl. Faster than you can say, "Old Saint Nick," James is mixing business with pleasure...and in real danger of forgetting that this is just a holiday romance.

Just as they're well on the way to having their peppermint sticks and eating them too, Sedgwick discovers the truth. James has been a very bad boy. And any chance Santa will bring him what he wants most is disappearing quicker than the Jolly Old Elf's sleigh.

Warning: This book contains an ocelot, songs by America, Stardust martinis, tinsel, long-lost manuscripts, Faith, Hope and...Love.

To All a (Very Sexy) Good Night

A Samhain Publishing, Ltd. publication.

Samhain Publishing, Ltd.
577 Mulberry Street, Suite 1520
Macon, GA 31201
www.samhainpublishing.com

To All a (Very Sexy) Good Night
Print ISBN: 978-1-60504-922-9
An Improper Holiday Copyright © 2010 by K.A. Mitchell
The Dickens with Love Copyright © 2010 by Josh Lanyon

Editing by Sasha Knight
Cover by Mandy M. Roth

An Improper Holiday, ISBN 978-1-60504-836-9
First Samhain Publishing, Ltd. electronic publication: December 2009
The Dickens with Love, ISBN 978-1-60504-837-6
First Samhain Publishing, Ltd. electronic publication: December 2009
First Samhain Publishing, Ltd. print publication: October 2010

Contents

An Improper Holiday

K.A. Mitchell

Dedication

For Mom and Dad,

Thanks for fostering a life-long love of books, history and Christmas traditions.

Chapter One

The tall mahogany clock made the customary ominous tick as Ian waited in front of the equally foreboding desk. Nothing good ever came from being called into the study, even if now the man seated behind the mahogany desk was brother rather than father. Standing at parade rest had lost the comfort of familiarity, as if the empty sleeve pinned back at his elbow created some sort of asymmetrical impropriety to the stance.

Ian supposed he could have interrupted Edward's shuffling through his books, but habit held him silent. The last time Ian had been peremptorily summoned to stand before the desk in question, his father had been behind it, and it was never to Ian's advantage to interrupt the old earl in his calculations when such calculations concerned how many strokes of the switch would correct Ian's behavior.

Edward—no, he must think of his brother as Rayne now. Their father had issued his final orders while his second son's own life danced with death on the edge of a surgeon's blade. Rayne rubbed a hand over his eyes and slapped away a ledger before looking up, dark brows shooting to his hairline in surprise. "God's blood, Ian. Why did you not speak? How long have you been standing there?"

"Not long. I—I suppose old habits are the hardest to break."

The corner of Rayne's mouth twitched, offering a fleeting

glimpse of his younger self. "Expecting ten of the best?"

"The thought crossed my mind, God rest his soul."

Edward made a brief nod of agreement, all trace of humor vanishing from his expression.

"Your sister tells me we have received an invitation to the Carleigh Twelve Night fete."

The very instant the word Carleigh entered Ian's ears, he wished himself on the receiving end of his father's switch rather than the brother's order he sensed would follow.

"I wish to cultivate the marquess's favor. He would be an ally in the House. You and the heir are of an age, are you not?"

"We knew each other at school." *And I mean that in every sense of the word, brother.*

Edward had barely paused long enough for Ian to answer. "Your sister desires to attend. You shall act as her chaperone. And while there, you shall canvass the marquess's leanings on several items that will be coming before us. Perhaps your prior affiliation will lend itself to influencing the heir."

I sodomized him just after Father purchased my commission, but I doubt that is the sort of influence you seek. Pain, tears and blood, and still Nicky had whimpered, "It's all right." And Ian, prick in such a hot grip, could no longer restrain the motion of his hips, even as Nicky's teeth sank deep into his bottom lip, cock flagging despite the attention of Ian's fist. That sort of parting might lend itself to awkwardness on a renewal of their acquaintance.

But Lord Rayne could command Ian to undertake any sort of awkwardness his lordship deemed necessary, and if Ian didn't care to accept the latest commission, he could make his own way in the world. Surely there was a yet-to-be discovered path for advancement available to a younger son with a missing limb and no familial support.

If he could face French artillery, he could face Nicky. Though he rather preferred the artillery. "When are we expected?"

"It is their usual Twelve Night gathering. I am sure you remain familiar with the customs of our country."

Of course, the twenty-fourth. Which meant he needed to get his sister Charlotte stuffed in a carriage as soon as possible. At this time of year, the journey to Carleigh Castle would take him perhaps three days on horseback. Traveling with whatever his sister would want to drag along would double or triple the time required. He had heard that females were difficult travel companions.

"Also, I wish you to encourage some sort of suitable attachment for her. Or at the very least, some respectable company. She is still a bit—"

"Hoydenish?" Ian suggested. He hadn't been home long, but the sister he remembered who was so often pleading with him to conceal that she had once again been climbing trees and riding astride did not appear to have become much more civilized. As he had dressed this morning he had seen her well past the bottom of the Italianate garden, tugging at something in the arbor and scribbling in a book.

"I think I should prefer headstrong." His brother's lips quirked again. "Damn me. Ian, I believe you may have smiled for a moment."

Stanton men were not renowned for a sanguine temperament, and Ian had found very little about which to be cheerful since his return from the Peninsular War. "I'll do my best to correct it in future, Rayne."

"See that you do. There are some papers I should like you to examine before you leave in order to familiarize yourself with the items that concern me." Rayne began digging through the books and ledgers.

Ian nodded and stepped closer to the desk. If he were busy with Lord Carleigh, perhaps he could avoid his son. A mountain of letters to rival the Alps melted into an avalanche, and he reached out with his hand to stop it, forgetting for an instant the moment when he'd awakened to find his arm a half-yard shorter. Phantom pain shot deep into his bones, a fire in flesh that had long since been tossed out to rot on a field in Spain.

"Does it pain you much still?"

"No," Ian lied. He had always lied easily. Except to himself. From what he'd been able to glean from conversations with other maimed officers both in the Second Fifty-second and others, the phantom limb would be with him until he joined it in death. His body couldn't remember what his brain knew: his left hand had been shredded by shrapnel, a tourniquet the only way a field surgeon could save his life. "I simply moved too suddenly. It will pass quickly." *Or it will throb for hours. But there is nothing to be done for that.* "I shall inform Charlotte of your decision."

On his return from the Continent, unable to face his family or friends, Ian had immured himself with distant cousins in Norwich. He preferred that damp time staring at marshes in England's arse-end to being trapped in this warm coach with plush upholstery if such comfort came burdened with searching stares from his sister. By the fourth day, those stares had grown more frequent, almost unceasing.

"Don't you have knitting or needlework? An improving book?"

Nan, Charlotte's maid, pursed her lips and stared out the

window. Ian had difficulty deciding whether the contortion of her mouth was to hide amusement or disgust.

Charlotte's laughter in no way resembled the drawing room titters Ian had heard on his brief forays in society.

"My dear brother, in my three and twenty years have you ever known me to engage in handwork or read an improving book?"

"Perhaps you should take it up."

"Perhaps you would care to share why you have 'such a February face, so full of frost, of storm, and cloudiness'."

"Ah, I see you have managed to plow through at least one work of Shakespeare. Father would be pleased to know your governess was not an utter waste of what funds he could rescue from the exchequer's clutches."

"And I see you are attempting to divert my attention."

"From the scenery?" Ian's arm ached as he fought the urge to gesture at the frozen fields with his missing hand.

"From my question. We are on our way to celebrate the most joyous time of the year with dear friends, yet from your expression, one would think you are being dragged to the hangman."

That was one possible outcome of his sinful relationship with Nicky. Or could he request the block? Was a more honorable execution possible for sodomites who were younger sons of an old and loyal house? He really ought to know the exact statute, even if he had sworn never to repeat the crime. "I am filled with a generous quantity of holiday spirit."

"Your glower is very misleading. Come now, Ian. You were not always so much like Father. Or Edward."

"Rayne," Ian corrected.

"Oh, of course, his lordship the Earl of Rayne. The same

15

esteemed lord who dipped my plaits in ink."

"That was I, Lady Charlotte. Lord Rayne would be the chap who preferred to replace the ink with a dozen small spiders."

"Ian."

"Still here, dear sister."

"And you are still avoiding my question. What is this sudden dread you have of Carleigh Castle? You and Lord Amherst always seemed to be such *particular* friends."

A chill took a tight grip on Ian's lungs. The emphasis as she spoke trod dangerously close to an insinuation. If Charlotte had been a man, he'd have considered resorting to violence to protect his—Nicky's?—honor. But a female, even one as hoydenish as his sister, could not be aware of the darker aspects of male desire. And she was waiting for him to speak.

"I find that a curious choice of words."

Charlotte's gaze was all too penetrating. "Dread?"

Ian clung desperately to the reprieve she had offered. "Yes. I am not dreading the party, merely my duty as your chaperone. With such a great beauty, I will have time for nothing but keeping your more importunate suitors at bay."

Charlotte's gaze had not wavered, but at last she smiled. "Are you certain there was no accompanying damage to your skull at Badajoz?"

One didn't refer to the casualties of war in mixed company, but Charlotte was still the girl whose braids had looked best when tipped with black ink. "As I remember very little after the mine exploded, anything is possible."

Her expression turned to sympathy and Ian looked away. This was what had kept him in Norwich long after he was fully healed. Useless sympathy when he felt consumed with anger. If he had moved more swiftly on the escalade, if he had not accepted assistance from the eager young Lieutenant Archer, the man would still be alive and Ian would be whole—or wholly dead. Either state preferable to his current existence as neither.

"Do you think it will snow?"

"I fervently pray that it will not." It would be bad enough to be trapped at Carleigh Castle by the weather, but a snowfall would provoke Ian's memories of the five days he and Nicky had spent penned in by man-high drifts at the marquisate's hunting cabin. It had been the first time they had dared to fully disrobe, the first time they could look their fill without fear of discovery. Five days of the same wretched stew turning to gruel over the fire, five days of Nicky's infectious laugh, five nights of hard flesh pressed together until they were bound by spit and sweat and spilled seed.

"You have the most bizarre look on your face, Ian. Does your arm pain you very much?"

He could not even school his features around his sister. How was he to look at Nicky, perhaps even at Nicky's betrothed or—bloody hell—Nicky's wife, without some untoward emotion starting in his face? Ian's guts writhed with a dread against which he had thought himself inured since leading his company to that breach in the walls at Badajoz. He could ask Charlotte about Nicky's state of attachment, even a female as peculiar as his sister would surely be aware of the alliances among the ton, but a newly found respect for her perception held him back.

"I am merely stiff from days in this carriage."

"You are wishing you had ridden."

"Of course not. I am pleased to keep you company."

"You are a terrible liar."

"I am an excellent liar. I told Rayne how much I admired that nag he spent far too much on, leaving him none the wiser. You merely have an unbridled imagination which causes you to see pain or frustration where there is none."

"Is that what it is?"

He met her steady gaze. Though she had yet to demonstrate the decorum Ian expected from a lady, his sister's acquisition of a dangerous perspicacity and immunity to his teasing boded ill for any future peace of mind.

He chose to exercise the familial option of ignoring a pestering female relation, focusing his gaze on the passing scene, wishing he could ignore the memories provoked by the lazy spiral of snowflakes that had begun to fall.

Amidst the deluge of inappropriate reminiscences, one item which had escaped Ian's notice was the memory of the Carleigh tradition of lavish hospitality. There were so many guests milling in the Gold Salon, with more arriving every moment, that avoiding Nicholas Chatham, Lord Amherst, was a mission at which even the most bumbling of soldiers could succeed. If the crush also ensured that no one had borne witness to Charlotte's precipitous departure from the carriage, nearly bowling over the footman who was trying to assist her, so much the better.

The last stretch of the carriage ride might have been especially designed for Ian's torment by one of Lucifer's more creative demons. The coachman seemed determined to catch the wheels in every rut, a constant reminder that he was utterly useless, as he could neither brace himself nor his sister against the sudden lurches that bounced them like India rubber within the confines of the coach. Then his gaze caught a familiar landmark and he was flung back into the bittersweet memory of the first time he had accompanied Nicky home to Carleigh.

Nicky had wagered his skill at satisfying Ian against the speed of the coach and four.

Certain he could outlast the final few furlongs, he had taunted, "I can see barns, Nicky, and yet—"

Nicky had shockingly, devastatingly put his mouth to the same use as his hand, an obscene and wonderful kiss, warm and wet around the head of Ian's prick. A rut jolted Ian deeper into the slick suction and there was no further need to mark furlongs, or even a yard. The heat of Nicky's mouth, the movement of his tongue, drew the sweet aching fire from Ian's spine, brought it boiling from his stones and out his prick—and into Nicky's mouth.

It should have been horrifying, but the notion that he had spilled between those wide, quick-to-smile lips only made his body clench again and again with pleasure. He had scarcely even cared when Nicky had wiped his face on Ian's formerly immaculate trousers.

With that fresh in mind, he had been nearly unaware of the present-day coach coming to a stop and unable to halt his sister's unladylike vault from the coach step. Intent on executing his chaperonage with a greater deal of success, he scanned the room, located her by dint of the towering yellow feather which graced her bonnet—easily recalled after the constant tickle against his nose as the coach jolted along—and cut a swath to her side like Major-General Picton into Ciudad Rodrigo.

Ian wished he could ply his saber for safe passage here. The manse in Norwich, the Stanton manor in Oxfordshire, even their London townhouse all were untenanted wastelands compared with the long narrow salon. Not since Badajoz had there been so many other bodies around him. And while the scents and sights of a nobleman's salon in Derbyshire were far

19

removed from the stench of smoke and entrails—or worse the vision of what had been men fragmented by shot and shrapnel—Ian's ears roared as blood pumped hard and fast, heating his skin, empowering his limbs. The voices around him faded under the drumming of his pulse, vision narrowing as if through a tunnel, the only sight not blurred that of the plume nodding on Charlotte's bonnet.

A hand fell on his shoulder. Blood full of heat, muscles warm and vigorous, he whirled, good right hand reaching for the saber he no longer wore at his waist.

"Ian."

If there had been a trace of shock and fear on Nicky's face, Ian's chance to study it was lost as Nicky used the hand on his shoulder to pull Ian into a half-embrace, which though entirely appropriate to the season and their outward familiarity, left Ian rigid. The thrum of battle-ready nerves still vibrated across his skin, but for an instant the familiar scent of the flesh just above Nicky's collar managed to penetrate the sensory blinders keeping him shuttered from the crowd.

In that instant Nicky became a bulwark, shelter and shield against the worst memories of the Peninsula. He was reaching to offer some reciprocation but Nicky had stepped back, hand sliding along Ian's arm to close on the empty sleeve.

Ah, there it was. Horror soon masked by pity. The dark blond curls that had slipped through Ian's fingers in countless caresses fell over Nicky's forehead, but the clear blue eyes still laid his feelings bare.

"Lord Amherst." Ian executed as correct a bow as possible with Nicky yet clinging to his sleeve and turned, wrenching free at last.

But although Charlotte's plume was still in sight, the path to her had closed and as he sought another, Nicky stepped around him again.

"Lord Amherst, is it? Are you not aware that in this bedlam no one would hear were you to shout, Captain Stanton?"

"I am a simple gentleman only, my lord. As I am of no further use to His Majesty, I have resigned my commission."

More sympathy, lashes lowered in grief, drawing Ian's gaze to the candlelight's sheen on Nicky's cheek, the wide curve of his lips. That mouth. The mouth that had—

Ian tore his gaze free of the fascination, a wrenching separation that shared the aching emptiness of his left arm with all of his bones. Charlotte's gold plume had moved off, nodding near a lacey cap adorning the head of a tall slender blonde.

"And at the moment, my lord, I am failing in my new commission. I beg your leave as I must see to my sister."

"Then as always, I shall stand aside and permit you to do your duty." Nicky's voice held a rough edge quite unlike any Ian had yet heard from Nicky's lips.

When Nicky turned and strode off without another word, Ian was forced to a surprising conclusion. Amherst was furious.

Chapter Two

Stiff-necked, infuriating, whoreson bastard. Nicky allowed himself eight strides along the gallery and back to try to contain his explosion of frustration. With Ian and with himself. He had convinced himself that Ian only stopped answering their carefully worded letters because of battlefield conditions, that Ian's feelings were still as strong as when he had acceded to his father's wishes and taken up his commission. Above all, Nicky had promised himself that Ian's injury, his dreadful loss, wouldn't matter. Instead Nicky had let show the terror and pain he had felt when he had heard the details of Ian's wound. *Well-played indeed, Amherst.*

Despite that cold intonation of his title, it was clear Ian was not entirely indifferent to Nicky. In the past five years he had learned to discern when a man regarded him with a certain sort of interest. But the past five years had also taught him there was a great gulf between simple companionship and the gratification of lust and what he and Ian had shared in those two years of sweet, slow discovery.

With the way Ian's gaze had moved to Nicky's mouth...no, Ian had not renounced his desire, even if he clung ever more tightly to his restraint. In that moment just past, Ian's hunger had been a nearly palpable yoke to bind them.

Had Ian learned as much as Nicky had these years apart?

The idea of another man lavishing on Ian the kind of attention that would bring the color to his cheeks, his throat, his chest, blasted Nicky with a surprising surge of arousal. He would have thought to find himself jealous. Instead, his too vigorous imagination provided a tactile and visual feast. Ian's back against Nicky's front, the prickle of hair over hard flesh as Nicky's hands stroked the broad chest, the heat between Ian's thighs as Nicky's cock slid through the tight space, pressing up against the heavy sac, driving Ian forward so that his own cock slid deeper into the throat of the faceless man kneeling before them.

There would be no returning to the salon now. A stubborn cock-stand was not at all the thing to introduce in a room full of family and guests, certainly not in trousers as close-fit as those he wore. Nicky strode down the gallery's full length to the portrait of the first marquess, wishing he dared run out into the snow to cool his face—and other overheated areas.

"Nicholas? Whatever are you doing out here? What is the matter?"

His four-years-elder sister Lady Anna had stepped into the gallery. Since their mother had passed away after giving birth to the twins who were still in the nursery, Anna had taken over running the household, maintaining her grip even after her marriage to the Bishop of Warwick several years ago.

"I am—" Hell, taking the air was something only females did. He could scarcely tell his sister he'd stomped off in a fit of pique because of a romance gone awry, and he certainly couldn't tell her he was trying to tamp down the pulse of blood in his cock. "I wanted exercise." Under the circumstance, it wasn't difficult to affect a limp.

"Exercise? Now?"

"I—it—I fell from a horse and—"

"When?"

"Last week."

"And?"

"Well, my—uh—I don't want the injury to—" *Ah, shit, don't think stiffen.* "To wither."

His sister regarded him as if he were mad, which he no doubt appeared to be, was, and would continue to be until the all-too-honorable Mr. Ian Stanton came to his senses.

"It is a most inappropriate time. Lady Rathmoore wishes you to make the acquaintance of her daughters. And Lady Susannah asked to be remembered to you. And Lady Charlotte Stanton was most insistent that you wished to renew her acquaintance." Anna's lofty brow furrowed. "She is a lovely girl, excellent lines and no small fortune, but uncomfortably forward." She gave him a pleasant smile. "Still, if your interest lies that way, I am certain we shall make the best of it."

His interest. Yes. He had just attained the quarter-century mark, but Lady Anna wanted him matched. As their father had come to realize, whatever Lady Anna desired would come to pass, another's wishes notwithstanding. The thought that if their plan failed he would find himself betrothed to a random female before the turn of the season was enough to quell his errant ardor.

He answered his sister's smile. "I would be most pleased to renew my acquaintance with Lady Charlotte."

His sister stopped him as he reached the salon doors, flicking imagined lint from his sleeves and pulling his hair farther forward onto his brow. "There, darling, better than even a plate from *The Register*. Doubtless you shall capture whatever heart you choose."

His own heart having long since been captured, he devoutly hoped her estimation would prove correct.

Anna led him to Ian's sister who was standing a great distance from the more dense clusters of guests around the fire.

He bowed over Charlotte's hand and she offered him an almost imperceptible wink. Having delivered Nicky to a marriageable female, Anna left to organize some other campaign.

"Lord Amherst, you must remember my brother, Capt—the honorable Mr. Stanton?"

Her eyes were full of laughter now. Sly minx.

"But of course, Mr. Stanton." He and Ian exchanged bows, Ian's handsome face more wintry than the wind battering the castle's stones.

Charlotte turned to the tall blonde in half-mourning beside her. "And you will of course already be acquainted with Mrs. Collingswood."

Ian's sister had the very devil in her. Emily Collingswood was his mother's cousin and had spent a great deal of time at Carleigh as a companion for Anna. Nicky no longer felt quite as put-upon by his meddling older sister. He would rather have Anna fuss over him than deal with someone as inwardly devious and outwardly guileless as Lady Charlotte.

The imp turned to her beleaguered brother. "You remember Mrs. Collingswood, of course. We met at another of these Twelve Night fetes. Just before my first Season?"

Just before Ian had been sent away. The Twelfth Night when Nicky had finally persuaded Ian to take full possession of his body—and damnation. He would be needing yet another stroll around the gallery if he allowed his thoughts to dally along that primrose path.

Nicky had been working so hard on that ultimate seduction, he should be surprised if Ian would have remembered if His Highness himself had been in attendance at that Twelve Night.

But Ian surprised him. "You were Miss Graves then."

"Yes, Mr. Stanton, how kind of you to remember me."

"Lady Charlotte could do nothing but sing your praises on our journey home. She was awed by your skills."

How Ian missed both Charlotte and Emily nearly swallowing their tongues, Nicky could not imagine.

"Mrs. Collingwood, will you be favoring us with your long-remembered skill at the pianoforte?"

His clarification was met with a slightly audible exhalation of relief. "I should be pleased to assist my hosts in any way possible."

Charlotte recovered her equanimity. "What would please me most at the moment is to rest before dinner."

Emily followed Charlotte's lead. "Goodness, Lady Charlotte, you must be greatly fatigued from your travels. If you gentlemen would excuse us, I believe I can show Lady Charlotte to her room."

Many of the guests had already excused themselves from the reception. Supper would not be served until after the midnight service and he expected most of the assembled party would take to their rooms to rest.

"Could someone be similarly dispatched to my assistance, Lord Amherst?"

Not "Would you assist me to find my room?" If Ian were not such an utter bloody idiot, they could be enjoying hours of rediscovery before the celebrations began this evening. Instead, all Nicky could expect was assuaging his needs alone or suffering the dull ache of unfulfilled want.

"Certainly." Nicky nodded at a footman near the door who immediately stepped toward them. "Merry Christmas, Mr.

Stanton."

The dark slashes of Ian's brows drew into a sharp *V* over his eyes. Had he expected Nicky to plead with him? To throw himself at his feet?

"And to you, Lord Amherst."

Ian had departed with the footman when Charlotte slipped back in through the doors to the hall.

Nicky held up his hand to ward off any more of her many alterations to their plan. "Please don't delay your rest on account of my lonely despair. Why should your holiday be bleak?"

"A brief word, my lord?"

Nicky nodded.

"My brother claims to value his solitude, but I have known him all my life. If there is one thing he cannot abide, it is being ignored."

After a glance around the nearly deserted salon, Nicky offered her a lightning-quick salute. "I yield to your superior strategy, General."

"Keep to the plan, sir, and all will be well."

Ian was trapped. Pinioned as surely as if in irons.

And quite utterly mortified by having been laid low by a tight-fitting coat.

Cursing himself and his missing valet, he stomped over to the pull cord to summon a servant. With both arms held behind his back, he was reduced to yanking at the cord with his teeth. As he waited, panting, he berated himself for leaving his valet back in Oxfordshire. Ian had been on the outs with Timpet since his return and couldn't say for sure whether the frost had ensued because Ian's maiming destroyed the cut of his coat or because Ian had dragged the chap to Norwich for nearly a year. He could say that as unappealing as this trip to Carleigh was, it would be far more so with Timpet's icy glare and glacial silences.

A slender man with silver hair and an elegant mien entered his room. Before Ian could even explain his predicament, the man slipped around Ian and freed his aching shoulders with a quick tug on his cuffs.

"Thank you. Thank you indeed...?" He let his intonation rise. He would definitely want to leave this fellow a generous vail.

"Simmons, sir."

"Thank you, Simmons."

Simmons brushed the jacket and placed it in the wardrobe with his other clothes.

Ian could manage buttons on his own, his right fingers having become astoundingly dexterous in the last eighteen months, but Simmons' quiet efficiency at finishing the small rows on Ian's waistcoat was so unlike the huffs of Timpet that Ian let his hand fall to his sides.

"There are several gentlemen enjoying whiskey and tobacco in the India Room, sir. Will you be joining that party?"

"I prefer to rest. I'll take my dressing gown for now."

"Very good, sir." Simmons turned up the left sleeve with far more ease and grace than Timpet. "While you're resting, sir, I could stitch up your shirts for you. Then you wouldn't need to risk a pin jabbing at you."

Why had Timpet never suggested such a thing? Ian

couldn't count all the pinpricks he'd received, or the number of times his sleeve had fallen into the soup or the marmalade or once across the face and into the generous décolletage of the vicar's wife in Mundesley.

"That would be much appreciated, Simmons. Tell me, how was I fortunate enough to receive you as an answer to my summons?"

"As Lord Amherst was aware that you did not travel with your valet, sir, he instructed me to stand ready to offer any assistance you might need."

"How thoughtful of him."

"Yes, sir. His lordship has a very generous spirit."

In plainer speech, Ian was such an invalid Nicky felt compelled to act as maiden aunt, managing Ian's life. He thought of telling Simmons he would need no further help, but it was apparent he did and such a pointless action would no doubt make Nicky feel further compelled to discuss the matter with Ian. That was something to be avoided. An end to future pinpricks and even more so any future embarrassment caused by the impertinent actions of his sleeves made Simmons' offer impossible to refuse.

Simmons had already draped most of Ian's upper wardrobe over his arm. "I shall return these before you'll need them for the evening, sir. Please call if you have any other needs arise." He slipped out of the door as gracefully as he had managed everything else.

Simmons' innocuous comment regarding arising needs brought Ian back to painful awareness of that moment when Nicky had touched him.

After his discharge from medical care, Ian had not expected an immediate return to his previous health, but as the months passed it seemed that Badajoz had cost him more than his arm.

Once he recovered from the fever of infection, his body had reclaimed its former vigor—save for one particularly vital organ. While Ian at first had enjoyed the respite from his prick trying to order him about, he grew alarmed when aside from an occasional dream, it seemed nothing sparked his particular interest.

An attack of impotence was hardly something to be discussed with peers. He could not even imagine visiting an apothecary to explain the difficulty. Apparently there was no need. His cure was at hand. That brief contact with Nicky accomplished what Ian's will had not, gifting relief and agony in equal measures.

It took only picturing Nicky's generous mouth and Ian fumbled to release the fall of his trousers. The joy he'd heard when Nicky said his name became Nicky groaning it as Ian sucked him to completion. His prick lengthened, filled, ached. He stared at the head pushing through the foreskin, almost amazed. One stroke of his hand and the sensitive shaft was bared. He took a grip, the pressure of his fist at once familiar and strange. Arousal pulsed down his legs, up his spine, blotting out sense.

Another stroke, tighter, turning his wrist. Deep rich pleasure rippled out from his belly until he had to bite his lip to contain a groan. How long? God, how long had it been? How had he gone without this delicious agony?

Those nights in Spain before Badajoz, as Ian lay awake imagining what horror or boredom the next day might bring, he had sought the lethargy release could offer. Some of his men, even some of the officers had turned to each other, and Ian himself had turned a blind eye to it all. He was scarcely in a position to reprimand them for acting on the memories that brought Ian gasping and shuddering in his fist. The grip of a man's body milking his prick, the act of domination, the exhilaration of another man's surrender.

It wasn't as if he didn't see a look in the eye of some of the other officers, or become aware of broad shoulders and narrow hips, whether the admirable physique was found beneath the pale complexion of his fellow countrymen or the swarthier cheeks of a Portuguese, and it wasn't only fear of a court martial and public humiliation or even a hanging that kept Ian from acting on the longing. It was fear that such an act would never measure up to the memories, and an equal part of fear that it would. That he would fall into such a craving for it he could never right himself again.

It was safer to live unaware and take his ease only in that best and worst memory, Nicky split wide on Ian's prick, the clench of muscles as Nicky's body shrank and tightened in pain as horribly right as it was exquisitely wrong.

Ian sped up his strokes, and just as it had those long nights on the Continent, the burn of shame in his gut somehow doubled the sweetness of pleasure filling his balls. He pressed hard with his thumbnail on the slit, the pain bringing him over the narrow edge. A moment to hope his aim at the chamber pot stayed true before his body seized and he jerked out that long, hot flood, legs wide, head flung back, mind's eye fixed on the image of his seed splattered across Nicky's face.

Ian might have done better without that brief release, for it only intensified his awareness of Nicky as the guests gathered in the hall to don wraps for their brief walk to chapel. Although were he not so attuned, he might have scarcely seen Nicky at all. Every time he sought a glimpse, Nicky was engaged in conversation with some gentleman or a lady, a conversation that usually ended in great merriment for both parties. On one occasion the conversation was with Charlotte, but Ian was too far away to hear what brought such a rosy hue to her cheeks. As Charlotte had taken up such respectable company as the Widow Collingswood, Ian had felt safe in leaving her side.

The lady glanced his way, and Ian averted his gaze. Collingswood. He remembered hearing about him now. Captain Collingswood had been with the Third Division, killed during the looting that followed the victory at Badajoz, killed—as Ian had heard it—by his own men. He felt her gaze upon him and offered her a bow, approaching them to offer his sister his arm as they went to the small church, but Nicky swept Charlotte away, smiling down into her face.

Quite at point non plus, Ian checked and turned the offer of his arm to Mrs. Collingswood. She accepted as graciously as if she had not noticed his faltered step, laying her gloved hand on his coat. "How very thoughtful of you, Mr. Stanton. Your sister speaks highly of you."

Ian had gone from reading classics in his purple robes to the buff and scarlet of a second lieutenant, with no time at all to learn how to converse with a lady. What did one say in such a case?

"Oh. Ah."

"And Lord Amherst also."

"She has known his lordship since she was just out of the schoolroom," Ian explained.

Lacy clumps of snow still fell, yet slowly enough that the cobblestone path was well-cleared by servants wielding stable brooms. Hundreds of candles in the chapel threw enough light to gild the small drifts with a gold luster. Such a view coupled with the light scent of horses from the brooms made Ian fancy the sight and smells recaptured the Nativity.

"Oh, no, sir, you mistake me. Lord Amherst speaks very highly of you. Though I am certain he is much in Lady Charlotte's esteem as well," Mrs. Collingswood said.

Ian glanced ahead. Now that Nicky was in the vestibule, he had surrendered his hat, and his hair gleamed with as bright a halo as any of the saints portrayed in the stained glass windows. But Ian knew the lie in that. He had seen Nicky with those very curls upon awakening, twisted up on his temples like a satyr's horns. An apt resemblance as Nicky was then wont to pipe a suggestion to lure Ian back into bed. Somehow the weight of his responsibilities, whether an examination or a translation to be given that day, never felt as pressing when Nicky looked like that. Pure devilry at great odds with his cherubic features.

Nicky escorted Charlotte directly into the family pew in front. When Ian would have stopped mid-nave, Mrs. Collingswood continued forward down the aisle until it was clear her aim was the same destination. Not knowing quite how to correctly steer a lady, he would have delivered her to her relations and found a seat elsewhere, but Nicky's father greeted him like a son, with a familial clasp of Ian's forearm, and ushered him into their pew.

Carleigh's face bore the deep grooves of age, but Ian sensed it was more from joy than cares. Lord Carleigh had always been as ready with a laugh as his son. The marquess's handsome weathered face might well be Nicky's someday.

At the thought, a hollow regret echoed beneath Ian's breastbone in answer to the last of the joyful peals summoning the party to church. He certainly would see no such future day. Whatever had happened that Twelfth Night past, he and Nicky could only ever meet as friends. Nicky had his duties to family and title, and Ian—well, he would have to find where duty lay now that he was neither fish nor fowl, not soldier, but without use to anyone.

Ian found himself between Nicky's sister, Lady Anna, and Mrs. Collingswood. Charlotte, seated on the widow's other side, appeared to be fighting off a giggle, so Nicky on her left must be keeping her amused. As they rose for the processional, Ian tried to fix her with a stern glare, but she only fluttered her lashes at him. Short of lunging across Mrs. Collingswood and laying his hand upon her, Ian failed to see how he was supposed to correct her behavior. He wondered what Edward had been doing to try to keep the hoyden from disgracing them all.

His own behavior was hardly a sterling example, since although they had been honored by a bishop as celebrant, he could not keep his mind on the joyful service. His attention and even his gaze strayed to where Nicky sat at the end of the pew, dark gold side whiskers angled as if to deliberately accent his lean jaw and wide soft mouth. How could Ian ever endure a week of not staring at Nicky's mouth, of not recalling all the things he could do—had done—with that mouth? It would be far easier if the recipient seemed conscious of Ian's gaze, if Nicky were embarrassed, disconcerted or even amused by it. Any response and Ian knew he would be free of this childish urge to somehow regain Nicky's attention, to seek his approval or disapprobation.

During the Eucharist, Mrs. Collingswood whispered, "Is something amiss, Mr. Stanton?"

Startled, Ian looked at her. "Not at all, madam."

"It is just that you are chewing on your lower lip with great industry. I have been known to unwittingly tread on a gentleman's foot."

"Nothing of the kind, Mrs. Collingswood. I apologize if I have given you distress."

"I know what it is."

Ian gave his lower lip further abuse while shielding his sudden inhalation at her remark. "Yes?"

"It is concern for Lady Charlotte. I assure you, sir, she is in the best of company. Lord Amherst would keep her safe against all the world."

Nicky—and Charlotte? The candle flames bent and blurred as Ian tried to reorder his world. The Eucharist turned to chalk in his mouth. What level of sin was vomiting the Host?

Nicky to be his brother-in-law? Was that why Charlotte had insisted on this trip, been so eager, so full of questions about Nicky? Was this to be Ian's expiation, to give his sister in marriage to the man who had been his lover?

He gazed at the Holy Family in the crèche, considering all that they had been required to endure for the world's salvation. How disgraceful that Ian could not even let this unnatural infatuation die a normal death. Of course, Nicky had been happy to see him, the greeting reflected the warmth and affection due the season and their long acquaintance. Now Nicky desired a deeper bond, one of family. If he were planning to offer for Charlotte, it was plain Nicky had put those illicit fumblings out of his mind.

It was past time for Ian to do the same.

Chapter Three

After a rich supper that would have tested even a royal larder—which in turn tested the strength of many a waistcoat button—the gentlemen of the house party showed every sign of continuing their celebration of the Savior's birth until well past dawn of that happy day. The ladies were all safely abed— Charlotte twice accounted for—and with his resolution to keep his unrequited lust locked safely in the back of his mind, Ian began to enjoy the party. During his recuperative exile in Norwich, he had mastered the ability to play whist aided by a small wooden-covered spring that held the cards for him while he drew to follow suit. With the other players deep in their cups, Ian grew tired of answering "What is trumps?" so he retired from the table and went to observe a billiards game.

In addition to his button-sized playing card holder, the clever craftsman he had met in Norwich had fashioned a wooden bridge for him so that he could aim the cue stick. Still no easy feat, play required pressure from his stump to keep the stick in the groove as he imparted momentum with his right hand. He thought himself no worse a player than he had been before. After watching the looks exchanged at the table, Ian decided he'd enjoy buggering that pitying stare out of Weatherby's eyes. As he crossed the hall, intent on retrieving the bridge from his room, he nearly collided with someone who stepped into his path.

"Oh, I beg your pardon, Captain Stanton." The interloper bowed politely.

Ian nodded in return then froze. He hadn't known Julian Lewes would be here. From all accounts, Lewes never left London, preferring to maintain a readier access to all avenues of debauchery.

They had never been formally introduced, but it was impossible not to hear stories of Julian Lewes, to not have seen him pointed out in loud whispers. Lewes took pleasure wherever he chose to find it and if his fortune and family were not enough to deter dangerous allegations, he was reputed a lethal duelist, though he never issued the challenge himself.

Ian would have a strong word of warning for Charlotte in the morning, though the *on dit* was that Lewes was inclined to make other men the targets of his seductions. How even having the Duke of Norfolk as his grandfather allowed Lewes to still move freely in society with such a reputation Ian could not fathom.

Ian could see how Lewes might hold a certain fascination for some. He was handsome, as classically beautiful as a statue. He put Ian in mind of a panther he had seen when his nurse had taken them to Astley's Exhibition. There was beauty in the pacing beast's graceful strength and clean muscle under the midnight coat, but not even the cage bars between them could spare Ian the fear of immolation he had felt from staring into the flame-colored eyes.

"Captain Stanton?"

Ian was still frozen, though he knew his ruminations could have taken but a second.

"Rather I should say Mr. Stanton then? I see you have forsaken the uniform for that handsome coat. It is quite an improvement from when I saw you last, despite the missing arm."

Not even the surgeon had made such bald-faced pronouncements about Ian's injury.

Lewes' smile brought Ian to an understanding of the allure of creatures like panthers and men such as Lewes. A desire to possess that power and grace, to revel in the illusion of control before being consumed in fire.

He tore his gaze free of Lewes' eyes to stare at the similarly colored topaz stickpin winking in the starched folds of Lewes' cravat.

"Merry Christmas, sir." With a nod, Ian endeavored a polite extrication from the repellent company.

"I do hope you are enjoying the holiday as much as I am. Lord Carleigh and his son are such wonderfully accommodating hosts."

Ian looked back at Lewes' face. If this filthy bastard was trying to say— "Yes, the whole family take great pleasure in celebrating the season."

"Lord Amherst in particular. I've been enjoying his hospitality tremendously. I came up last week, you know."

Something tried to break free under Ian's breastbone, prickling like fire on the inside of his skin. The animal within fought for release, the creature of pure instinct which had lent him the strength to plunge his sword forward until the resistance of cloth and skin yielded to the liquid grip of guts and blood, the strength to withstand the shock vibrating up his arm as he swung at head and neck.

No saber here, his fist would do. The clarity of battle-readiness would direct his arm to connect precisely with the mole on the side of Lewes' mouth.

But he stopped short of planting his fist, a mere breath

away from that irreversible action. Perhaps it was the amused tilt to Lewes' black brows, the way the lip so near the mole lifted in a half-smile of success.

Dragging his animalistic rage back under lock and key, Ian forced the tendons in his hand to relax. "I am surprised you could tear yourself away from Town. You must find the country dreadfully dull."

"Oh, the right company can enliven any setting as I am sure you are aware, Mr. Stanton. And the current company is most enervating, indeed. In fact, I am planning on some rousing cheer at this very moment, if you will excuse me." Lewes nodded. "Again, my compliments to your valet. If I hadn't known, I wouldn't even have noticed the disfigurement."

Lewes turned for the doors to the India Room, leaving Ian alone in the hall. As he wrestled his rage for control again, he was forced to admit that what had nearly earned Lewes a fist and Ian a dawn appointment had less to do with outrage at the insinuations and much more to do with the bitter twist of jealousy in his heart.

Nicky was full to bursting with Charlotte's advice. To have Ian here, to have him close by at last and yet be unable even to look at him was nothing short of hell. Safely obscured by Ian's concentration on his whist game, Nicky had dared enter the India Room to observe Ian for a moment only to find him forced to use a device even for as simple an activity as a hand of cards. A fist of anger and pride gripped the breath in Nicky's lungs, along with a soul-deep determination to see that the fool never again felt the need to get blown to pieces just to prove himself good enough.

Charlotte could take her advice and use it to stuff a goose. Before the night was out, he would see Ian and have his reasons on why he had cut off all contact.

Intent on his cause, Nicky took up a flanking position just inside the gallery doors. The lookout provided a view of the main stairs Ian would have to take to go to bed, a venture Nicky suspected he would soon undertake as Ian had never been a candlewaster. Nicky kept ready an excuse, fiddling with the ties on his breeches in case anyone else who happened by wondered what Lord Amherst was doing lurking behind doors.

At a violent burst of noise behind him, he snapped his head up, striking it on the doorknob. Vision somewhat blurred, he turned to see Ian pop out of the salon doors like a clockwork toy. Excuses, advice and caution lost their foothold in Nicky's dazed brain. He had rehearsed a speech as eloquent as any his father had delivered to the House of Lords, but when Ian strode toward him, those words took mount and cantered off as if the last hunt of the season had just been announced. Flushed by his own quarry, he bleated, "Ian?"

Striding closer, Ian grabbed Nicky's arm and shoved him aside before swinging the gallery door shut. At first, the loss of light from the main hall left Nicky nightblind, but as his eyes adjusted to what little light filtered in through one of the gallery's narrow windows, he thought darkness might be preferable to beholding the fury on Ian's face.

"Ian—what—?"

"Lewes?" The name seemed to choke Ian. "What are you thinking? That foul abomination is no doubt poxed and if you—" Ian swallowed and ran a hand through his hair.

The condition of his hair and cravat suggested both had born the brunt of Ian's distress. Nicky was still trying to piece together Ian's complaint when his hand shot forward and grabbed Nicky by his own cravat, hauling him forward and crushing their mouths together.

The rough, angry kiss was unlike anything that had ever passed between them. Ian used Nicky's mouth, teeth and tongue, forcing his lips apart. Nicky gripped Ian's shoulders, pulled him close and let him take whatever he sought to find with his tongue sweeping deep inside. Ian's groan was barely more than a harsh breath, yet Nicky felt the change in the kiss. No less demanding, but it no longer felt like punishment. Ian drew Nicky's tongue back into his own mouth with a suction so sweet and strong the pull might have been on his cock.

It didn't matter why Ian had stopped answering his letters, why he had disappeared so soon after his return, because this thing between them was still alive, could still make Nicky willing to risk anything simply to bring a smile to Ian's lips, to hear him laugh.

This time they would do it. They'd go to Italy and live in sun and smiles. Where the wrong whisper wouldn't mean their necks.

Ian made that groan again, the sound still soft, but his hard cock jutted against Nicky's. Something brushed his hair like the touch of Ian's hand when it had so often pushed the curls from Nicky's forehead.

But such a feat was impossible. Ian's only hand still gripped Nicky's cravat.

As suddenly as he had kissed him, Ian released him— shoved him into the door.

Their breaths came heavy between them, wisps of steam visible in the unheated chill of the gallery.

Then of all things, Ian executed a perfectly formal bow. "I beg your pardon, Amherst," he said with no more feeling than if he delivered an inadvertent elbow in a crush at a soiree.

There were a million things Nicky should have said, but what came from his still-burning lips was "What for?"

"For far too much," Ian said, revealing a ghost of his old self, the unexpected humor that came up like wildflowers between cobblestones. Then he bowed again and left.

Thirty-six guests were staying for the full party, but Father and Anna might as well have decided to host the entire *ton* because the elusive Mr. Ian Stanton confounded all of Nicky's efforts to catch him alone Christmas morning despite a bitter north wind that imprisoned everyone in the castle. Nicky had been driven to considering the extreme of hiring someone to bind and gag Ian in the hayloft just so they could have a private conversation, when Charlotte rallied round to propose a riding party as soon as the wind let up.

It was for the best. Nicky didn't know how to get in touch with any criminals, though he would daresay Simmons might be of some help.

Several other gentlemen and ladies were keen to escape the indoors and a party of ten set off in the early afternoon.

In deference to the ladies, they maintained a decorous pace. Nicky's Galen kept twitching his ears and shaking his head as if he could not believe he had been dragged from a warm stall to mince along the fields instead of flying over fences. Galen was only too eager to take up the trot that brought him side by side with Ian's mount.

Ian immediately glanced about as if he sought rescue in larger company, but Nicky had timed it well. The path narrowed through a copse, forcing them to keep to no more than two abreast, and the party spread out long ways. Charlotte and a few ladies were behind them, all of the gentlemen and the Dowager Duchess of Coventry rode ahead. Ian's gaze sent a final appeal to the impassive hemlocks and beeches before staring straight between his mount's ears, his spine as fixed and rigid as his gaze.

"You never answered my letters," Nicky said.

Ian's head didn't turn. "There was nothing more to say."

"After all you swore to me?"

Dark red stained Ian's cheeks, more than could be attributed to the frosty air. "We were boys."

"And five years later we are men who no longer feel that passion."

"As it should be. That is all in the past."

"And my best stud's an untried colt. You bloody kissed me last night."

That at least sparked something. Ian's head shot 'round, eyes wide with alarm. Although no one could possibly be in earshot, Ian's voice lowered till it was scarcely audible over the ring of hooves on frozen ground. "And I have apologized. My judgment was impaired by—"

"Don't try to tell me you were in alts. I know you, Ian. You had barely a sip of whiskey."

"Nevertheless, I express deepest regrets for my—"

"Regret? Of all the stupid, doltish, empty-headed—I wanted you to do it, you unmitigated ass."

Ian shook his head. "Nicky—Amherst. Even the Greeks knew there was a time when a man had to put aside his *eromenos* and undertake a man's obligation as a citizen and head of a family."

Nicky remembered the papers he had found behind lock and key in the college library, how he had brought them to Ian

43

for translation, aching with joy to hear love between men not only accepted but celebrated.

"There are ways of meeting the expectations of both heart and duty. What of the lovers described by Aristophanes, the ones who forever seek to join themselves to their missing halves, whether it is man to woman, woman to woman or man to man? Are you not the same man who finished the translation and looked straight at me to whisper, 'He is so right, Nicky. That is what I have found with you'?"

Ian looked away. They approached the edge of the copse. Rejoining the others would end the conversation.

When Ian looked Nicky's way again, there was little of that remembered joy to be seen on Ian's sharp features. "But we do not live among the ancients. Such physical union risks our necks. And as I recall, you found little to enjoy in our attempt."

They had reached the field. Nicky read imminent flight in the tension of Ian's hand on the reins, the shift in his seat. He was going to urge his mount to a trot, catch the others up and vanish into the crowd where further direct speech would be impossible. Nicky reached out and gathered Ian's reins, forcing the mare to stop.

"For a man who could read Greek as easily as many do plain English, you are incredibly lacking in native intelligence. We didn't know what we were doing. Of course it was uncomfortable. But I have learned—"

Ian snatched away the reins, wheeling the mare so tightly her eyes showed white. "How?"

"I beg you will not take your idiocy out on my horses, Ian. Rowena has a soft mouth."

Ian eased his grip on the reins, but his voice was still cold enough to rival the air. "How?"

"How do you think, you bloody fool? The point is there is

much we can share. The pleasure is boundless and with proper caution—God, what I will show you."

Ian dug his heels into Rowena's sides and urged her off at a canter, flying across the field, far from the riding party, headed for—oh Sweet Christ, the folly. The ditch that kept the picturesque image of grazing sheep in sight of the castle without the actual sheep shit to litter the lawn. Most of the snow had been swept from the high field by the morning's wind, but it surely filled the ditch. If Rowena and Ian took flight there unaware, the fall would break both their necks.

He heeled Galen after them, calling out a warning, but he was sure his voice would be lost under the wind and pounding hooves. Even if Ian remembered the exact location of the folly, or it was miraculously clear of snow, could he take the jump with only one limb for balance? A low try for certain, but the folly was wider than any fence Nicky had taken on a hunt. As if aware of pursuit, Ian's path veered, no longer on a trajectory to the folly but to the style in the fence farther upfield. Rowena was a good hunter and could easily clear it, but if Ian lost his seat...

Nicky's own heart and stomach parted ways, like he could sense the power gathered beneath him, as if he too made the dizzying leap into space on ninety stone of horse in flight. As Rowena cleared the style and landed in the next field, the man atop her pitched dangerously forward onto her neck, nearly dangling off to the left. Nicky's pulse echoed in his ears, loud even over the thud of Galen's hooves. He counted off the beats...one-two-three...before Ian righted himself and sped into the distance. Nicky drew a deep breath and turned Galen back to the rest of the riders. If Ian didn't come to his senses soon, Nicky might break the man's neck himself.

Chapter Four

Ian tugged at his cravat, itching to be free of the starched cloth and the high collar of his coat. What the devil was taking Simmons? Every bit of sinew and bone—both real and phantom—ached for a chance to settle into the mattress and forget the whole blasted holiday.

He wished he could lay the fault for his pains on the ride this afternoon, but Rowena had a softer gait than he deserved, especially after his dash pell-mell for land unpeopled by the heir to Carleigh. Upon his return, he had stayed with a groom to be sure she had not suffered from his ham-fisted treatment and seen to her getting a soft warm mash as a reward for the exercise.

No amount of mash or currying could excuse either his behavior toward a creature under his care or his assault on Nicky. Whatever the provocation—and Ian should have realized a man like Lewes could scarcely be counted on to speak the truth—Nicky hadn't deserved the violence of Ian's temper any more than had the gentle bay mare.

When at last the door opened, Ian spun 'round to be relieved of his coat, sufficiently irritated by Simmons' delayed arrival to forgo his usual greeting.

Perhaps the fellow had been overindulging in whatever libations were being offered to celebrate the day in the servants' hall because the valet was clumsy rather than deft, struggling just to ease the coat from Ian's shoulders.

"And I shall be retiring, Simmons."

Instead of the expected "Very good, sir," the man left his arms pinned behind his back and brushed his fingers beneath Ian's cravat. The unanticipated contact awakened Ian's skin, his flesh alight with delightful ripples of sensation.

"What the devil?"

He would have turned to face the man, but Simmons stepped closer, hands moving to remove the starched tie while pressing his hips intimately against Ian's arse.

The shock and terror in his gut, even the pain of his confined shoulders, could not dampen the rush of arousal evoked by the touch, by the strength of another man's embrace.

"Simmons. I must ask that you remember yourself." Ian twisted free, retreating to place a wall at his vulnerable back, but his all-too-vulnerable front was exposed to—Nicky.

The identity of his assailant did little to mitigate Ian's dismay.

"Are you mad?" Ian struggled with his coat, anger lending him sufficient strength to tear one of the sleeves from the body.

Nicky locked the door and removed his own coat. "It is Boxing Day, after all. Simmons has the evening off, as do almost all of the servants. Surely you would not deprive the man of his well-earned holiday."

"It is not Boxing Day for another hour," Ian asserted as the solemn toll of the chapel bell made him a liar. He flung his torn coat to the floor.

Nicky's cravat parted company with his shirt, revealing a neck still defined with the strong tendons Ian had once traced with his tongue. Quelling thoughts of other flesh his mouth longed to revisit grew more impossible with each piece of clothing Nicky dropped onto the Aubusson rug.

"What are you doing?"

"I am preparing for bed. That bed." Nicky indicated the four-poster in the center of the room.

"Is the castle so crowded the son of the house has been turned out of his rooms?"

"If it pleases you to think so." Nicky straightened, torso bared to Ian's gaze.

Firelight gilded Nicky's skin, gleaming on the fine hairs of his breast, drawing Ian's eye to the waist of Nicky's breeches where the hair thickened and darkened. The garnet on his signet ring flashed as Nicky's hands moved to those buttons.

Ian shut his eyes. "No."

"No?" The amusement in Nicky's voice had Ian looking again, forgetting what imminent danger had prompted his action. But Nicky only bent to remove his shoes and stockings, gifting Ian with the sight of the firm curve of his backside under the tight kerseymere breeches.

Nicky brought his hands to rest above his hips, fingers disappearing under the waistband. "Is it truly no or is that what the good soldier, the dutiful second son, feels compelled to say?"

Ian's throat burned as it tightened, but he could not look away.

"Whom do you seek to save with your denial, me or you?" Nicky persisted. He stepped closer, but made no move to touch Ian. "Why are we to be denied pleasure when you must know how precious and brief life is?"

"The risk of—"

"You threw yourself against a wall of French rifles in service to your father's idea of honor. Can you not permit yourself something your own honor knows is right? How can it be wrong when we both desire it?" Nicky shoved his breeches down and stepped free, the proof of his desire standing proud and hard.

As swiftly as snow falling off a steep roof, Ian's body dropped into a pit of raw need. He made a last effort to find any handhold which might keep him from the abyss.

"I do want..." *you* "...this, but only what we did before. We cannot, I will not..." He tried making a gesture to communicate the specific deed.

"Bugger me?" Nicky grinned. "Fuck me?"

Despite Ian's shock, the coarseness of Nicky's words brought a faster beat of blood to Ian's prick. That unabated grin suggested Nicky knew damned well what effect he had wrought. His next step brought Nicky close enough to try the truth with his hand. Fingers traced the outline of Ian's prick beneath a layer of wool and linen, a light pressure that offered nothing beyond exquisite torment. A quick hard rub against the crown, dragging the linen across the damp skin until heat pulsed from the tip, the touch as unerringly accurate as Ian's own.

Pleasure stole his breath as surely as a fist to the stomach. Sucking the air through his teeth, he reached a hand to Nicky's shoulder, hips tipping into the caress.

Nicky leaned forward until his breath moved against Ian's ear. "While I find your concern utterly charming, what makes you believe you could take my arse if I didn't allow it?"

Ignoring the wail of protest from his prick and balls, Ian transferred his grasp to Nicky's wrist to still the motion of his palm. "I am well aware that many now consider me less a man, but with all your protestations, I would have thought—"

Nicky laughed. "Christ, Ian, try not to be more of an ass than the good Lord intended you to be. You couldn't best me even when you had four inches and two-stone advantage."

"I've never had two stones on you, you country-fed beast." The retort came unbidden to his lips, their long habit of verbal sparring impossible to amend.

"By God, how I've missed you." Nicky chuckled and yanked Ian's cravat free.

Ian felt his own lips curve in answer. There had always been so much laughter between them. For years, that absence cut as keenly as the loss of Nicky's touch.

Shoving away bolster and counterpane, Nicky flung himself onto the bed. "Now. Kindly divest yourself of those clothes and get up here before I am forced to seek other amusements."

Nicky arranged himself in a gloriously naked display, familiar laugh and cornflower-blue eyes at odds with the strangeness of a body more heavily muscled, more thickly pelted, but no less enthralling than the one that had filled Ian's dreams as he slept in tents on the edges of battlefields. Longing clawed deeper hollows than all those years of denial, until again Ian was deprived of sufficient breath.

Such was the assault wrought on his senses by Nicky's sprawl across the mattress that Ian had stripped away waistcoat and shirt and unfastened his breeches before Nicky's last words attached themselves to a meaning. The haze of lust clouding Ian's mind took on a red veil of anger.

"Other amusements?"

Nicky sighed and leaned forward, taking Ian by the arm. "I swear to provide you with a detailed history of the past five years in writing and affix the bloody Carleigh seal to my testimony. But if I don't have you right now, one of us will end up dead."

Nicky pulled him with a force too gentle to be compelling, but it was easier by far to let Nicky drag Ian onto the bed than to make the decision himself.

Nicky rolled, trapping Ian beneath, the press of hard warm skin such a shock Ian had to close his eyes against the sensation. When he opened them, there was Nicky, the achingly familiar blue eyes and full lips all Ian could hope of heaven.

"Which of us?"

"Does it matter?" Nicky rocked against him.

Ian thought again of Aristophanes and Phaedrus and their tales of separated lovers. Of Achilles' terrible grief for Patroclus. "No."

Nicky kissed the word from his mouth in a gentle press of lips, but Ian brought his hand up to tangle at last in those curls and pinned Nicky tight, an upward thrust of hips to feel the harder, wetter kiss of Nicky's cock on Ian's belly.

Nicky wrenched free and reared up, hands working to finish his duty as substitute valet, shoving away Ian's breeches and small clothes until at last their pricks slapped together. Ian thought he had exorcised it from his memory, but there was no forgetting that sensation, the silky heat of Nicky's cock against his.

Adding his spit to slick the way, Nicky held them together, rubbing the thick ridges against each other, washing the whole shaft with heat and pressure. Sweet enough to die from but not enough. God, not enough.

Ian reached up with both arms to pull Nicky down against him, and then let his good arm drop as the left hung useless, withered stump bared to Nicky's gaze. Nicky caught Ian's half-arm as it fell and bent to press a kiss on the scarred folds of skin. Although the wound was ill-repaired to the point of numbness, the intimacy on his maimed flesh sent a shock of sensation up and down his arm, making his ghost fingers tingle.

Suddenly Ian was ashamed of the way he had made Nicky coax him into this, as if he were somehow unmoved by what Nicky offered.

"That part about not having you or dying. Nicky, now, please."

Nicky dropped down, stretched out. Ian flattened his palm against Nicky's back, urging him on. He slid forward an inch and their pricks aligned, trapped together in hard heat and driving friction. No tenderness now, Ian couldn't have stood it. Nicky seemed to understand that only violence could tear through Ian's hard-won restraint, meeting each thrust of hips with matching force.

Openmouthed kisses, shared breath and—as an errant tooth met an eager lip—shared blood, but Ian couldn't make himself care whose blood had spilled. All that mattered was the rut of rigid flesh, and the sound of Nicky's groans trapped between them as they strained together.

A plea rose in Ian's throat, though what more he would demand he could not say. Much as he wanted to ride the sharp, sweet edge of satisfaction forever, he needed the completion that would burn away what remained of the distance between them, bind them with slick seed.

"Now, Nicky." Ian's palm slid on sweat as he pressed lower, hand wide across Nicky's arse to draw him even closer. "Come to it."

Nicky gasped, a short choked sound, and spilled hot and slippery across their bellies. The first splash of warmth from inside Nicky's body on Ian's prick took him over, dropping him into long spasms of blissful relief.

Uncaring of the solid bulk sinking down on him, Ian would have surrendered consciousness in favor of heedless sleep, but Nicky lifted himself away, forcing Ian's attention to the clammy state of his belly.

He sat up, catching Nicky under the chin with his stump.

"Ow. What the hell?"

"My breeches. The linens."

Nicky rubbed his chin. "Bugger your breeches."

Ian couldn't say who broke first. The laughter came almost immediately, great gulps of it, until they were breathless and their faces wet with tears. He collapsed on his back. Nicky swiped his thumb across Ian's cheek. "I did miss you. And all this."

Ian knew what he meant. No one had ever known him better. Since they had first met Nicky had been the brighter half of Ian's heart, sharing the joy that followed in Nicky's wake. But that had never been just Ian's; Nicky shared his light with everyone.

Those thoughts linked darkly, one to the other until the twinned pleasures of laughter and sexual satisfaction were buried under a cold weight beneath Ian's ribs. Perhaps knowing would be worse, but he could no longer stand the uncertainty, could not face Lewes until Ian learned the truth to outface the man's lies.

"You swore you would tell me of the last five years."

Nicky's laughter disappeared as swiftly as the sun behind leaden clouds. "You cannot allow us even a moment to savor our reunion? You are without a doubt misery's most ardent suitor, Ian Stanton."

Ian turned his head from the hard look in Nicky's eyes, making busy with kicking away breeches, reaching down to wipe at the cloying seed with soiled smallclothes. What if there was truth to Nicky's accusations? Ian never asked for unhappiness, but avoiding it served no good purpose.

"And if I am, what does that make you?"

"An utter fool." With a long sigh, Nicky retrieved the bolster and propped himself upon it, apparently unconcerned with his nudity.

Ian longed for a nightshirt. His stump was not the only disfiguring souvenir he had brought home from the Peninsula. An ill-knitted scar the size of a fist blossomed over his ribs to mark where the shrapnel that had taken his hand had also sought his heart. After envisioning himself trying to wrestle the shirt over his head while Nicky laughed from the bed, Ian contented himself with hunching over a pillow placed on his lap.

"What is it you feel you must know?" Nicky's voice was still heavy from his sigh.

"Lewes." The name rushed from Ian's lips. "That filthy bastard told me—"

"That filthy bastard is a good friend."

"What sort of friend could such a man possibly be?"

"I'll tell you if you stop shrieking like a fishwife."

Outrage drove Ian's fist into the pillow. "Fishwife?"

"An aggrieved peacock then." It wasn't quite up to Nicky's usual smile.

"Lewes," Ian said again. He would not let Nicky bait him to a false trail, though Ian suspected he already knew the answer.

"You truly wish to know?"

"No. But I must."

"What a quiz you are. Very well." Nicky settled farther back against the bolster. "Julian had a younger brother who was a year ahead of us at school, do you remember?"

Ian shook his head.

"Julian came up to visit. You had been gone for more than a year."

"I wrote you."

"Yes. A few terse passages on the ineptitude of the quartermaster was definitely the sort of thing to keep the fires burning." Nicky glanced away and then looked directly into Ian's eyes. "Julian was—well, Julian. You've met him. He spoke to me. He was charming, older and beautiful. He said he wanted to show me his new tack, but I knew why he summoned me to the stable."

Ian had demanded this, but with supper curdling in his belly, he couldn't bear anymore. He turned away.

Swift as a hawk, Nicky snatched Ian's chin, forcing his gaze up.

"I have heard enough." Ian tried to pull away, but Nicky had a bruising grip.

"No. You wanted this. I dropped to my knees and sucked his cock in that stall. He gave me his direction in London and when I managed a visit, I learned more than you and I could ever find in those missing dialogues of Plato's Symposium. He fucked my arse until I could barely walk and I loved it. He showed me a club—"

A hard shove freed Ian's head at last, the force causing his head to snap on his neck. He was free for an instant then Nicky followed after, pinning Ian to the bed. "You asked. You bloody well insisted, so stop acting like you didn't want to hear every damned word."

Ian stopped struggling. Not because Nicky was right, but to fend off fresh humiliation. Every breath filled his senses with the mingled smell of their sex and sweat, and Ian's lust, so long mewed up, tore free again. Nicky's weight against him, the heat of skin, the rub of ballocks and prick against his own. Anger and disgust were an insufficient barrier as need came roaring back.

He tried to lock it away. "I shall never be able to look at him—or even at you—without seeing—"

"Then prepare to start a new fashion for wearing horse blinders. Half the men in London have probably had Julian's cock in them one way or another." Nicky shifted and Ian's prick made an embarrassing twitch as it filled anew.

Nicky's narrowed gaze widened abruptly. "Is it like that, then? You like to watch others at it? Get a cock-stand from watching them fuck? A man at Hylas House watched his friend buggered by half the room and said he'd pay a thousand pounds to watch again."

Shame and desire coiled like snakes in Ian's belly. Not to watch Nicky, no. But the idea that there were others, that they sought it. Wanted it. Wanted and freely took that which filled Ian with terror and need.

"Is that what you want? Shall I invite Julian to join us? Do you want to see me split wide open on his cock?"

"Stop your mouth." Ian yanked Nicky's head down again. Ian meant the kiss only to silence Nicky, but he greeted Ian's assault with open passion. The slick pass of Nicky's tongue between Ian's lips licked deeper inside than just his mouth until Ian burned with an all-consuming need to stamp Nicky with ownership, brand him until Julian Lewes and everyone else alive knew this skin, this taste, this man was for Ian alone.

Ian rolled, dragging Nicky beneath, hand holding his chin, thumb rubbing across the full wet lips. Nicky flicked the thick pad with his tongue then drew it into his mouth. An overwhelming sight and sensation, never was there anything as astonishingly lewd as Nicky's tongue and lips suckling Ian's thumb.

Blood filled his prick in a painful rush, and he drove it against Nicky's belly, Nicky returning the rough embrace thrust for thrust. Ian pulled his thumb free, scraping it across Nicky's cheek before swiping the curls back from Nicky's brow.

Pinning him flat with full settled weight between his thighs, Ian demanded, "And what now?"

Nicky blinked. "Now? Are you asking for instructions?"

"What is between you now?"

"Lord, but you are a contrary animal. Friendship. Nothing but friendship. Anything Julian had to offer me was long ago."

"Good. Because I swear, Nicky, if Lewes dares try anything with you again, I'll geld the bastard."

"I am not exactly a helpless female in this, you know."

Ian watched the bob of the apple on Nicky's throat, barely resisting the urge to set teeth to it. "Then I'll damned well geld you both."

Nicky swallowed again. "Very well." But there followed a quick flash of his smile. "But before it comes to that, suck my cock, will you?"

Chapter Five

Nicky waited to see how Ian would react. Would there be more outraged protests? Or would he unleash the furious caresses Nicky would never have anticipated and certainly would never have expected to find so arousing?

He had forgotten how much fun there was to be had in baiting Ian, teasing him from his dark moods, challenging his painfully rigid views. That such action also brought forth a wildness in his lover that seared them both with its heat was a *bonne bouche* atop the sweetest meal.

What Nicky's demand wrought was an echoing groan before Ian bent to bruise Nicky's lips. There was so much he had dreamed of showing Ian when he finally succumbed, yet all Nicky wanted to do now was lie back and let Ian take what he would from Nicky's mouth before moving onto his jaw and throat. A moment's hesitation, the tingling scrape of teeth, and when Nicky whispered, "Yes," Ian's mouth latched onto the tight skin beneath Nicky's ear and sucked the blood to the surface until Nicky moaned and arched.

Ian had ever been a quick study and he applied the lesson down Nicky's collarbone and even to his nipples, blending teeth, tongue and lips to bring hot pressure hovering at the edge of pain. Nicky lent encouragement with a hand on Ian's head, willing his mouth lower, but as usual, hurrying Ian was pointless. He left marks across Nicky's belly, and no amount of trying to move his cock closer to Ian's mouth brought satisfaction.

For all that Nicky had gained in experience, Ian could still drive him to despair. Frustration added a harsh note to his voice as he gasped, "Whoreson bastard."

Ian's hand squeezed Nicky's hip. "My father would be grieved to hear it."

The laugh happily perished in Nicky's throat as Ian wrapped his lips around the head of Nicky's cock at last. Certainly there had been men with far more experience performing this task for him, but this was Ian, and when he set himself to something, he would have nothing less than perfection.

Perfection played out in the wet caress along the shaft, hand and mouth exciting every nerve, driving Nicky's hips to press upward, seeking more, *please* more. Instead Ian moved, dragged his tongue and then his chin across Nicky's ballocks, a scrape of rough evening whiskers tingling the sac.

Ian had audacity by the score to play the hurt faithful lover. This was practiced skill woven to drive a man insane.

Nicky's throat ached from swallowing back cries and pleas, sounds he feared would crack the oldest stones in the castle were he to free them, when Ian took the shaft in a firm grip and applied his mouth. Ebb and flow of hard suction and comforting laps with a wet tongue, sensation alternately an agony of need and the sweetness of fulfillment.

As much as Nicky longed for the soft heat of Ian's throat, his rhythm carried Nicky swiftly to the edge. His body trembled with tension, the flood gathering in his balls, when the cursed fiend raised his hellborn head.

The blaze in Ian's dark eyes stilled the protest firmly behind Nicky's lips.

"When he took you did it feel as good as this?" Ian's breath fell hot against the head of Nicky's cock until he was sure he would weep.

He shook his head and then dared the word. "No. No. But—Christ—Ian—" How to tell Ian that he longed for that full possession, the intimacy of bodies connected, all bundled with the gift of Ian's single-minded attention?

Ian growled and dove back onto Nicky's cock, swallowing, pulling him deep into the shocking heat and slick, velvety caress of tongue, mouth, throat. Ian growled again, the vibration rippling across Nicky's cock, piercing him on that blade-sharp moment from which there was no return.

Nicky reached down, scrabbling for a hand to grasp as the spasms racked his body, forgetting in that perfect moment that there was none to spare. His hand closed around the end of Ian's arm, the struggle as Ian sought to free himself making warmth sting the backs of Nicky's eyes even as his hips pumped, shooting his seed deep into Ian's throat.

When Nicky had ridden out the last of the shudders, Ian wiped his face against Nicky's thigh, twisting out of his grasp.

"No." Nicky reasserted his grip. This was a part of Ian now and damned if he would let him hide it or be ashamed when there was already so much Ian kept from those who loved him. He tugged Ian closer. "Kiss me."

Ian dragged the back of his hand across his mouth. "But—"

"I don't care."

Ian's kiss was tentative, resisting all of Nicky's efforts to coax his lips apart. In the end, Nicky had to relinquish Ian's arm to make a grab for the hard staff jutting between them.

Ian gasped and Nicky licked into his mouth, tasting himself layered with the familiarity of Ian.

Ian pulled away, his chiding "Nicky" at once familiar and frustrating.

Nicky could feel his own grin down to his toes. "You will never change. And I am the happier for it." He licked his lips. "Climb up here and feed me your cock."

Ian shook his head, backing away and taking his shaft in hand.

Nicky looked askance, for he could not imagine how one's own hand could surpass a willing mouth, even for Ian, but as Ian's hips jerked and his lids fluttered over his eyes, Nicky decided he would not complain about this course of entertainment.

After only a few quick strokes of his hand, Ian's cock spurted, streams landing from Nicky's chin to his navel. Ian folded from the waist as he spent himself and then looked up, trailing his fingers across the creamy drops. Nicky watched in astonishment. Ian had always seen bodily emissions as something to clean away as soon as possible.

"Ian?"

Ian stroked his hand across Nicky's chest again. "Wanted to cover you with it." Ian's smile was rueful. "As if I might leave my mark."

"Noddy fool." Nicky tapped Ian's temple. "You already have done."

Icy, predawn air bit at the tip of Nicky's nose, and he squinted at the fire. He hadn't been a very good valet.

Unbanked, the fire had burnt itself out. Ian had ever been a heavenly bedmate in the winter, body radiating enough heat to thaw a glacier, but as soon as Nicky put his foot out on the floor he knew he'd be perished. He'd heard it was warm in Italy and Greece the year round.

Ian didn't stir, but Nicky felt the body beside him shift to wakefulness just the same. At school, the all-male environs had offered something of a shield. The masters were lax and some students even managed to smuggle in their *filles de joie.* Carleigh Castle was another matter entirely. Nicky must need to start the day from his own bedchamber.

He slipped one leg from beneath the bedclothes and held off a groan. Knowing a dilatory effort would only prolong his agony, he vaulted out and began to haul on his clothes as swiftly as his benumbed fingers could manage.

Ian remained silent, though Nicky could feel the weight of his gaze. He expected a lecture, expected recriminations, and was surprised by a deep chuckle from beneath the quilt.

"You could scare children with that head of hair, Nicky."

He brought both hands to his head and peered into the glass on the washstand. Half of his curls were flattened, but for one that twisted out like a billy goat's horn. As for the other side...who knew what he had slept in to create the resemblance to an angry badger. He reached into the washbowl and cursed as his fingers cracked through a thin film of ice.

"What?" Ian's voice was the deeper from recent sleep.

"The blasted water's frozen. I'd rather hang than coat my head in it." He cast an eye to the window, trying to gauge the time. Nothing but darkness, broken by a hissing clatter slashing the glass. Finding it too cold to snow, the heavens were hurling ice at them. "Even the pig-swiving snow is frozen. We won't be hunting this morning either. And it's Boxing Day which means cold meats and old bread. Damn it."

"I don't recall you being quite such an ill-tempered riser."

"Then there is some fault to your memory." Nicky shivered violently, sending the icy water on his fingers flying into his face. "Shit."

"Be grateful for the fortunes of birth. If you'd ever had to stick out a day of soldiering I think you'd be cashiered before nightfall."

"And be glad of it. Didn't you have a batman? I thought all officers were assigned one."

"Father said we couldn't afford it. Not with Charlotte's come-out. I was treated to a lengthy letter on how her court dress alone would have kept three profligate households flush for a year." Ian's voice deepened another octave until it was positively sepulchral. "No one to bring your tea. Boxing Day, every day, Nicky. Imagine the horror of it."

Perhaps it was the chill or perhaps it was the remnants of sleep still wrapping Nicky's head with wool, but he finally latched onto the realization that Ian was not carrying a millstone of shame this morning. He'd half-expected Ian to deny what had happened and then Nicky would need to spend yet more time convincing him to resume their physical relationship. Yet with this morning's familiar exchange, the intervening five years might have been a dream from which Nicky had just awakened in Ian's bed as he used to do. One thing was true, when Ian committed to a course, it took a labor of Hercules to deter him from it. Nicky should know. He'd undertaken the labor twice now. With sweeter rewards than the gods could dream.

After shrugging his coat onto his shoulders, he sat on the bed and brushed a thumb across Ian's rough cheek. "I'd kiss you, but I'm afraid our lips will freeze. Of course, I'm sure we could find a way to thaw them. It might be fun to have my mouth stuck fast to your cock."

Ian gave him a stern look.

"In the absence of a fire, I could stand some bracing before I make my bitter journey."

"For God's sake, your room is just across the hall."

"Don't you think I arranged it so? But in this air, I could catch my death without something to warm me."

"Your complaints are too fatiguing. Get to bed and speak to me when you are fit for company."

"What sort of company?" Nicky offered him a leer.

"You know whose it had best not be."

Nicky smiled. He had never received a better gift than such narrow-eyed proof of Ian's devotion. "I'll see you at breakfast, Mr. Stanton. And do try not to issue any challenges to my friends before then."

Nicky's mother had begun the tradition of a Twelve Night party when she had been a young bride, and Nicky had enjoyed every one, even when he had to sneak out of the nursery to spy on the goings-on just as his twin brothers were doing when he caught the lads skulking on one of the tower's stairs. When they'd been in leading strings it had been impossible to tell them apart, but now at eleven, Richard had an inch on Robert and Robert's hair was showing a tendency to the wildness that had plagued Nicky just this morning.

He considered dragging them by their ears back to the nursery, but he was feeling a considerable amount of charity toward all mankind this morning, though it resulted more from how he had spent the night than from the joyful Christmas season. Besides, he was owed a respite from listening to everyone decry that it was by far the coldest winter England had ever seen, following hard on a bleak summer. If he heard one more suggestion of impending doom for all humankind, he was likely to lose his head.

Dickie, older by several hours, immediately offered up a denial. "Nurse said as long as we stayed on the upper floors—"

Robbie gave him a sharp elbow. "Shut it. Annie told us we may."

Their sister Anna had mothered them as best she could when Mother failed to recover from birthing them. Nicky supposed he felt an awkward affection for them, but they had been born when he was at school, and his first memory of them was a jumble of burial, christening, condolences and mourning. He remembered little of it except that it had been the first time he'd ever seen his father cry.

He knew less of his brothers than he did most of the guests at the party. With himself at school and then in Town, Nicky scarcely saw his brothers, would see even less of them now that they were going away to school.

Robbie's question came out in an awed whisper. "Is it true Weatherby just lost two thousand at hazard?"

"Probably." Without any outdoor pursuits, stakes were edging higher. If this weather did not let up, half the guests would be in dun territory.

"I wonder if his wife knows," Dickie said.

"I wonder what he'd pay to be sure she doesn't," Robbie added.

At first his brothers' enterprising natures were a source of pride tempered with concern over exactly what their tutor had been covering, but a sudden shock of alarm sent Nicky's bonhomie cowering. "How on earth did you hear that? Not from Anna, I'll wager."

"There's that spot on—ow!" Dickie's answer was again foreshortened, this time by a hard stomp on his instep.

But Nicky was able to finish the sentence. There was a disused medieval privy in the tower, and depending on how close one stood to the wall, it was possible to hear conversations from the north end of the gallery and the hall. Sweet Christ. If they'd been out early Christmas morning they might have heard him and Ian in the gallery.

The gallery wouldn't be used until New Year's Eve, and Nicky would remember to hold any future tête-à-têtes elsewhere. In the meantime, perhaps he could discourage the budding blackmailers. Disused or not, it took a certain willingness to disregard the lingering odor of its prior incarnation to make use of it as a listening post.

"Ahhh." Nicky wrinkled his nose. "That's what I smell. Best change or Nurse will think you still need swaddling."

They ran off, though Nicky suspected they would find their way back—or happen on another method of subterfuge. If he weren't trying to secure his future happiness, he would have applauded their ingenuity. But when he thought of what was at stake, all he could manage was to swallow back a cold lump of dread.

Nicky had good reason to be wary of his brothers' skills at reconnoitre when Ian herded Nicky into the gallery from the Gold Salon. In deference to Ian's temper, Nicky had avoided Julian's company all day, and while that might have kept the peace, Nicky's head ached from a day of feminine chatter and the attar of too many different massacred flowers.

He wished Ian's sudden desire to converse intimately was born of passion, but it was born instead of his sister's perverse sense of humor. Charlotte had been at her worst, simpering as she asked Nicky to fetch her a cup of rack punch, and then to engage in minute adjustments of the fire screen to suit her comfort. Each of her demands wrought darker and darker looks from her brother until Nicky thought he'd enjoy strangling the blasted chit. Couldn't she see the way Ian was tying himself into knots of guilt because he thought Charlotte had truly set her cap at his lover?

When Charlotte asked Nicky if he would be so gracious as to retrieve her fan from the gaming table, Ian popped to his feet as if the sofa's upholstery were afire. Nicky just had time to gift Charlotte with both fan and glare before Ian bowed. "A word, Lord Amherst?"

Nicky snatched up a candle before following Ian through the doors.

Why the hell had Nicky's mother settled on winter as a good time for a lengthy house party? The foul weather meant that there was no sure retreat from an out-of-control game of blind man's bluff or another guest seeking a change of scenery. Or from Nicky's budding spymaster siblings. Nicky thought of bringing Ian up to the nursery since the twins had no doubt abandoned it in search of damaging information they could use to extort money from unsuspecting guests.

"Do you mind if we walk?" Nicky set off at a brisk pace toward the south end of the gallery. He'd only gained a few yards when Ian stayed him with his hand.

"What are your intentions toward my sister?"

"Your sister? How can you even ask that after last night?"

Ian resumed walking. "I know you will soon wish to marry."

"Wish to?"

"Must, then. But Charlotte has no female relation to advise her save Rayne's wife and she is unable to travel."

"I am afraid I have lost the trail, Ian."

"What I mean is, Charlotte is not well-versed in the way things are done. She was gently reared."

Nicky fought back a bark of laughter until it turned to a cough. Ian's look of concern only made him cough harder until he was forced to lean against the wall next to the painting of the third marquess.

"Perhaps you should get out of the chill," Ian said.

"I'm fine. A little desperate for a proper meal, but well enough to sustain further conversation."

"Very well. I simply do not wish to see Charlotte hurt."

"I believe your sister may have depths which remain hidden even from those who know her well."

Ian nodded as if he understood. "I only recently discovered she is quite fond of Shakespeare's comedies."

This time Nicky thought the effort to suppress his laughter would lead to genuine asphyxiation. He assumed a serious expression. "Let me see if I have this full. You insist that I marry, when you know that any woman will of necessity find herself neglected since I will always choose to take my affections elsewhere, yet you balk at this lucky woman being your sister."

Ian paused, mouth slightly agape. Unassailable logic. It would always be Ian's defeat.

"Well, yes," Ian said at last.

"Perhaps I won't marry."

"But you must. You have a duty to your title and your family and—"

"I have two brothers who will no doubt be willing to leap at the chance of title and duty."

Ian's expression of slack-jawed horror would have been amusing if Nicky weren't so fond of the dolt.

"Aren't you worried your face will freeze like that? Of course, I know I must marry."

"And will you?"

"That all depends."

"On what?"

"On you."

"No. There is no possible say I could have in the matter. I know—I know I was a bit off my head where Lewes was concerned but this—I will always regard you warmly, Nicky, and I will treasure what time we have here, but—no. You must do your duty to the title."

"Warmly. It seemed far more than tepid to me last night."

Two dark red spots appeared high on Ian's cheeks, but he lowered his gaze.

Nicky pressed on. Charlotte had been the one to caution him against rashness, claiming Ian would bolt if they revealed too much too fast, yet her actions today had precipitated this. "And if my choice is Charlotte, do you have any say in the matter?"

"I have a brother's say and that is to refuse the honor."

"And what will *your* brother say?" The new Earl of Rayne wouldn't have been more delighted with the match than if he'd learned to piss gold, and they both knew it. Nicky gripped Ian's arm, holding tight enough to keep him from fleeing. "Ian, I swear to you, on my honor, I will not marry unless you approve my choice."

"Then it will never be Charlotte."

69

Hiding a smile felt at least as difficult as standing in for Sisyphus and taking a turn with his rock, but Nicky managed it. "Just as you say."

Chapter Six

Though Simmons appeared hale and hearty each morning when he brought Ian a cup of tea and helped him to dress, it was no surprise that Nicky claimed to be aiding an ailing Simmons by taking his place each night when it was time to prepare for bed. Ian accepted the pretense, though he did not know why Nicky insisted on maintaining it. Each night Nicky had barely locked the door before they were divesting each other of clothes as if their very speed would bring about the release they sought in each other's arms.

Ian tried not to think about how easily he had been converted to hedonic pursuits. Somehow he had managed to convince himself that this indulgence was only for a week's time, and if they refrained from actual sodomy no one's soul or life would be irreparably harmed. What was hardest to banish from his mind was consideration of how painful the inevitable separation would be.

Their parting would sting less if a physical release was all they shared, but after that exquisite moment, they still lay together, talking. Nicky seemed to delight in lavishing kisses and caresses on Ian's scars.

"Tell me what it's like," Nicky whispered one night, thumb rubbing gently across the folds of skin at the end of Ian's stump.

Some sensitivity had returned, an odd patchwork, so that Nicky's touch danced in and out of Ian's awareness.

"War?"

Nicky nodded.

Ian settled more firmly on his back. "The smell gets you first. And you can't see from the bloody smoke. If you aren't deafened by cannon, you'll wish you were when the screams start. Half the time you don't know where you are or where your men are or what they're shooting at."

"And this?" Nicky's warm kiss tickled across the wrinkled skin. "Tell me."

"I don't remember much." And sometimes he remembered too much. Lieutenant Archer's surprised face. A sensation of movement. The gut-wrenching separation from earth. Pain and red-tinged darkness. "We were ordered to the breach in the walls. To take out the defenders. The escalades were soaked with blood from the last company to try. I slipped. The mine went off. I woke in a field hospital."

"Thank God you slipped."

Ian doubted Lieutenant Archer's family would say the same.

Nicky shifted and looked down into Ian's face, moving the arm so the stump rested over the beat of Nicky's heart. "Did they ask you about taking it? Did you have to decide?"

There were flashes of it. Hearing the discussion. A tiny protest buried under the cowardly majority that prayed he would bleed to death and be done with it. The blessedly uncaring embrace of opium. He was far more aware when they removed the fragments imbedded in his chest.

"I never really was conscious enough. Even after, I had a fever. It was more than a week before I truly knew."

Nicky leaned down to kiss the lump of flesh over Ian's heart. As he did so often, Ian reached out with his missing hand, seeking the softness of Nicky's curls. Pain shot up Ian's arm, and he clenched an imagined fist.

So real, the memory of it, he could see it, knuckles, tendons, fingers. "I still feel it. As if it's there."

Surprise widened Nicky's eyes.

"I know it sounds mad. It's long healed. Long gone."

"No. I thought I was mad. Sometimes I swear I can feel it. I thought I was just remembering."

"That's probably it. There's no way you could feel it."

Nicky held up his own hand, fingers spread wide. "The Haunted Hand. A perfect tale for a dark December night."

"You are mad."

Despite the concern from his family, the quiet understanding of his cousins in Norwich, there was no one who simply accepted it. Who spoke of it without fear or pity. Who touched without horrified curiosity. Who even now could make Ian laugh.

"It still hurts." Nicky's tone made it statement rather than question.

Ian wanted to look away, but Nicky held his chin and kissed him.

"Then I must needs take your mind off it." Nicky licked the side of Ian's neck.

There were moments without words too.

And if in those moments Ian dared believe nothing could be more right than when they strained against each other, cocks rubbing together, mouths fused with shared heat, the truth came rushing back each morning when Nicky woke while it was still dark, dressed and slipped from the room.

The penultimate day of the year was the first that the weather deigned to permit decent hunting. They were out well past breakfast, only returning when the hounds floundered in deep drifts and lost the scent. Exhausted from the sudden increase in exercise atop little sleep, Ian dropped into oblivion that night with his hand still wrapped around Nicky's spent prick, damp forehead pressed into Nicky's neck as they lay on their sides.

He woke to Nicky's tongue lapping at him as if Ian's cock were made of sugar and cream, deep sounds of satisfaction echoing from Nicky's throat.

"Somewhat of an improvement over rising to reveille."

Nicky made a long wet swipe up Ian's prick with an accompanying smacking sound then looked up. "And rise you did."

Ian groaned as Nicky chuckled and returned to his task with an eager and meticulous commitment. Lips tight around the head, tongue flicking in unpredictable rhythm. Ian threaded his hand through Nicky's curls and dragged him forward. Something akin to shame but far more thrilling beat under Ian's skin at this use of his friend as Nicky groaned and swallowed, the soft tissue of his throat pulsing around Ian's prick.

Nicky took Ian to the back of his throat again and again, tongue and mouth working a magic that turned Ian's bones to liquid. He scarcely noticed what Nicky was about until he felt the rub of Nicky's finger—there.

Ian shuddered, and the tip of Nicky's finger slipped inside.

"What are you doing?"

Nicky raised his head. Without the slick bob of his mouth, Ian was all the more aware of the intrusion. It didn't hurt. It simply was. A sensation of pressure utterly neutral.

"I believe I am engaged in a practice Aristophanes called

74

sucking the sugar stick."

"He never said—"

Nicky sucked again, finger wiggling farther inside. The pressure was no longer indifferent. Ian's nerves could not seem to choose a side between pleasure and discomfort, a desire to pull away and the yearning to sink deeper into sensation, to capture Nicky's finger with his body.

Wrapping his hand in Nicky's hair, Ian tugged. "I mean what are you doing with—" Damn. He hadn't needed a word to refer to that particular location since he stopped needing a nurse. "—my nether eye."

Nicky's laugh tingled along Ian's most sensitive flesh until at last Nicky raised his head again, blue eyes locked on Ian's.

"Nether eye?"

It was hard to summon the tattered shreds of his dignity in a situation that transported dignity as swiftly as a ship of convicts to Botany Bay. "Well. The term is certainly as applicable as sugar stick."

Nicky rubbed his chin across Ian's ballocks, the unruly hair on his forehead tickling Ian's prick. "Oh, Ian. Only you could make use of a word like *applicable* with a mouth on your cock and a finger up your arse."

Ian thought of pointing out that there was no longer a mouth on his cock, but that would not answer the more...penetrative question. "What do you plan to do?"

Nicky looked up, his fixed gaze unnerving as his finger glided in and out as easily as if oiled. Each time he thrust it in, a sweet jolt raced along Ian's prick.

"I plan to frig your arse with my fingers while you use my mouth with your cock."

Almost against his will, Ian's hips moved to widen his legs.

He should stop this, but he couldn't. Because there was something bewildering about the sensations coursing through him and he might be damned forever, but the trip to hell was astonishingly sweet.

As if Nicky sensed capitulation, he wedged Ian's legs farther apart with the brace of broad shoulders before returning to plunge that heavenly mouth up and down Ian's prick. Nicky's finger tapped against something inside that seemed to be the very root of Ian's cock, and he clutched at the sheets, at Nicky's hair, anything that could ground him against the pleasure spiraling outward. A flush of scalding fluid gathered in Ian's balls.

"I will—must—Sweet Jesus—"

The flood took him and his hips snapped, prick ravaging Nicky's mouth and throat. Ian knew he would need to beg for forgiveness for the way his hand held Nicky fast, permitting no quarter until Ian had spent himself between Nicky's lips.

As his heart and lungs calmed, Ian composed the apology to be uttered as soon as he freed his bottom lip from the grip of his teeth, but he was distracted by the strangest scent. Engaged in a struggle against the lethargy that sought to pin him back beneath sleep's hold, he could only manage one question. "Why do I smell lavender?"

Ian awoke that morning to the sounds of Simmons stirring the fire, panic accelerating Ian's heart rate so suddenly he thought he might cast up the contents of his stomach. Had Nicky forgotten to return to his own bed? Every other morning Ian had awoken when Nicky did. He glanced around the room, but there was only Simmons, busy with a tea cup and toast rack on a tray.

"As you've missed breakfast, sir, I brought you something. His lordship suggested you might wish to sleep undisturbed."

Oh, did he? Ian shifted his body on the mattress. There were no lasting effects from their wildness last night, other than a pleasant lassitude preying on his limbs, and the strange scent of lavender lingered which had the unsettling result of making Ian's prick twitch. He prayed the odd association would not continue or he might have trouble in feminine company.

He intended to seek out Nicky and make clear the necessary boundaries to continuing their dalliance. Dalliance. That was not a word Ian had ever thought to apply to himself. He had always been so certain of the correct course, but Nicky had ever been able to lead him astray. First when they were boys, and even now with all that Ian knew of the world.

Despite what resuming physical relations cost Ian's sense of propriety, it grew harder to imagine their coming separation. To lose Nicky after having him again—it would be easier to part with another limb. The phantom pain of absence would be greater than it had with a physical amputation.

The dance on New Year's Eve was the high point of the Carleigh house party, so it made sense that Nicky would be so busy with preparations he could not be located, no matter how many of the bustling servants insisted they had "just this minute seen him, sir." Despite those assurances, Ian began to wonder if Nicky was avoiding a meeting because he knew last night had been beyond what Ian could in conscience offer.

That evening, Simmons' attentions had Ian looking fairly well-turned out in black coat, white stock and silver-embroidered waistcoat. The adjustments the valet had made to Ian's sleeves ensured that they hung better from his shoulders, drawing attention away from what was no longer there. Ian felt quite smart as he joined the other untitled bachelors waiting in the hall.

It took a single remark to cut him down as surely as a blast of grapeshot.

"Mr. Stanton, my, you look all the crack."

Lewes. Of course. Ian turned and offered a stiff bow. "Thank you, sir."

Julian Lewes wore almost the same clothes, black coat and embroidered waistcoat and formal knee breeches, but as he returned Ian's bow the polished elegance of the man's clothes and form made Ian feel about as well-turned out as if he had stopped to roll in shit on his way downstairs.

"I must say I am looking forward to this evening's entertainment."

Ian tried to stare the other fellow down. "Country dances and a child's game?"

"You do not care for Snapdragon? I find the treat sufficient compensation for the risk."

"I hardly think a few pieces of fruit are worth the cost of self-immolation."

"You mistake me. While I enjoy brandied raisins and almonds, I refer to the opportunity of becoming King of Misrule. I have several...creative ideas I look forward to acting on. The king's rule is absolute, after all."

Being able to decree what costumes were to be worn for the Twelfth Night party and making guests perform various forfeits was hardly as salacious as Lewes made it sound. After all, the Bishop of Warwick was a member of the party. Ian had been retiring early to steal more time with Nicky, leaving Charlotte under the watchful eye of Mrs. Collingswood who had assured him Charlotte's company was a joy. What if the evenings had grown licentious?

"You still have to select the golden raisin."

"I consider myself quite skilled at Snapdragon, Mr. Stanton." Lewes raised his fingers and waggled them. "Dexterity can be damned useful in tight places."

Before last night, Ian would have had no idea what prompted the leer that accompanied Lewes' words. Now they provoked a hot flush on Ian's cheeks.

Lewes reached out and plucked at something on Ian's left arm.

"A spec of lint, Stanton. I hate to think of something marring Simmons' magnificent work."

"You know him?"

"Oh yes. Recommended him to Lord Amherst myself. Of course, I knew Simmons before he took up valeting. Used to see him quite often in Betham's apartments. You'll have heard of Laurence Betham? Has the audiences in Drury Lane absolutely enthralled."

There could be no doubt of what Lewes was suggesting about Simmons, and the open pronouncement left Ian speechless.

"Of course they have parted brass rags since. Some dustup over an Italian painter who caught Betham's eye." Lewes buffed a nail against one of his cuffs. "Despite the merry dance His Royal Highness and his brothers carry out in public, they cannot match the lower classes for the absolute theater of relationships gone awry. I understood you could hear Simmons' reaction to finding them *in flagrante* all the way to Highgate." Lewes seemed to run down. "Oh, sorry, dear fellow, didn't mean to cause such consternation. Nicky said you were—ah, one of the lads, if you follow me."

The idea of Nicky sharing their intimate connection with Lewes, who was clearly as inveterate a gossip as any matron could hope to be, had Ian clenching his phantom fist again.

"No ill will meant, Stanton. It seems Lady Anna has managed to sort out the precedence at last." He nodded at the gallery doors. "Ready?"

Chapter Seven

Ian took up a post against the dark wood paneling and remained safely unnoticed through the first few dances, but Charlotte and Mrs. Collingswood found him while the musicians had paused for refreshment.

Charlotte's cheeks were flushed from exercise, dark eyes alight with merriment. Nicky had not danced with her once, so if she had formed some sort of attachment or hopes in that direction, she seemed unaffected by the loss of his attention.

At their request, Ian fetched cups of the Negus punch, tucking the extra cups safely between his right arm and his torso, dodging those who had already partaken of too much cheer and would be greeting the new year with an aching head.

Charlotte was laughing as he returned, a look of such joy on her face Ian could only hope that whoever had put her in such fine spirits would be more suitable for her than Nicky.

"Oh dear, Mr. Stanton. I should have considered the difficulty before adding my request to your errand." Mrs. Collingswood stepped forward to take a cup from him, handing it off to Charlotte.

"Not at all, Em. Ian prefers when people forget."

"My sister is quite correct. Though she knows better than to employ such familiar address."

"I don't mind, Mr. Stanton. Lady Charlotte and I have had such a very long acquaintance."

"Indeed?" He studied the widow. He supposed she might have been close to Charlotte's age, though her more reserved manner had led him to think she was older, even before her marriage. Marriage did seem to have an aging effect on females.

"Yes," Charlotte added. "After we met here at that Twelfth Night before you went away, Em and I saw each other quite frequently during my first Season. Nick—Lord Amherst and Lady Anna were kind enough to take us both under their wings."

"Though I was already quite on the shelf," Mrs. Collingswood said with a laugh.

"Never." Charlotte's defense was a trifle heated for loyalty to an acquaintance.

"Well, those days are past us now." Mrs. Collingswood gave Charlotte a beseeching look.

"And good riddance to it all."

Lord, Ian hoped Charlotte did not mean to bid farewell to her own days of seeking a proper match. Rayne had charged Ian with her well-being. If she returned to announce her intention to simply molder on the family estate, Ian was certain he would bear the brunt of the blame. He was considering how he might best remind her of her obligations when Mrs. Collingswood spoke.

"Now then, Lady Charlotte. Surely not all of it."

Charlotte softened. "No. Not all."

Ian brought his own cup to his lips, the hot spiced wine filling him with a relaxing warmth. Seeking out Nicky was something Ian had put off until he could be certain his temper would not get the better of him. Perhaps the Negus would soften him as well to the point where he might address Nicky without bringing Lewes' gossiping tongue into the conversation.

Ian had not noticed the opening bars from the musicians until Lord Anthony Montrose bowed to Charlotte. "Lady Charlotte, would you do me the honor?"

Some sort of glance passed between Ian's sister and Mrs. Collingswood, and then Charlotte nodded and placed her gloved hand in Lord Anthony's. Again the gaps in Ian's social training came glaringly to the fore. Although Mrs. Collingswood was technically out of mourning, she might be offended if he asked her to dance, and a missing arm made some of the steps awkward. Perhaps she would prefer to be escorted to a seat.

Placing his drained cup on a nearby tray, he offered the lady his arm.

"How thoughtful of you, Mr. Stanton. I would be honored."

Unwittingly, it seemed Ian had acquired a dance partner.

Although their form was burdened with Julian Lewes and a young lady Ian didn't recognize, and Mrs. Collingswood did indeed demonstrate a propensity for stepping uncomfortably close to a fellow's toes, Ian enjoyed the set. Mrs. Collingswood adjusted quickly to having a partner with one arm, both of hers gripping his one when the steps called for it, or placing her hand in an approximation of where his would be to avoid contortion. Even more satisfying, the young lady partnered with Lewes had a laugh like a bugle blown underwater. Ian hoped Lewes was saddled with it and her company for the rest of the night.

As injurious as this fortnight was to Ian's *mens sana*, it was a boon to his *corpore sano*. His body had not seen this much activity since his return from the Peninsula. When they had finished the set, he deposited Mrs. Collingswood on one of the sofas lining the gallery and quenched his thirst with another cup of Negus, draining it just as the musicians struck a dramatic flourish from their bows.

Nicky's father stood in the center of the room holding a single candle. Two footmen brought a scarred table and placed it in front of him while two others entered with a wide shallow bowl. As Lord Carleigh spoke, the wall sconces and chandeliers were extinguished until only his face was visible in the light of the candle.

"As the year draws to a close, we will choose our King and Queen of Misrule to guide our merriment through Twelfth Night. Her Majesty will be she who braves the dragon's flames to find a fig. His Majesty will be he who manages to select the single golden raisin from the bowl."

The back of one of the servants was just visible as he finished preparing the bowl. Ian had played many times as a child, the memory of scalded fingers and burnt tongue rather vivid, but those games were never for the stakes the Chatham family held as tradition. He had no particular desire to be responsible for entertaining bored members of the party for the final five nights, but possessed a strong will to see that whoever was so charged, it was not a reprobate like Julian Lewes.

"Now." Lord Carleigh raised his candle and began the chant. "Here he comes with flaming bowl." He lowered the flame and ignited the bowl of brandy.

The rest of the guests took up the chant as blue flames spread across the surface. "Don't he mean to take his toll. Snip! Snap! Dragon!"

Lord Carleigh took the privilege as host to be the first to try. His face looked demonic wreathed with eerie shadows as he reached in quickly, snatched a piece of dried fruit and popped it into his mouth to smother the flames. He held it up to show it was only an ordinary raisin and everyone clapped. A line formed on either side of the table, mostly younger guests, unwed ladies and gentlemen.

The chant went on as others risked scorched fingers and mouth to pluck out a sweet prize. "Take care you don't take too much. Be not greedy in your clutch. Snip! Snap! Dragon!"

Ian took his place in line. Lewes had already made one pass, netting a candied almond instead of a raisin for all his boasts of dexterity. Ian saw Charlotte's hand dart in just as he came to the table.

"The fig," she cried.

"Our queen." Lewes and Nicky and Lord Anthony surrounded her with deep bows.

Charlotte blew on her fingers as if to cool them. "Your queen commands you to fetch her more punch, you knaves."

Lord Anthony scurried off. She waved her fingers at Ian as if to show she was unharmed.

His turn had come.

"With his blue and lapping tongue, many of you will be stung."

Across the table now he could see Nicky, a fiery archangel in the blue light from the bowl. Ian reached out and plunged in his hand. Hot, but not burning, the oddest sensation of passing through fire without paying the price. He tried to examine the raisin as he brought it to his mouth, and it scalded his fingers. Black as pitch. He closed his mouth on the fiery treat, the liquor and the burn making the raisin all the sweeter, even as its juice scorched Ian's tongue.

"Snip! Snap! Dragon!"

Many players ceased to find it worth a longer exposure to the flames to seek any remaining treats. Ian took another turn. If pressed, he could claim he did not want Charlotte spending time as Lewes' consort, no matter how playful the circumstances; but he could not hide the true reason from himself. Ian could not bear the idea of Nicky at Lewes' beck and call, couldn't bear to see that arrogant bastard win.

Ian's fingers were tingling from near burns, bristling under the skin as if he were touching nettles. Lewes and Lord Anthony also refused to miss a try at the bowl.

"Do be careful, Stanton," Lewes remarked while biting down on another almond. "You know you've just the one hand left."

"Yes, Stanton. It's hardly sporting of you to keep Lady Charlotte's company all to yourself. You are her brother after all," Lord Anthony added.

Holding his back teeth together so tightly they ached, Ian ignored the idiots and plucked out a dried cherry, blowing on his fingers with burning lips as if such action could salve the sting.

"For God's sake." Nicky plunged his hand through the flames, rooting about for the space of a full heartbeat, during which Ian envisioned Nicky's sleeve afire, the blue tongues leaping up to his curls.

Nicky safely pulled out a handful of burning fruit and closed his fingers around them to smother the flames licking across his palm. He opened his hand again to show the golden raisin.

"All hail His Majesty, the King of Misrule."

Though Ian lent his voice to the acclaim, he felt far from cheered. He should have known relief that Charlotte would not be paired with such as Lewes, that she was safe from even Lord Anthony who might be inspired by the merriment to take liberties. Instead, he felt as ill as if the fruit he had ingested had been charred rather than sweetened by the brandy.

He should not have been surprised by losing, and at Nicky's intervention. How could Ian ever hope to be recognized as even as much a man as Lewes when other men were what he was not? Whole.

The sconces were once again lit, gifting Ian with the sight of Nicky sucking the sweet taste of brandy and fruit from his fingers.

Ian turned and grabbed one of the steaming towels a footman was circulating among the guests. As soon as he had wiped his hands, he found himself face to face with Nicky who took the towel, though after such a lewdly thorough tongue washing, Ian could not imagine why he needed it.

"Better now?" Nicky asked.

"Why? Because you were forced to rescue Charlotte from that man you call friend when I could not?"

"Think of her position, Ian. If you wish to get her married— only not to me—she can hardly show her light if you keep it veiled."

"But why you?"

"How dog-in-the-manger you are. Not Julian, not me. What was wrong with Tony? Is there a man here who could meet your ridiculous standards?"

It was fortunate Nicky had taken the towel or Ian might have flung it in his face like a gauntlet. "There is nothing wrong with seeking the best in oneself—or others."

"Maybe. But for we lowly mortals here, it's bloody exhausting to keep taking a fence that does nothing but grow higher with each try."

With that, Nicky quit his company, drawing Charlotte aside for a private conference. After a few moments, Nicky's laugh remained anything but whispered as it rang to the rafters.

"Your gracious rulers have declared a pleasant occupation for the morrow," Nicky said. "We will have a procession around the castle in a sleigh."

There was a murmur of approval.

"The sleigh to be drawn by our devoted subjects," Charlotte added.

"What? You would use us as horses?" Lord Anthony demanded.

"But of course." Charlotte favored him with a smile. "How better to serve us?"

Further refreshments were furnished for the guests, but as soon as the New Year had been dutifully sung and toasted in, Ian made for bed.

When the hair on the back of his neck prickled pleasantly, Ian knew who followed at his heels.

"Your king has a special request of you, Mr. Stanton."

"I am fatigued, Nicky. Perhaps tomorrow." Ian turned to face him. "And I promised your father I'd first foot."

Nicky's face held all the disappointment of a schoolboy seeing his favorite treat snatched away in the last instant. If there was a man who could turn a cold heart to such an expression, he was not Ian Stanton.

Ian bowed. "Very well, Your Majesty. What is it you desire of me?"

Nicky's grin was alarming.

Of course the royal request began with subject and king naked in bed. Ian's again.

"And now?" Ian might be unable to master a simple child's game, but at least he knew he could still offer pleasure to the man straddling his hips. Ian reached out and grasped Nicky's shaft, stroking him, lavishing the attention of his thumb on the slick head as the foreskin retracted.

"Your king desires you to lie there while he takes his pleasure."

"Oh, he does? And does his gracious majesty no longer enjoy this?" Ian favored Nicky with a faster stroke, a twist that brought a soft grunt before—

"Wait."

Ian stopped and Nicky swung off, moving to the edge of the bed and leaning down, arse up. The lump in Ian's throat weighed two stones as he swallowed it down. Why could he not control this desire? His fingers longed to trace the curving flesh, to seek out the entrance to Nicky's body, to find again the hot embrace of that channel. But he had made the limits clear. And for good reasons. No matter how pleasurable Nicky's finger had felt, there was a world of difference between finger and prick, even in the most modest of men. His reading had suggested even the Greeks disdained the practice as it turned the very idea of masculinity on its...well, on its arse. He would not ask that of either of them. Pain, history and the law all bespoke the risks.

Nicky's face returned to view, somewhat reddened from his previous position. "Here." He held a pretty little vial such as might be found on a lady's dressing table.

"What is it?"

Nicky removed the stopper and handed it off. "Oil."

This time the odor of lavender was overpowering.

"Perfumed oil," Nicky admitted a little sheepishly. "I pinched it from Anna's room. It was either lavender or roses, and I thought you would prefer the lavender."

"For what?"

Nicky put a generous drop or two on his fingers and then coated Ian's prick. "This." Nicky's hand glided, the warm and slick strokes positively maddening. "'Tis far better than spit alone."

Ian could scarcely gasp. The only thing akin was Nicky's mouth, his throat, hot and wet, but this was tighter, harder, a knowing, familiar grip.

"Trust your king." Nicky's hand moved faster, then slower. "Have you never tried something to ease the dry rub of skin? Did no one ever show you?"

Ian grunted then bit his lip. "Show me?"

"Come, Ian, you surely did not spend all your time soldiering without any release. I have confessed my sins."

"Some of them." Ian meant it to be a deep growl, but the harder Nicky stroked, the more difficult it became to contain the whimpers that sought escape on the backs of his words.

"What of you? Camp followers, a dutiful lieutenant, a fellow captain?"

Ian shook his head.

"You would lie to your king?" Nicky stopped the rhythm of his hand, fingers a tight ring over the base of Ian's prick.

"No. No one. I—" Ian closed his eyes. He could not face Nicky. Not with this between them, the truth that no one had ever touched Ian intimately but the man above him. Eyes still shut, he shook his head.

Nicky's unoiled fingers were gentle on Ian's chin, then his cheek, thumb light across his still-burning lips. "I would not have minded."

"I would have." Ian opened his eyes.

Nicky's eyes glittered in the candlelight, moisture gathering in the lower lashes. Ian thought Nicky might speak again, but he brought both hands to Ian's shoulders, holding him flat as Nicky lowered his head for a long, thorough kiss. Never rough or demanding, his lips and tongue offered, worshiped, celebrated. Despite the one drop of moisture that fell to Ian's cheek, he could feel Nicky's smile against his mouth. "You stupid, ridiculous, amazing man." Nicky raised his head for an instant and then kissed harder, tongue licking inside Ian's lips until Ian strove to move away.

"My mouth is still cursed raw from Snapdragon," he explained.

"As if I needed more proof." Nicky rolled his eyes heavenward, the lift of his head and neck driving his hips against Ian's, demonstrating again the usefulness of that oil. Ian's prick slid against Nicky's hard belly, pressure bringing insistent need to the fore.

"Nicky." Ian didn't care if he was pleading. Desire had a painful grip on his ballocks, pounded spikes into his thighs.

"Do you trust me?"

"As king?" Ian smiled.

"As king. As a man. As the man who wishes to share the heights of passion with you." Nicky was so rarely serious that his words acted as a rope tied to Ian's spine, pulling him in with the promise of safe harbor.

"Yes."

"Then simply lie there."

In that moment, determined not to break any more commandments than necessary, Ian could admit the truth to himself. He knew well what Nicky had planned, no matter how much Ian might pretend otherwise, no matter how much he wished he had the strength to refuse.

Nicky grabbed his glass vial again, thoroughly coating Ian's prick in the scented oil. If he spilled now from the pressure of Nicky's hand the decision would be taken from them both—but Ian held himself in check. As he watched, Nicky reached behind his body, eyes drifting closed, mouth going slack. Then he lifted himself and the head of Ian's prick was surrounded by wet, textured warmth. He could feel the space there, the muscles that sought to repel him even as Nicky's downward motion forced those muscles to yield.

Nicky groaned, the sound deep and low. Although Ian's grip on his will was as slippery as if his hands bore the coat of oil, it was strong enough to keep his hips flat against the mattress. He would not give way again. Would not surrender to the incredible force that drew his cock deeper. Would not force the issue no matter what Nicky claimed he wanted. As he sank lower, he caught his lip in his teeth, eyes twisted shut. Ian reached for Nicky's hips, forgetting again that one arm would lack enough force to move him off.

Nicky pushed down until his arse landed on Ian's thighs, sheathing every inch in hot, fluttering, slick sensation. His prick inside Nicky's body. Every breath and movement Nicky made licked like the brandy's blue flames across Ian's cock. How could it not be a consummation to pleasure Ian's very soul?

Nicky's breathy complaint brought a return to mundanity. "Christ, Ian. Move."

"But—"

"Of course it hurts, you wantwit, your fat cock is up my arse. Now do what I said and move."

Ian held Nicky's hips and rocked upward.

"Yes. Again." The furrowed concentration on Nicky's face relaxed.

Ian tried lifting him as he thrust his hips upward. Nicky's expression softened more, lips curving, eyes wide, the laughter they always held ready to burst free.

"C'mon, Ian, put your ballocks into it."

May as well be hanged for a sheep as for a lamb. Ian wrapped his arm around Nicky's back and somehow kept his berth deep in Nicky's body as he rolled him to his back.

Nicky looked up with his fallen-angel smile, and Ian drove his hips forward into that amazing clench of muscle and soft skin. A shudder rolled up his spine. "Sweet Jesus."

Nothing could ever match this, Nicky's legs wrapped high on his back, the sweet groans from his throat, the incredible pressure of his body on Ian's prick.

He wanted to stay here forever, deep steady rhythm of pleasure from the drag of Nicky's arse on Ian's shaft as he lifted his hips, the tight sucking kiss as he pushed back in. He raised his upper body, bracing his weight on his good arm and stump, and pumped slowly until Nicky shoved at his chest.

"Damn." Nicky's back arched as his hand found its way to his prick. His next words came out in gasps punctuated by Ian's thrusts. "You're. Too. Quick. A. Learner. By. Half."

Pleased, Ian arched his own back and the resulting cry Nicky bit off behind his hand inspired Ian to rise to his knees. It seemed only natural to pull Nicky closer, dragging his arse onto Ian's thighs with Nicky's enthusiastic help. His hand too, seemed to know to rest on Nicky's hip to steady him against the way Ian's body demanded a harder, faster, rougher pace.

"Yes." Nicky's hand on his prick matched the increase in speed, and Ian was torn between watching Nicky's hand and his face, desiring in equal measures to see pleasure take hold on his expression and the proof of it in the explosion from his body.

The first of the spasms that rocked Nicky's body were accompanied by a hoarse cry that had Ian casting an eye for a pillow to drop over Nicky's head even as pride burst from Ian's chest that he could cause him to make such a sound.

He was unprepared for the consequences of Nicky's satisfaction. As the first creamy burst shot from his prick, the muscles in his arse clamped harder on Ian's own cock. Nicky's release pulled Ian's into that warm body, a hot rush of seed shuddering from him even as Nicky continued to fire streams onto chest and belly. The force of the contractions sapped the strength in Ian's spine until he could only fall forward onto Nicky, feeling more beastlike than human and oddly uncaring of the distinction.

Nicky shifted beneath Ian's weight until the mattress bore its fair share and then stroked a hand down Ian's sweaty spine. For once, Ian knew words were superfluous and he allowed himself to be soothed into sleep with the caress.

When Nicky woke, it was nearly the blue of night, the sky giving a hint of warning that dawn was not far off. Sometime during the night, Ian must have gotten up to drag the quilt over them. Nicky luxuriated in their warm nest, stretching his limbs, feeling a twinge of hard use in his arse and thighs. He smiled and teased Ian's side whiskers with a finger, slipping his hand out of reach when Ian swatted at it. A light touch on his nose brought a frown, but Ian still did not wake. A kiss on his neck wrought a sigh and Ian rolling away.

With his own lips pursed in a frown, Nicky slid off the bed and pulled on his breeches and shirt then walked around the bed to face Ian.

"What?" Ian opened his eyes.

Nicky smiled. "Ha. Caught you faking."

Ian tugged the counterpane over his head. Nicky shoved it back.

"I say again, what?"

"You're rather testy. Didn't you sleep well?"

"I was enjoying a blissful rest. Until now." Ian's usual stuffy tone held a chill instead of the trace of humor Nicky often found in it.

A kernel of apprehension took root in his gut. "It's almost morning." He brazened it out. "I just wanted to wish you good morning and a Happy New Year."

"Which could not be done at breakfast."

"Well, not with a kiss."

As he suited deed to words, he found Ian's lips hard and unresponsive.

"I see. You have had your use of my body and now it's fare-thee-well. I suppose this is what one can expect of soldiers. What a libertine you are."

"I'm a libertine?" Ian sat up, face dark and hard in the dim glow from the fire. The kernel of apprehension in Nicky's belly sowed a full field of dread. He stepped back.

Ian swung his feet to the floor. "I told you how I felt about that. And yet you insisted."

A smarter man might have left his lover to boil himself in his own ill humor, but Nicky's wits were losing ground to his temper.

"And you were so very unwilling your cock could not even rise to its duty, is that it?"

"It was under orders, King of Misrule."

Ian's rigidity could be frustrating. It could and did make Nicky need to vent his feelings with a quick bout of exercise before he could manage to keep a civil tongue in his head. But this. It was as if Ian was so very bound to his own cross that he sought to blame Nicky for nailing him there.

"That was play." The heat of Nicky's anger froze under an emotion too powerful to name. "If you wish to cry rape, make your accusation plain. Say it and damn yourself."

Ian looked away.

Nicky stepped to the fire and took a deep breath, but nothing could warm the cold that ate away inside. If he stayed, if they kept this course, the emotion would have its name, the worst in the world: hate.

He turned back. "It was play," he said again. "I thought if you had the excuse, it would make it easier, just as I claimed Simmons was ill each night."

Ian pulled the quilt across his lap.

Nicky turned his lips in, but his feelings would have their bent. "God knows I've done everything I can. And I have embraced all that you are, because I would not have you any other way, but this is more than a saint could bear."

Without a single blink, Ian's dark eyes met his. Even then Nicky's heart wanted to drive him to his knees and beg Ian to understand what he was so eager to cast off like old linens. If he would only offer the smallest sign... But he merely accepted Nicky's words as if they had no meaning.

"I will not allow you to twist this thing between us into something ugly and obscene to salve your misguided conscience. If you cannot accept it, so be it. I had rather none, than to let you make me loathe myself too."

Ian's hand gripped the counterpane tight across his lap, but he offered nothing.

"A Happy New Year to you then, Mr. Stanton. I hope it brings you all you desire."

Chapter Eight

New Year's Day brought Ian more solitary freedom than the most devout of hermits could wish. When he made his excuses to their majesties, claiming he felt unable to draw a sleigh given his injury, Nicky responded with a curt nod that offered no insight into his feelings. Charlotte was more forthcoming with a roll of her eyes, but no one in the party demonstrated any particular distress at his absence. The game went on with no abatement of joy. Even the Dowager Duchess of Coventry was taking a pass, the four-in-hand on her sleigh made up of the company's most handsome bachelors.

It appeared all the ladies were going to get a turn, as Nicky hopped down after his first ride and acted as whip to the slower teams.

Ian turned away from the windows in the study to find Mrs. Collingswood beside him.

He bowed. "I had thought you would be enjoying the sleighing party."

"Oh, I cannot. I suffered a...fall several years ago and the cold weather endangers my breath. I can only enjoy the briefest moments outdoors in the winter." Her expression grew wistful.

"I am sorry for your injury, madam."

"I am too." She smiled, but her gaze seemed distant, fixed on remembered pains.

His own chest exceedingly heavy this morning, he forgot himself enough to ask. "Do you miss him?"

Mrs. Collingswood started from her reverie. "My husband?"

"I beg your pardon for presuming on our brief acquaintance. It is certainly not my place to inquire." But he thought he would rather like to know. Did the weight ever ease? Could you draw deeply of the air in a month? A year?

For all the pain his words brought, Nicky had the right of it. What they had shared would have run its course in a matter of days. There would be no logical reason for Ian to remain at Carleigh, or for Nicky to visit Ian in Oxfordshire. Indeed, an attempt to rekindle something best left behind in youth had been doomed from the start. The sooner desire was reconciled with reason the better off they would both be.

Mrs. Collingswood searched Ian's face and appeared to come to a decision. "Would it distress you very much to hear that I do not?"

It did not, and he said so. He had heard nothing but ill of Captain Collingswood, and he was pleased to know that this good woman did not grieve unnecessarily.

"It is curious, though," she said. "Sometimes the memory is fresh and other times it is as dead as last autumn's leaves."

As it was with Badajoz. Sometimes he could recall every second, and other times he could not even remember whether the day had been cloudy or fair. Could no longer call to mind Lieutenant Archer's features or the slippery feel of blood on the escalade.

"I believe I have some experience with that," he said.

They both watched as the dowager's four floundered in a drift, Nicky railing over them and slashing a buggy whip that fell nowhere near their backs.

"Is there nothing that can be done for your complaint?" Ian asked.

She gazed at him directly, blue eyes serene. "I was told my rib pierced my lung. I consider myself fortunate to have any breath not tainted by grave dirt."

Taken aback by her frank pronouncement, Ian struggled for words. None seemed to come.

"But then I imagine we both know how precious life is." She offered him another smile, but her intent tone was at odds with her placid expression. "I for one intend to seize the second chance I have been given."

Although the lady clearly spoke from her heart, Ian felt her words like a rebuke.

But what if you cannot? What if the act of seizing your chance requires you to set aside honor and duty? He could not ask, even if she could answer.

"I beg your pardon, Mr. Stanton. Lady Anna is abed with the headache and as I am cousin to the family, Lord Carleigh asked me to stand in her stead to be certain the riders and horses were offered proper warming when they returned."

Ian looked back through the glass. The four "horses" had overpowered the "groom", tackling him to the snow while the duchess gesticulated from her sleigh. Ian knew that no matter how cold the snow, with Nicky in the thick of it, the whole party was laughing.

Nicky cursed the leather strap that was supposed to be holding his ice skate on his boot and pushed unevenly against the ice to find an out-of-the-way spot to adjust it. Charlotte was presiding over races, the losers threatened with elaborately humiliating forfeits to be meted out following dinner. A large section of the pond—which bore the generous title of Green Lake—had been swept free of snow by servants and some enthusiastic guests to permit a skating party. Nicky was about to rejoin it when the strap slipped off his heel again.

"Pig-swiving shit."

"Is that still your favorite appellation?" Julian Lewes skated up next to him, offering the brace of his arm as Nicky wrestled with the strap once more.

Julian skated the way he did everything, with the grace and beauty that had left a younger Nicky breathless with hunger. Now he was only grateful for a sympathetic ear.

Julian's voice was dry. "What has the poor piece of leather done to suffer such calumny?"

"If you're not going to be helpful, Julian, you can take your wit elsewhere."

"Oh. It's that way, is it?" Julian looked across the ice to where Ian hovered like a petulant crow at his sister's side. "The irreproachable Mr. Stanton has remained true to form. The whole family has ever been a sanctimonious lot, dear Lady Charlotte excepted, of course."

"Of course," Nicky gritted out. The trouble was not with the heel after all. The cross straps had shifted. Nicky tugged them down hard enough to nearly cut through his boot.

"Now do you see the value inherent in being an uncaring bastard?"

"Because you are a bastion of joy?"

"At least I'm not savaging my foot with a piece of leather."

"I'm not. Shit." Nicky gave up on trying to balance on one foot and dropped to his knee to work at the straps.

Julian chuckled. "Deeply conscious of the honor, Amherst, but I have sworn never to marry."

"Bugger off."

"Ahh. I should very much like to. Do you think Lord Anthony could be persuaded to sample richer tastes? I'm afraid I've run through all the qualifying members of your groomsmen."

Nicky was never sure whether he could believe everything Julian said. "You are incorrigible."

"And why not? I possess the three things guaranteed to make life pleasant: wealth, power and a big cock."

In spite of himself, Nicky laughed. Certain at last his skate would not part company with the boot and send him sprawling, he rose to his feet. They skated slowly back to the rest of the group. "There are other things to enjoy."

"Name one."

"Companionship."

"Love, you mean."

Nicky shrugged.

"If love possesses all the power with which the poets endow it, why has it not solved your dilemma with the erstwhile Captain Stanton?"

There was no answer, so Nicky offered none.

"You see? You will never witness me chase after some imagined bond that men use to justify their most ridiculous behaviors."

"And what of women?"

"As I am not one of those delicate creatures I cannot speak to their motivations, though I suspect were they permitted honesty, they would be just as guided by pleasure as men."

Nicky knew one in particular who would let nothing stand in her way. "Charlotte, damn it." Nicky had been putting off telling her.

"Insulting his sister now?"

"No. May I beg a favor?"

"Are you going to your knees again?" Julian arched a brow.

"Would you take over the races? I need to speak with Lady Charlotte."

"An appointment as Prince Regent? Is this some sort of insinuation about the fit of my waistcoat?"

"You are slender as a rail, as always. Will you?"

"I suppose. If you give thought to what I said."

"I will. And you give thought to this. Someday you're going to be twice as wretched as I and I will laugh to watch you fall headlong into the abyss."

"I shall look to see Lucifer buying his own pair of ice skates on the self-same day."

Nicky had scarcely expected Ian to crawl into his bed and beg for forgiveness, but rather hoped for something besides a blank look as they joined Charlotte near the start of the races.

Feel something, damn you. Argue. Create a scandal to keep the gossips buzzing for a year.

Ian lowered his gaze.

Nicky glared a hole right through the top of that bowed head. Ian could make love to his blasted honor and duty and much good would it do him on a cold lonely night. Nicky would take Julian's advice. Maintain a pretense of sangfroid until his blood cooled in truth. And when the cold bothered him, he'd fuck it into another man's body, slam it down someone's waiting throat, and at the moment when his body flooded with ecstasy, he'd still hate Ian for destroying what could have been perfect between them.

He led Charlotte over to the far side of the pond, where a spot of shade might shield them from the blinding sunlight reflecting off ice and snow.

She tilted her chin at him, heart-shaped face nothing like the lean one belonging to her brother, but they shared the same expressive brown eyes.

Faced with such a look, he spoke in fits and starts, at last stammering out, "The plan has failed. We won't be getting married."

Her eyes immediately filled with tears, but their softness disappeared behind an iron will as strong as her brother's. "You promised."

"I know, but how could that serve us now?"

"You told me, you swore while I sobbed my heart out on Emily's wedding day that you would make certain I never had to undergo such a fate. That you'd do everything in your power to help me." If she had not been on skates, Nicky was certain she would have stomped her foot.

"And you in turn would get me word of Ian. I have not forgotten. But, sweet, can't you see how impossible this would be now? Do you truly want a household where your brother will not set foot?"

"Right now I don't care if the both of you go straight to hell where you belong." She shoved at him, and he maintained his balance on the thin blades with wind-milling arms. She had surprising strength for a tiny creature muffled in fur scarf and bright red mantle.

There was a reason he had put off telling Charlotte. She was free with all the passion her brother held in check.

"Do you know what I believe, you foul perjurer? You think

you'll find another man with a biddable sister for your *arrangement*." She made the word sound as licentious as an advertisement for a brothel.

"You know that's not true. I just think perhaps with cooler heads we can find some other way to ensure your happiness. One that doesn't involve Ian becoming my brother-in-law."

She wiped her glove across her face. "There is none. Do you have any idea what these last years have been like? The waiting? You give up in a week when you told me that nothing would stop you from having Ian."

"Nothing but Ian it seems."

"You're just a—a—"

"Pig-swiving?" he suggested. Perchance he'd have more luck appealing to Charlotte's better humor than Ian's.

"Wastrel."

She turned away, but not before he saw the tears flood her eyes again, sparkling spurs to his conscience. In that moment, he wanted to lavish on her all the comfort her brother rejected, soothe and pet her as he would one of his horses.

"Very well. I will honor my promise. We will marry and Emily shall come to live as your companion."

She tilted up her chin again. Would that appealing look work as well on Ian's face? Nicky would have given his own right arm to see such an expression used to implore his forgiveness, though he expected he had a better chance of sprouting wings.

"Truly?" she asked.

"Yes." He glided closer, near where she drifted into the shade of a thick stand of evergreen.

The sound of a pistol echoed across the ice. Charlotte's head shot up looking for the source, but Nicky knew it came from under their feet. After such a bitter cold week who would think the ice could crack?

He glanced down. "Charlotte, come toward me. Slowly."

Fear dried her tears. "Nicky?"

"Just start to skate. Come on, sweet."

She looked down at the cracks around her feet, but she was Ian's sister and brave and smart. She took a few careful gliding steps.

"That's it." There was another booming crack, rolling long and hard as thunder. Nicky dove for the bright red cloak before it vanished under the ice.

Ian had thought to skip the skating party, but with Mrs. Collingswood staying behind, someone had to look after Charlotte, so he fitted the skates to his boots. Skating without the counterweight of his arm proved far more difficult than relearning to ride or walk, so there was naught to do but stand about awkwardly and try not to think of anything at all. Sometimes it almost worked.

Lord Anthony and Sir Timothy Neville had insisted on a best two out of three, racing away at the signal to start, which Lewes had supplied with exaggerated ennui.

As Lewes' gaze remained fixed on the swing of their morning coats as they dashed away, he startled Ian with sudden speech. "Do you know why you despise me so, Stanton?"

"Does it matter?"

"Not to me. But it seems to matter a great deal to you."

Ian wondered which of the two options would be most humiliating: to listen to Lewes impugn his character or to skate away, single arm flailing about for balance. There was a third choice. He could offer enough of a public insult to institute a duel, let Lewes kill him, and put an end to a miserable existence.

He took the most cowardly way out and stood there. "Nothing you could say would be of any possible interest to me."

"You loathe my existence because you envy it."

So be it. He would let Lewes kill him. "Why would I envy a poxy whore?"

Lewes simply laughed. "Because I enjoy nothing but pleasure as I choose to take it. And you hate having such an example when you are terrified to have the smallest bit of joy for yourself. I pity you."

"Do not waste it on me. I am certain there are others who would—"

At the first boom, Ian's senses took him straight back to Badajoz. Blood, smoke, screams. Screams. He searched the ice frantically for Charlotte's bright red cloak. He found it just as the second crack reverberated across the sky. This time the scream was here, not in his mind, and the flash of red disappeared, as did a darker patch beside it.

He started for them immediately, faster than he'd thought his balance could manage.

Lewes skated beside him. "Off to drown yourself as well?"

Lewes spoke no more than the truth. Ian could not hold Charlotte and swim, and no amount of wishing in the world would make it otherwise.

"Hoi!" Lewes called back to the figures in the distance. "Bring a broom, a stick, whatever you can find." His voice dropped back to normal speech. "Yes indeed, some fine specimens of English pluck there. Half of them have already scrambled to the bank."

Ian didn't care. Everything he held dear in the world was somewhere under this ice, and he was going to get it back or die trying.

Squinting against the sun's glare, he saw an arm wave.

"There."

He dashed off. The ice shuddered once more, no loud crack this time, a rumbling groan. Ian calculated the distance to the dark patch on the ice and launched himself in a dive, sliding across on his belly, muttering a swift prayer that his momentum wouldn't carry him in.

There were two of them in the black water. Alive, but struggling in heavy wet clothes. Nicky held Charlotte, their faces dead white, their breath shallow and quick.

At first Ian thought Nicky refused the hand Ian thrust forward, but then realized Nicky was handing off Charlotte. Her icy hand slipped from Ian's fingers and he gripped her hood instead, hauling with every fiber in his body. His breath, his pulse, every minutiae of sound enveloped in the frosty clouds of air as he labored to pull his sister free of the water's grip.

Movement at last. Or perhaps just the ice breaking apart beneath him. Then there were hands gripping his legs, tight as shackles.

"Pull, Stanton. Pull, you blasted ox." Lewes' final word was a barely heard grunt.

Ian gathered everything inside him for another effort and Charlotte was out, sliding back with them.

He was dimly aware of Lewes wrapping her in his coat, but all Ian could see was Nicky, still struggling like a fly in treacle.

Each time he put his hand on the ice to push himself out, it broke away.

Ian crawled toward him, shoving his stump against the ice for traction as he held out his hand. The ice heaved beneath him and again Lewes grabbed at his legs, hauling him back.

Nicky was closer now, but so were the cracks in the ice.

"It's breaking apart. We'll have to wait for the broom." Of course Lewes would turn caitiff now.

"We can't wait." Ian glanced about. "Charlotte. Your scarf. What is it made of?"

Shivering and almost blue, Charlotte seemed to not understand. Ian crossed over and grabbed it.

"My tippet? It's mink." Her fingers fumbled as she tried to help him unwind the scarf that was more than twice her height in length. "Please save him. He would not have gone in but for me."

Ian made no complaint as Lewes reached in and pulled the scarf free.

"Put that coat back on and crawl out of the way. Don't stand until you hit the bank. Lewes, get her safe." Ian didn't even look back to see if his orders were followed, as he wrapped the sodden fur in a coil. Pinning one end under his stump, he sent the rest spinning toward Nicky.

"Caught it," Nicky called back but his voice was weak with strain. Any longer and he'd freeze to death, even if they saved him from drowning.

Again Lewes took Ian's legs as they tried to haul Nicky out of the icy water. Ian kicked away the grip. "I have to get closer. We'll never pull him out from here."

"If you cut my face with your skates, Stanton, I'll let the both of you drown."

There was perhaps a yard of stretched mink between them now. Nicky's head and shoulders became visible for an instant and then sank back. And again.

Ian had ever thought the color of desperation was red. Blood spilling from his fingers as he fought to staunch a wound. Blood pouring from the shattered end of his arm. But now he knew it was white. Cold and empty and eternal. He was not leaving Nicky here in this frozen void.

Ian pulled until it felt like the sleeve on his coat was all that held his arm in the socket.

Nicky's torso flopped over the edge of the hole. He kept his grip on the scarf, but made no further move to save himself. And the ice still groaned beneath them.

Lewes gave a sharp tug to Ian's legs. "Come on, you useless sodding cripple. Or do I have to do this for you too?"

Ian reached down and found a strength he never knew he had. Even his phantom arm lent its invisible power as Ian risked rising to his knees to haul them backward with all that he was. All that he would ever be. Because if he failed this, he was joining Nicky in that icy blankness.

Ian fell back onto Lewes and Nicky came with him. Aching with every beat of his pulse, Ian reached down, and between them, they dragged Nicky to safety.

At last people seemed to have been jolted into activity, running toward them, brooms and coats in hand.

"I still hate you," Ian said.

"Thank God for that." Lewes' answer was as fervent as a prayer.

Chapter Nine

The local doctor had been enjoying a cup of cheer with Lord Carleigh, so there was no need to send for him. There was no medicine for a chill but warmth. Outwardly with blankets and hot stones tucked in about them, and inwardly, with brandy and broth.

When Ian left Charlotte an hour past sunset, she was sitting up against the pillows, sipping a cup of chocolate. Mrs. Collingswood had not left Charlotte's side since she was brought into the house. Indeed, Ian wondered if the lady might not take a chill by association so closely did she affix herself to his sister. Assured that Charlotte showed no signs of catarrh or fever, not even a sniffle, Ian went again to check on the other patient, but the word was the same, his lordship was resting.

Nicky had roused briefly as they hauled him onto a farm sledge to bring him home, blinking about and coughing out some water along with the single question, "Charlotte?"

"Safe, thanks to you," Ian assured him, and Nicky sank back under the pile of coats and blankets. Ian and Lewes rode with him on the sledge. Lewes cultivated an image of insouciance, but Ian could tell it was a façade from the frequent glances directed at Nicky's too-pale face.

Ian also suspected Nicky was aware of what was happening around him, but too exhausted to do anything about it. Ian remembered that state all too well, one's body so abused it fell out of charity with one's spirit, issued the cut direct, and sank inward past conscious control. A familiarity with the state did not ease concern to see it on one so dear, however.

Heedless of Lewes' presence, Ian slipped his hand beneath the pile of coats and found Nicky's, squeezing warmth into the cold limp fingers. "Come, Nicky. Who will remind me what an unmitigated ass I am if you don't?"

"I shall be happy to perform the office at any time," Lewes said, but the words failed to cut.

The corners of Nicky's mouth twitched and the two watchers let out pent breath in perfect unison. Ian was certain it was the last time they would ever be in such agreement.

Now Ian hovered outside Nicky's room, unsure if he should knock. Lord Carleigh and Lady Anna were within. Neither had been anywhere else since Nicky had been carried upstairs, despite his reassuring though weak-voiced protests that he could walk.

Simmons came out carrying a tray.

"Still asleep, sir. But I'm sure they wouldn't mind if you were to go in."

Warmth crept into Ian's cheeks. Since Lewes told him of Simmons' affair with an actor, Ian had tried to banish the idea to a frozen wasteland in his mind, especially since such experience probably left Simmons all too aware of why Nicky visited Ian each night. Standing here now with Simmons, Ian felt the nature of his and Nicky's relationship couldn't be more plain.

Ian swallowed. "Thank you, Simmons."

"He'll pull through, sir. Lord Amherst has always enjoyed the best of health."

Ian offered his gratitude again and tried to school his face into something appropriate for Nicky's family before he tapped on the door.

Lord Carleigh's deep voice invited him in, but since he addressed Ian as Simmons, Ian simply stuck in his head. A blast of heat nearly knocked him back a pace.

"Ian, lad, come in." Lord Carleigh launched himself from his chair and strode over to grip Ian's hand and shoulder, shaking both roughly. "Thank you. They told me you and Mr. Lewes pulled him out. That no one else would risk it."

"Ni—Lord Amherst is the one deserving of praise. If he had not acted, I would have lost a sister."

"Nonetheless, you have my gratitude. I knew when he first brought you to visit you would be good for him. Just the sort of sober chap to keep him from getting in over his head."

Ian looked down at the carpet. He had made up his mind to beg forgiveness from the man so still in the middle of that big bed, to seize what they could of happiness between them, but Lord Carleigh's words brought home the audacity of such a decision. They were not beholden to only each other. The bonds of family were strong.

Lady Anna came around from the other side of the bed. Her greeting was less effusive, but still warm. "Mr. Stanton, it seems we have made an even exchange, a sister for a brother. Thank you."

"The praise is undeserved. Anyone would have done as much."

"Anyone didn't. Great lot of profligate scoundrels eating us out of house and home." Lord Carleigh stomped over to poke at the fire.

"Father..." Lady Anna turned back to Ian. "It has been a terrible strain. Father hates feeling helpless." Voice lowered to a

113

whisper, she said, "I think he should rest. And he must have something to eat. Could we impose on you further and ask you to sit with him?" She nodded at the man under the pile of blankets. Her manner suggested she was more troubled than her father. Her hands kept twisting in front of her, and her brow remained furrowed.

"It would be no imposition at all, my lady."

"Father, Mr. Stanton will stay with Nicholas. You need to take some dinner."

"I am perfectly well as I am."

"Of course you are. But a bit of dinner will elevate our spirits."

Her managing ways, though couched with a maternal air, reminded Ian of Nicky at his most high-handed.

"If he wakes, if you need anything at all, just call," she said as she shut the door behind them.

He had to say that Nicky's color was much improved, skin back to its warm tones, cheeks and lips regaining their cherubic pink. After five minutes, Ian was so warm he had to remove his coat, a feat Simmons' clever tailoring had made easier to perform for himself. He was definitely letting Timpet go. It would be too heart-wrenching to suffer such a falling off in quality.

After ten minutes, Ian unbuttoned his waistcoat. No wonder Lady Anna had been so eager to vacate the stifling heat. He swung his chair around, availing himself of the chance to study the patient. Nicky's breathing was even, and every so often the tip of his tongue flicked between his lips, an activity Ian found so amusing and endearing it made his breath catch each time he witnessed it.

The gold curls were glued to his forehead with sweat, so Ian reached out and brushed them back. Nicky's eyes opened. "Come to eulogize the remains?"

114

"I'm sorry I woke you."

"Why are you half-dressed?"

Before Ian could answer, Nicky began shoving at the pile of quilts and blankets heaped on him. "Christ. Get these bloody things off me before I suffocate."

Ian helped him but insisted on leaving the last few. "You'll thank me when the sweat starts to cool."

"In this room?" Nicky glared at the fire as if it offered a personal affront.

"You were rather chilled."

"I expect so. The ice broke. And Charlotte went in with it."

He seemed to be asking Ian for confirmation so he gave it. "Yes."

"I went after Charlotte and you got her out and then pulled me out with some fur scarf?"

"A tippet of mink. She says it should recover."

"Well, it's a good thing you've those two extra stones on me."

"I think rather my arm may never be the same."

"Stretch out a few inches, did it?"

Ian lifted both his arms out straight. "Lacking a source for comparison it's hard to say for certain. Feels as if that might be the case." He dropped his arms at his sides.

Nicky shivered. "Perhaps one more of the quilts."

Ian dragged up two and Nicky tucked them around him. "Charlotte is well. She was not in the water as long as you were. Thank you."

"Thank you," Nicky returned gravely.

Ian reached up and tugged at his cravat. He wished he dared untie it. At last he looked at Nicky. "You were right. I am an unmitigated ass."

"I heard you. In the sledge."

"I thought you might have done." For once, Nicky's expressive features offered Ian no clue about how to proceed. "Can you forgive me?"

Nicky didn't speak, so Ian leaned down, pressing a kiss to his lips. They were both slick with sweat, but Ian didn't care. Nicky's lips were warm, alive, and sliding open to the light pressure.

When Ian raised his head, Nicky's expression was unchanged.

"Is this some wild gesture at a life and death moment? Will your behavior be once again explained away by an excuse so that on the morrow you will claim duress?"

It was appalling to hear his actions described so, but at the moment, Ian could find no grounds for disagreement. "No. You were in the right before you nearly died."

"Comforting to know."

"But as I am speaking the truth, what you ask—" At Nicky's frown, Ian clarified, "What we both want, can't you see that it fills me with fear?"

"Of course I can. But if we were to ever let fear control us, how could any of us seek happiness, to touch on the betterment you aspire to?"

"I know Phaedrus had the right of it with his army of lovers. You make me a better man, Nicky. You make me feel whole."

Nicky reached out and gripped Ian's maimed arm, pulling him forward into an embrace. Ian exhaled into Nicky's skin. If only it were as easy to bury all cares, all fears and pain. Nicky's hand fell on his head and held him tight against his neck.

Ian let out another long breath. What good did it serve, to

cling to an ideal that excluded the person he most wanted to please? "I thought I had lost your regard."

Nicky's hand stroked through Ian's hair, landing heavily on his neck as a soft laugh rumbled between them. "Regard? Ian, only you could come home from war wounded in body and spirit and still sound like a classics scholar. You hold that always. And my honor and my passion and much more."

Ian swallowed and lifted his head. "I don't deserve it."

"Who could?" Nicky began with a joke and then his face became serious. "But you do, Ian. You are more deserving than most. Whose face did I see peering at me over the ice? Who was brave enough to risk his neck to save mine?"

"Julian Lewes came to your aid as well," Ian admitted with scrupulous honesty.

"God, I am sure to hear of that. Is he no longer a disgusting bastard, then?"

"He remains so. But he also saved your life. I could not have done it alone."

"You would have found a way."

There was a tap at the door and Ian pulled free, sitting upright in his chair, dragging on his coat.

"Yes," Nicky called in answer to a second tap.

Simmons stepped in, carrying a tray. "My lord! It's good to see you looking yourself." He set the tray on the bed, and Nicky made a face at what was clearly sickroom fare. Thin soup and something steaming and clotted, though how anything could steam against the heat of the room Ian could not say.

Simmons put the tray on the washstand. "I'll let his lordship and Lady Anna knows you are awake and see if I can find you something more hearty in the kitchen." He nodded at Ian as he passed on his way to the door. "It will only be a minute, sir."

Ian understood the warning. He buttoned his waistcoat, nursing a deep resentment that this interlude should not end with them embracing through the night. It was unfair and it was maddening, but the one thing it wasn't was shameful. The notion came as such a surprise it must have shown on his face.

"What?"

Ian shook his head and looked at the door.

"Come to me tonight?" Nicky whispered.

"Your rest...?"

"I have had a sufficiency. And I assure you all parts are in working order. Besides, what could warm me more?" Nicky made a salacious waggle of his eyebrows.

Ian had never been more anxious for nightfall in his life. Despite the events of the day, it seemed the house would not quiet enough for him to risk the quick trip across the hall. When at last he was certain he would not be observed, he darted into Nicky's room and locked the door behind him.

The fire still blazed and lamps were lit on every surface. The room glowed, but for Ian all the warmth in the room was waiting in the bed.

"I thought it would be morning before you were here." In his nightgown, Nicky looked years younger. He stripped it off, revealing the man beneath, then held the covers open for Ian.

"Are you certain you are well enough?"

"Come over here and ask again."

Ian moved to the foot of the bed.

"I think you have mistaken this party for a masque. The invitation was to come in your finest." Nicky crawled forward and opened Ian's dressing gown.

"It is my best nightshirt."

"But your finest features—" Nicky gave a sharp tug to lift the long tails of Ian's shirt. "Ahh. There they are."

Ian let Nicky finish pulling the nightshirt over his head. As it dropped behind him, Nicky's palm rubbed across Ian's cheek.

"You're freshly shaved."

"Simmons offered." Ian felt the heat in his cheeks. "I think he sensed I was in great anticipation."

"Of what, I wonder?"

"Now who's an ass?" Ian shoved Nicky to his back and climbed on top of him.

Warm. So warm. Skin gold in the light. With Nicky spread out beneath him, Ian had never cursed his missing arm more. He wanted both hands to cover that flesh, both thumbs to rub across the dark pink nipples, wanted a double grip in those wild curls as he lifted Nicky up for a kiss.

"Don't. Please, Ian."

"What?"

"Glower."

"I'm not—I just want—"

Nicky reached up and rolled him down onto the bed so they were on their sides, facing each other. "Name it."

Ian couldn't put a name to all his wants, and he had precious little time. This was a farewell as much as it was a celebration. In two days, he and Charlotte would be southbound in their coach. A year would scarce be long enough to sate himself on all he wanted of Nicky.

Above all, he wanted to humble himself in worship. Let mouth and hand and body speak to his regret at not recognizing the gift Nicky had offered sooner. To show he knew, even if in future all they shared were a few stolen moments, those moments could make life so much more than the passing of time in service to one ideal or another.

He ran his hand over Nicky's hip.

"You want my arse again?" Nicky's smile held a warmth Ian felt in his bones.

"No. I want you to take mine."

Nicky drew back as if to afford a better point of observation.

"Don't do that."

Nicky cocked a brow. "Do what?" But the amusement in his face was clear to read.

"Make me any more nervous, you bastard."

Nicky rolled overtop of him, kissing the very taste from Ian's mouth. When it seemed they would have to part or suffer asphyxiation, Nicky dove back for more, the tingling pressure of lips and tongues making blood beat hot and thick in Ian's prick.

Nicky's own cock rubbed hard on Ian's hip, and Ian bucked against him.

"This." Nicky raised his body enough to make a deliberate thrust of his hips, prick sliding in the groove of Ian's thigh. Drawing back, Nicky made another surge forward, so that the head of his cock rutted into the skin beneath Ian's balls. Ian's eyes screwed shut in anticipation.

"This," Nicky said again, and his prick pressed into the cleft below. "This is going inside you."

The knowledge was already sending pulses of readiness to dampen the head of Ian's prick even as it made his muscles tense. "Ah. Yes. But we will be using that oil again, yes?"

Nicky buried a chuckle in Ian's shoulder. "Yes, indeed. Allow me to worry about the details. I believe you have enough on your mind."

There was no question of trust, and Ian did not particularly fear pain on his own behalf. He worried only that an undignified arrangement of limbs would provoke the sort of feelings antithetical to passion, such as the fit of unmanly giggles building in his throat.

Nicky straightened up and dropped his weight to the side. "Roll over."

Ian complied with alacrity. Not having to see Nicky would go a long way to easing Ian's mind.

When he felt Nicky loom, Ian tensed, awaiting an intrusion of oil, but Nicky's hands merely stroked Ian's shoulders, fingers soothing the knots in the muscles under the skin, moving down each side of his spine until reaching the curve of his backside before starting at his shoulders again.

"You will send me to sleep," Ian said.

"I rather doubt that to be the case." Nicky reached beneath him and wrapped a hand around Ian's hard cock. "I believe I still have your intently focused attention."

"You do. But..." What was there he could not admit to Nicky now? "But I am starting to think that my dread is making it worse than the reality."

"Dread is it? I offer you a heaven on earth and you dread it?" But Nicky's voice held a smile. "You will sing a different song in a moment."

Again Nicky's touch began at his shoulders, but this time the comforting rub of his hands was accompanied by the flick of his tongue making its way down Ian's spine. He yearned to roll up into that light touch, to offer more flesh to be so caressed. When the tongue reached the end of his spine, the hollow at the

121

top of the crease of his arse, Nicky gave a slow deliberate kiss, stirring the skin with lush heat before blowing his breath on the wet spot until gooseflesh dimpled Ian's skin.

When the scent of lavender filled the room, Ian's prick ached. He would have to sequester himself until he learned to disassociate the scent from the expectation of pleasure lest he go about in company with his prick acting as tent pole in his trousers. Nicky oiled the crease, thumbs kneading the skin to a slippery softening that ended as soon as Ian felt the touch at his entrance.

"Relax your arsehole. This is the part where you get to help."

"'Tis easier said than done, you know."

Nicky laughed against his shoulder. "Yes, I do know." He pressed and retreated, then again. "I want to be inside you, Ian. My cock in you as you shiver around me." His thumb worked its way in, startlingly larger than a finger.

Ian stretched his arms—arm—above his head. Nicky made slow deep nudges with his thumb until he reached the limit of flesh and bone. After an initial twinge as his body opened, Ian accepted the sensation. A little violating, a little uncomfortable, but when Nicky moved his thumb, swirled it, drove it in and out, Ian's prick pulsed with pleasure.

In the moment when Ian thought he might learn to like it, Nicky stopped.

"Up on your knees."

Ian scrambled to get his legs beneath him.

"Ever the dutiful soldier. You like having your orders." Nicky whispered the words into Ian's ear, hot breath brushing the skin. "Orders make everything easier."

Ian shook his head.

Nicky entered him again with something, couldn't be his prick, but God, it burned. Ian wanted to fall back into the mattress, the fire in his arse sapping the strength from his legs.

"Push back on my fingers."

Fingers. "Christ, how many?"

"Two." Nicky sounded amused.

Ian groaned and pushed into Nicky's thrust. The action seemed to open up space inside him for Nicky's fingers, space that Ian wanted touched.

"Yes, you like your marching orders. Saves you from thinking."

"No." He didn't care for being ordered around any more than the next man, but somehow here, when it was Nicky, Ian's will gladly suborned to Nicky's commands.

Nicky reached around Ian's hips, fingers wrapping too damned loosely about his prick. "Then why is your cock like marble? The skin's that tight I think you shall spill before I can get my cock in you."

"Please, Nicky."

"Perhaps you should give the order."

"Do it."

"If you truly want it, give voice to it. Then you cannot say I made you."

"Nicky."

First Nicky stopped the light friction on Ian's prick, then Nicky's fingers fluttered inside, rubbing deeply before they withdrew.

In an agony of suspended sensation, Ian ground out the words. "Will you bloody fuck me?" He licked his dry lips. "Please?"

"Ever the gentleman."

Ian buried his face in his good arm, trying not to think of how Nicky had learned to push a man to the point where he was desperate to be taken. How many times he must have done this to show such patience.

Nicky's cock rubbed along the crease, nudging at the flesh that now seemed to want to capture that blunt pressure, drag it in to touch all the newly discovered places inside.

Nicky leaned down, his breath a damp kiss at Ian's ear. "I will try to be slow, but I confess the very thought of this makes me slightly mad."

"Glad I'm not the only one."

Nicky huffed a laugh against Ian's skin. "Together then."

"Yes."

Pressure, insistent steady pressure. Ian could bear this, it was—God, it was too much. No wonder Nicky had cried that first time. Even with the oil, Ian felt scraped, torn.

Nicky held still within for a moment and then withdrew, leaving Ian panting into the pillow.

"You actually reach satisfaction with *that* occurring?"

"I do. Some men can climax with naught but the stroke of a cock in their arse."

Ian took another deep breath. "I wish to give you this, but I do request you hurry matters along."

Nicky's hand made another soothing trip down Ian's back, then gripped his arse cheeks. "We'll see."

Perhaps it was because it was expected, but the pressure had eased somewhat. Still painful, yes, but if Nicky wanted to have Ian's body this way, he could manage. Nicky withdrew again and this time thrust swift and deep, seating himself so completely Ian felt the slap of ballocks against his arse.

He bit his lip. No wonder Nicky had demanded movement. The sooner Nicky took his satisfaction the better. Taking as deep a breath as he could, Ian said, "Please take your pleasure, but I beg you to recall I undertake a long carriage ride in a few days."

Nicky's laugh made the oddest sensation inside Ian, but before he could decide if he wished a repetition, Nicky gripped Ian's shoulder, shifting them. The prick lancing his guts shifted as well, and Ian remembered how enjoyable Nicky's fingers had felt. Sparks of pleasure intermingled with the pain. Nicky began to thrust, holding Ian with a hand on his shoulder, hauling him onto that thick slam of a prick inside.

Ian groaned and pushed back, almost disbelieving his body should crave more.

"Yes." Nicky dropped a kiss on the back of Ian's neck. "With me." Nicky's hand gripped Ian's cock, dragging him toward completion.

He slapped at Nicky's hand. "Can we wait?"

"If you wish." Nicky's arms wrapped around Ian's chest, hands stroked his back, his sides, his jaw. Nicky gave his fingers for Ian to kiss.

This was right. Nothing could be more so. Sharing pleasure, bodies climbing together. Why would God have created bodies capable of scaling such heights if they were not meant to experience this?

His fingers twisted in the sheet. "Now."

"No." Nicky shook his head on Ian's back and withdrew, leaving Ian aching. Punishment for all his doubt, all his fears?

Nicky grabbed Ian's leg and urged him onto his back, lifting Ian's legs high. "Like this." Nicky drove back in, a swift tearing burn that subsided as he began his thrusts. "Couldn't at first." He smiled down. "Thought if I watched your face, I would be off before the race."

Like a lodestone, Nicky's cock seemed drawn to the spot inside that spilled forth exquisite sensation, almost the very paroxysm of climax, but drawn out until Ian was drowning in it.

"Now." It was Nicky demanding it this time.

Ian wrapped his fist around his cock. One stroke had him gasping, ballocks primed, prick ready to fire.

"God, Ian, please. Come."

He did, body launched through that fiery space, where all he knew was the heat bathing both of them with each jerk of his cock.

Splash of warmth inside as well, Nicky shuddering, pouring his seed into Ian, the thought making his prick twitch again.

Nicky's breath crooned softly in his ear as he folded them together.

Ian's head settled on his maimed arm, and Nicky tried to wedge his head into the same spot.

Ian tucked in closer to his own shoulder.

"Do you often sleep like this? I mean to say, pillowed on this arm?"

"What an odd question."

"I was just thinking. Sometimes my own arm is twisted beneath me and goes to pins and needles. I thought in that at least, you might be fortunate."

"Yes, Nicky. You are mad indeed."

"Truth told, I didn't want you thinking too much."

"Fear me not." Ian leaned in and kissed him. He suffered neither guilt nor doubt for what they had done. "Can I take you like that? I mean, on your knees?"

Nicky smiled. "What, now?"

"Well not precisely now," Ian said with a rueful chuckle.

"Mr. Stanton, you may take me on my knees, against a wall, over a table, on my back, on my side, on the sofa—"

Ian had lost himself in imagery somewhere around "over a table" as he thought of Nicky reaching out to hold the edge as Ian slammed deep into his arse. "Well, perhaps not all that tonight."

Chapter Ten

To Nicky's delight as well as his despair, once committed, Ian could not be turned from his path. At the moment, his devotion to his chosen course gave Nicky blinding pleasure and what was sure to be a sore arse in the morning.

He buggered Nicky on his knees for what felt like an hour, arm around his waist with a hand stretched to his shoulder, bracing him for every hard thrust.

Nicky rose to his own knees, clutching Ian's foreshortened arm for balance, riding the cock that drove him to madness.

Ian lifted him slightly and withdrew.

Nicky released his grip. "What happened? Did you spend? Is it your arm?"

Ian's chin rubbed the top of Nicky's spine as he shook his head. "No." His voice was hoarse. "I know, I know there will be long stretches when we are apart."

Ian had interrupted coitus for conversation? Of course he had done. With that iron will, he had kept to a lonely bed for years.

Nicky sought to concentrate on Ian's words instead of the demands of a body which ached with the sudden severance of completion.

Ian continued, "I would never ask that you not seek

pleasure elsewhere, but could this—" his hand squeezed Nicky's hip, meaning plain, "—be mine alone?"

Nicky ached now with more than just pent-up seed. How could Ian have come to believe himself unworthy of fidelity that he should couch his request with such diffidence? Nicky would rather Ian's jealous passion, his threats and fierce kisses. He twisted to pull Ian down onto the bed beside him.

"I would swear any oath to you, Ian. There is no part of me I would not keep for you alone."

"An oath is unnecessary. Your promise will serve."

Ian looked so grave, the *V* between his brows as deep as a valley. Nicky wanted nothing more than to erase those lines. "You have it. Besides, didn't you threaten to geld me?"

"I did." Ian spoke with solemnity, but Nicky could see the smile start in Ian's eyes. He reached down and stroked Nicky's cock back to full attention. "And what a shame should it come to pass, but I would keep my word."

Nicky gasped as Ian's fingers lifted the sac beneath, the touch a teasing brush of feathers on skin drawn tight with need. "Fuck me, Ian."

"With deep and abiding pleasure."

Nicky woke to a rush of cold air as Ian eased out from under the covers. A shiver rolled down Nicky's spine. He wanted Ian back in bed, wanted warmth and then heat all over again, proof that Ian's surrender was unconditional.

"Are you going to issue another retraction?"

Ian had his nightshirt on when he turned around. "No. Not at all."

"So come back to bed. I'm cold."

Ian bent to build up the fire.

"It's hours till dawn." Nicky knew he sounded petulant but he had faced death a few hours earlier. Didn't that entitle a fellow to a little comfort? "I know Julian spoke to you. Simmons would not bat an eyelash were he to find us together."

Ian sat on the bed with his back to Nicky and pulled on his dressing gown. "And are we to live with one servant? Constantly fearing for our necks?"

"I thought you had come to an understanding."

"I have done. But there are practical matters to consider."

"Well, as you say, I must marry."

Ian turned to face him. "And that will make matters easier?"

"There is always the Continent. We could live in Italy. Like Byron." Nicky shivered again. "I think it will be sometime before I regain my fondness for winter sports."

"But how will we live? On my half-pay? My fortune amounts to scarcely eight hundred pounds, Nicky. Will your father support you if you turn your back on your responsibilities?"

"He may."

"Even if there was some way, what you said would hold more truth. If you abandon your family, you would come to hate yourself and me as the cause."

"Would you believe me if I told you that there is a simple solution to our problem? One that will bring much happiness to all concerned?"

"I am ever at your service, Nicky. But I'm afraid your reign as King of Misrule has gone to your head."

Now that Nicky came to it, the bald pronouncement was

130

bloody difficult to make to a man's face. He and Charlotte had never quite covered this part of their plan. Nicky ran a tongue along his teeth in contemplation. Perhaps something like this was best said without words. That Charlotte would be furious would only serve the minx right for the way she had tormented Ian. Nicky only wished he could be there to witness it firsthand.

"Off to your cold bed then. But I warrant you'll sing a different tune before Twelfth Night."

Stammering concerns about the weather, Lord Anthony and some of his friends departed into a clear blue sky the next morning. Ian thought the storm they feared was the one presaged by Lord Carleigh's icy glare as he contemplated their reluctantly rendered aid on the ice. With the party in smaller numbers it was difficult to avoid Lewes' company, but the man's mere presence no longer chafed. Ian would never like him, but he no longer could hold him up as an antithesis of decency. Not when his own soul seemed wedded to those same desires.

Charlotte and Nicky were forbidden to leave their rooms for breakfast, though both professed perfect health. Ian's private knowledge of Nicky's capacity for exercise was nothing which could be offered in Nicky's public defense, so in their rooms the pair of misadventurers remained. Ian's treacherous prick thought Nicky confined to bed was an excellent way to spend a day, but a lengthy disappearance would no doubt be marked. And if someone went in search of him... He shuddered in consideration of the potential disaster. Yes, it would take more than a simple decree from the King of Misrule to ensure a merry Twelfth Night.

When Lady Anna declared that dinner would be the final

formal entertainment of the evening, Ian looked forward to the opportunity to be abed—Nicky's—early. He escaped the post-dinner rituals as quickly as possible and was surprised to find Simmons waiting for him in his rooms.

"Ah. I'll have my dressing gown, Simmons. I may...wish to do some reading before I retire."

"Very good, sir." Simmons made quick work of Ian's coat and cravat and then hesitated.

"Yes, Simmons?"

"I don't like to repeat gossip, sir. But as it may be of particular concern to you, sir, I thought I must."

At the word gossip, ice filled Ian's veins, a rapid freeze to shattering, one shard lodging just under his heart so that a breath ached. How great a disaster? Would it be the Continent or gaol?

Surprised he could still speak, Ian said, "Go on."

"Or rather it concerns Lady Charlotte, sir."

The shock of relief offered a cushion against initial understanding. Charlotte? The ice roared away under a spring thaw, bubbles of rage erupting in his blood.

"Tell me."

"It seems that she has been, to put it delicately, entertaining one of the guests in her room."

Despite his missing arm, there would be no need for seconds or a dawn appointment. He would kill the man with his one hand. Heedless of his state of undress, he walked past Simmons and into the hall, heading for the south tower.

Had she asked for a room so far away from others to carry out this dalliance or had some vile rake taken advantage of the distance to seduce her? He took the steps two at a time. There would be no pause at the door, no warning, no quarter. He flung open the door to Charlotte's room.

At first, his brain could not discern what his eyes reported.

A woman's bare shoulders, nightdress down to her waist, but the hair was blonde, blonde as—yes, with the face turning toward the door it was Mrs. Collingswood. The figure recumbent on the bed was female as well and even as he placed his hand over his eyes he saw his sister, her own nightdress open to the waist.

"Ian," Charlotte shrieked. "What made you—? I'm going to kill him."

"I—I beg your pardon." Still covering his eyes, he backed out of the room.

Signaled by Simmons, Nicky made it to Charlotte's room in time to intercept her as she barreled onto the tower stairs in her dressing gown. "You! Why on earth would you send him here?"

"Were you going to tell him?"

"I thought you would."

"Ah yes, just blurt it out. Your sweet innocent sister has taken a lover," Nicky said. "Leave the worst of it to me again."

A quieter voice broke in. "Lord, anyone would think you were already married. Perhaps we could continue the discussion in tones that don't carry to the stables?" Emily stood between them. Nicky recognized a militant eye when he saw one and subsided. "Now. However misguided my cousin has been, someone has to speak to Mr. Stanton."

Simmons glided up the tower stairs like a ghost. "Mr. Stanton has sequestered himself in your father's study, my lord. From the sounds of it, he means to make the acquaintance of a great deal of your father's cognac."

Nicky started past him and then came back up. "Is the door locked?"

"No, my lord, but I do have the key." As he held it up, three hands reached for it, and Emily's slender fingers proved the most deft.

"I am the most sensible choice as I am bound to him neither by blood nor affection. Indeed, I may be the only one he will speak with. You'll see that they don't disturb us, Simmons."

"You have the only key, madam."

After Emily had gone out of sight around a corner, Charlotte turned on Nicky. "I can't believe you would do something like this. I'm going with her."

Nicky stopped her. "You just want to listen at the door. I have a better idea. Though you may want to go back to your room to secure a scented kerchief or something to cover your nose."

Ian welcomed the fiery cognac into his throat and poured a fresh glassful from the decanter. Such abuse was no doubt shameful given the expense of procuring the stuff during the war, but he needed something to blot the image in his mind. Another man might have been able to dismiss what he had seen in Charlotte's room as girlish curiosity, but not a man with Ian's experiences.

He had not known women felt that way too.

Another half decanter of cognac and Ian wouldn't care. This was why Charlotte hadn't married. Could a proclivity for one's own sex be something they had inherited from their mother?

Though Lord Carleigh's library was well-stocked, Ian doubted he would find the answer on its shelves. He might however find something less costly in which to submerge his thoughts.

Intent on his search, he ignored the first three taps on the door.

"Mr. Stanton? It is I, Emily Collingswood."

Maybe she had come to ask for Charlotte's hand. As long as she hadn't come to remove the strong spirits, they could exist in harmony. He stalked over and yanked open the door.

He had kept the room dark to match his mood, but after she closed the doors again, she slipped over to a wall sconce and lit it with her candle. Ha! A bottle of single malt was next to some political tract. He grabbed it.

"Mr. Stanton, I am sure you have suffered something of a shock."

A shock. Yes. Finding his sister engaged in...he didn't know what she had been engaged in and he didn't particularly wish to examine it with any scrutiny. He opened the bottle and started to raise it to his lips, but despite what he had seen, there was a lady present and Ian was still a gentleman. He poured a generous amount into his glass.

"I love Charlotte very much, Mr. Stanton."

Maybe she was asking for her hand. "Are you pleading her case or yours?"

"Neither. I believe you are entitled to an explanation."

"An explanation. That would be rather an accomplishment. Would said explanation cover the ease with which the three of you have subscribed me for the fool in your little bit of theater?"

"You are a proud man, Mr. Stanton, if you will not take my saying so amiss."

"And you are a direct speaker, Mrs. Collingswood."

"Then we know where we are. May I?" She nodded at the decanter.

He shrugged. He had the whiskey. He was content. Not nearly foxed enough yet, but content.

She poured out a measure for herself and took a sip. "My husband preferred gin. But then again he was a beastly man." She took another sip. "Very well. To begin, Charlotte and I became well-acquainted after we met here. We—"

"I believe that fact has been duly noted, madam."

"Then I will tell you what you do not know. I did not wish to marry. And Charlotte was adamant about it, as you might expect. But my family was intent on the match. No funds, four girls, a man willing to forgo a dowry, I'm certain my tale is in no way original. Charlotte begged me to reconsider, but I did not have her courage. I yielded to the will of my family. I believe you may have some understanding of that?"

Ian refilled his glass.

"Arthur was a dreadful man. Or perhaps all husbands are. I had only the experience with the one. He drank too much, and when he did he was violent."

"Your fall?"

"Yes. He pushed me down the stairs over some imagined insult. The wrong kind of tea or something. I suppose he might have finished me off, but his regiment was sent to Spain. And I lived. I do not know what you thought of when your body ached with mending until death seemed preferable, but I thought of Charlotte. And then she was there. She nursed me through it. Led me back to the land of the living."

Her words were soft and measured, but held the force of her feelings. Ian could not have interrupted her even if he could think of something to say.

"When I was finally able to leave my bed, I was determined not to suffer without her company again. By now, I'm sure you have suspected that we had hoped that by finding yourself similarly bound by affection, you would see that a marriage between Lord Amherst and Charlotte would enable either of us to frequent the household without exciting comment.

"I am sorry for any deception, but as I have said before, you are a proud man, Mr. Stanton, and not one who is easily swayed. You must follow the dictates of your conscience, but I do not intend to be parted from Charlotte again."

"You speak as if such an end were simple."

"It is. As simple as love itself."

"I assure you, madam, love is neither easy nor simple."

"But it is. Love is a very simple thing. I pity anyone unable to see that." She nodded at his glass. "But perhaps you will find that sufficient companionship for the rest of your days." She left him in the study.

Nicky sucked in his breath, nearly choking on the redolence of the former privy. The one at the south tower provided excellent hearing for the study and summer salon. "Of all the blasted stupid things to say. Christ. I never should have let her be the one to speak to him."

"But she's right," Charlotte objected. "It is all so simple, if only Ian would see that."

Nicky shook his head. "You have never understood your brother. I must get to him."

✧

Ian drank off the glass's contents and set it down with great care. Not care enough, however, for he knocked it sharply against the edge of the desk, and it separated into three pieces, sharp and thick as the icicles on the eaves. As he picked one up, it sliced deep into his palm, cold at first, but then the blood met the whiskey and it burned. Since he was reeling from the injudiciously applied alcohol and the implications of the tale from his sister's...lover, the pain was negligible. He held it up to examine the wound on the hand he had left. In his typically imperfect fashion, he had not made a clean slice, a notch made a V at the bottom in the deepest point. Blood ran down into his cuffs, a dark trail across the white. He flexed his fingers, found them still functioning, and the blood came faster.

It smelled like battle. Smoke and cries and cannons. He remembered the stillness of cold white as he pulled Nicky free of the ice. His blood felt warm where it ran over the back of his hand, cool as it flowed down his wrist. Hot or cold. Happy or sad. Honor or love. No. Such decisions were as far from simple as this study was from the Pyramids of Egypt.

"Sweet Christ, Ian, your hand." Nicky rushed forward, tearing off his cravat and wrapping it around Ian's palm before Ian could drag his thoughts back from wherever they had ventured on their river of whiskey.

"I don't want to be cold."

"Of course you don't. What the hell is wrong with you, letting it bleed like that? What happened?"

"I think you already know. You were the engineer behind the entire deceit."

"Actually, Charlotte was the one with the plan." Nicky tied off the cravat.

138

Ian pulled away. "Was it truly necessary to inflict the sight on me? I may never recover."

"That was my idea, I'm afraid."

"Mrs. Collingswood has the mien of Lord Wellesley. Perhaps we should send her to make short work of the Emperor."

"You will have to be the one to explain that to Charlotte."

"Marriage? You would marry Charlotte and—"

"Haven't you been urging me to undertake the blessed state?"

"It cannot be that simple."

"God, Ian, why on earth would you think it simple? Look at you. Has anything about this been simple?"

"No."

"Love is neither simple nor easy, but for such a man as you, I consider all the effort most worthwhile."

Ian felt he might have swallowed a candle. Nicky's earnest devotion radiated from him like the light and heat of a midwinter bonfire. But his words were curiously familiar.

"You devious bastard. Where were you hiding?"

Nicky grinned. "I don't think you want to know."

Ian took a step toward him and stopped, brought up short by the odor emanating from Nicky's coat. "What is that smell?"

"You prefer lavender?"

"By far." Ignoring the old stable floor smell of him, Ian took him by the shoulders, with both real and phantom hand, then leaned in until their foreheads touched. "But above all else in this world, I have come to prefer you."

The King and Queen of Misrule had declared Ancient Greece as the theme of the Twelfth Night celebration, placing the bedding supply of the household in grave jeopardy as everyone sought to drape themselves in sheets.

As they headed for the musicians' platform in the gallery, Nicky leaned in to whisper in Ian's ear. "I can't wait to see Father go out and pour Negus on the trees dressed like that."

Lord Carleigh had wrapped himself in what looked like gold velvet bed curtains. Ian suspected Simmons had no part of Lord Carleigh's costume, though Simmons had aided both Ian and Nicky by providing passable chitons cut from nightshirts, cloaks pinned to their shoulders. In Nicky's case, the cloak was a blue woolen blanket, since Lady Anna felt he was still susceptible to chill.

Charlotte and Emily met them at the platform, Emily nodding as Charlotte placed her hand in Nicky's.

Lord Carleigh and Lady Anna had been told ahead of time and waited to lend their support. Nicky raised his cup as they stood on the dais, and the party fell silent. "I wish our friends to be the first to hear that Lady Charlotte Stanton has consented to be my wife."

"A toast to the future marchioness." Lord Carleigh raised his own cup.

Nicky turned to offer his cup to Ian who drank and then passed it to Charlotte.

As they accepted toast after toast, Ian felt something brush his hand where he stood at Charlotte's side. He looked down to see Nicky's fingers reaching out from the arm he had around Charlotte. Ian put his own arm behind Charlotte and they locked hands. At first the touch was simple reassurance, and then Ian had to pinch his lips closed against a gasp as Nicky's fingertip teased the inside of Ian's wrist. In such a public moment, there was no way to stop him without creating undue attention. As he caught sight of Nicky's grin, Ian suspected he would spend much of his life in similar straits. The thought had him smiling.

After the toasts, Nicky led Charlotte in the first dance, and Ian watched from his spot near the dais.

"I wish you many months of happiness before Nicky's better sense asserts itself." Julian Lewes had managed to find something dark red to use as a tunic. With a gold belt and a coronet of evergreen, he looked impossibly fashionable for a man wearing a blanket.

Ian smiled. "And I wish you many months of happiness before it rots completely and falls off."

Lewes laughed. "I must say, Stanton, you surprised me. I would have laid steep odds against such an amiable arrangement."

"Then I am sorry I did not lay a bet on the other side."

"And what of all your protestations of honor and duty?"

Nicky strode toward them, cloak swinging with the force of his hurried movement. "Please tell me I am not too late to prevent a dawn appointment."

"Not at all." Ian forestalled another spur of Lewes' wit. "I think I will leave such matters to those who feel they need to prove their honor, as it is not apparent to an outward gaze."

"You wound me to the heart, Stanton. If you are still looking to lose some of your hard-won earnings, stop by Hylas House. There will be a book on those months we spoke of."

"I look forward to collecting my winnings." Ian held the other man's gaze.

With a slight twist to his lips that might have been disgust or approval, Lewes nodded and quit the field of engagement, pausing briefly at the spot where Charlotte was surrounded by excited feminine company.

Whatever Lewes offered as he bowed over Charlotte's hand brought a sharp laugh from Charlotte and a deep blush to Mrs. Collingswood's cheeks. She stepped closer to Charlotte, and Lewes bowed over the widow's hand as well, sending Charlotte into peals of laughter.

As delighted as Ian was in his sister's happiness, he did wish she would make less of a show about it. He could see Lady Anna bearing down on her at that moment, as swift as light cavalry. Mrs. Collingswood took up a flanking position and Ian thought Charlotte might be able to stand her ground. He knew just having Nicky beside him was as reassuring as the backing of the best of His Majesty's artillery.

"I thought to rescue you, but it appears there was no need," Nicky said.

Scoring one off Lewes had been surpassing fine. Ian smiled in triumph. "No. You will have to redeem your obligation at another time."

"Then perhaps we could retire someplace private to work out the particulars of the marriage contract?"

"If you think you can be spared." Ian had already started for the side doors.

"Somehow I don't think I'll be missed." Nicky looked back at the group buzzing about Charlotte. "The hunting cabin is in good repair and very well-provisioned. I think the first thing we should do is plan a proper holiday."

The thought of having Nicky to himself for several days had Ian fervently wishing for the foulest of weather. "Well-provisioned, is it? Even down to a dependable stock of that lavender oil?"

"You'll have to take that up with the quartermaster."

"And where would I find him?"

"I'll show you."

Ian paused briefly to look back at the party.

Nicky beckoned him on with his smile. "All will be well. Can you trust that?"

Ian could trust the man before him to hell and back. Indeed, Nicky had already led him back the once. "I believe your sovereignty has a few hours left. Does the King of Misrule have any final edicts?"

The hall Nicky had led them to was damp, dark and chill. "I hope I have already secured the future of my kingdom."

After a quick glance about, Ian pushed Nicky against the wall. "Then might I crave a boon, sire?"

"Crave away, Mr. Stanton."

About the Author

K.A. Mitchell discovered the magic of writing at an early age when she learned that a carefully crayoned note of apology sent to the kitchen in a toy truck would earn her a reprieve from banishment to her room. Her career as a spin control artist was cut short when her family moved to a two-story house, and her trucks would not roll safely down the stairs. Around the same time, she decided that Chip and Ken made a much cuter couple than Ken and Barbie and was perplexed when invitations to play Barbie dropped off. An unnamed number of years later, she's happy to find other readers and writers who like to play in her world.

To learn more about K.A. Mitchell, please visit www.kamitchell.com. Send an email to K.A. Mitchell at authorKAMitchell@gmail.com.

Look for these titles by
K.A. Mitchell

Now Available:

Serving Love Series
Hot Ticket

Custom Ride
Diving in Deep
Regularly Scheduled Life
Collision Course
Chasing Smoke
An Improper Holiday
No Souvenirs

Print Anthologies
Midsummer Night's Steam - Temperature's Rising

The Dickens with Love

Love

Josh Lanyon

Dedication

To my editor, Sasha Knight, who gave me a new publishing home and brand-new subgenre to write for Christmas. Thank you and Happy Holidays.

Chapter One

"Anything you have to do," Mr. Stephanopoulos said, pouring sherry. "I *must* have that book."

"Anything?" I repeated carefully.

We stood in the spacious living room of his Century City penthouse. The Palladian windows looked out over a city alight and twinkling on this rainy afternoon four days before Christmas. In one corner of the room was a large and particularly vulgar Christmas tree that managed to convey all the holiday charm of a sequined dildo. In the other was a plasma television set, sound muted. *It's a Wonderful Life*—the scene where Clarence explains to George Bailey how angels get their wings—played a silent background to our conversation.

Stephanopoulos smiled, handing me the fragile amber glass of sherry. "Short of murder, of course."

"Of course." Was that supposed to be funny? What a prick he was. What a godawful, odious *prick*.

"I don't want to know details. I want results."

I sipped the sherry. It was probably excellent sherry, if you liked sherry. I prefer brandy, but Mr. Stephanopoulos hadn't asked. The Mr. Stephanopouloses of the world don't.

"Well?" Mr. S. demanded when I didn't immediately answer.

I said lightly—although the mockery was more for me than

him, "Have I ever failed you?"

"No. You have not. And no one knows his Dickens like you do, James."

He managed to make it sound lascivious. That was unlikely his intent; Stephanopoulos was staunchly heterosexual. One more reason to be glad I was born gay.

I watched him savor the sherry, wet glistening on his plump red lips. He looked like a Tim Burton version of Father Christmas.

"Crisparkle. That can't be this professor's real name."

"Why do you say so?"

I quoted, "'Mr. Crisparkle, Minor Canon, early riser, musical, classical, cheerful, kind, good-natured, social, contented, and boy-like.' Canon Crisparkle is a character in *The Mystery of Edwin Drood*. He helps Neville Landless escape to London when he's suspected of killing Edwin Drood."

"That's right. How could I forget?"

How? Beside the fact that Mr. S. had never read *The Mystery of Edwin Drood*? Actually, I doubted if Mr. S. had read much of any Dickens. I don't suppose he even liked Dickens. He thought Boz was a smart acquisition. And he was right. The previous week an 1859 first edition of *A Tale of Two Cities*—illustrated by H.K. Browne and bound by Birdsall & Son from the original seven monthly serial installments—went for $6,950 on the Advanced Book Exchange.

Though Mr. S. ruthlessly and relentlessly collected Dickens for investment purposes, his personal preferences ran to 1920s erotica. Primarily naughty pictures and, ideally, French. Hey, *c'est la vie*.

"I believe it's his real name, though," Mr. S. said. "Sedgwick Crisparkle. He's a Professor of Chemistry at the University of

London."

"*Sedgwick?* He's having you on." As in totally yanking the fat man's chain. Still, what did it matter to me? I would be paid for my expertise whether the article in question was genuine or not.

"And how did this professor of chemistry get hold of a lost Dickens manuscript?"

Mr. S. said vaguely, "That's all part of the mystery. Not that I give a fuck how he got hold of it so long as I get first crack at it—assuming it's the real thing."

I smiled politely. When it came to ethics, Mr. S. made the House of Medici look like the Waltons. Say goodnight, John Boy. Only I couldn't say goodnight. If I didn't want to live in a cardboard box under Los Angeles River Bridge come the New Year, I had to have this commission.

"You'll have to be discreet, though. If Crisparkle knows you're acting as my agent he won't sell the book to you. Regardless of the money involved."

Interesting.

I said only, "Discretion is my middle name."

Stephanopoulos smirked. I resisted the temptation to dash my drink in his face. Desperation makes ugly bedfellows. Anyway, a thimbleful of sherry was a ridiculous gesture. He'd probably just lick it off.

Stephanopoulos handed me a slip of paper with a phone number. "He's staying at the Hotel Del Monte. It's crucial that you get a look at the book and, assuming it's genuine, that I'm able to make an offer before LAABF on Saturday."

LAABF was the Los Angeles Antiquarian Book Fair. The fair was held every other year. It was neither the largest nor the most prestigious of such book fairs—not in the state and not in the country—and I wondered why Professor Crisparkle had decided to auction his valuable manuscript here. It seemed one more indication that all was not kosher. Not my problem.

"Hotel Del Monte. He must be expecting to make a killing," I remarked, examining the phone number.

"With good reason."

I made a noncommittal reply. Well, however things went down, I'd treat myself to a few hours in the Hotel Del Monte's legendary Champagne Bar. It was one of my favorite places in Los Angeles though generally right out of my price range. The good thing about working for Mr. S. was that he paid promptly and well.

Mr. S. said jovially, "To Dickens' Christmas books. God bless 'em every one!"

We clinked the crystal glasses. They made a brittle chime. Somewhere a disheartened angel tumbled off a Christmas tree.

This is for all the lonely people...

America's *The Complete Greatest Hits* was blasting from the apartment next door to mine. Darcy, my neighbor, was—in her own words—a HUGE fan of the English-American folk rock band. Actually the greatest hits album was an improvement over *Holiday Harmony*, the group's Christmas album. I'd heard that album at least twice every single day for the past month. Now I understood why so many suicides happened around this time of year.

Darcy's door flew open as I was quietly inserting my key into my door lock.

"James."

"Hey." I smiled distractedly and turned the lock.

Darcy was a few years older than me. She was a chubby, dishwater blonde with a fondness for baggy jeans, plaid flannel shirts and animal-shaped barrettes. I liked Darcy. She was a good neighbor and a kind and conscientious person. But despite the fact that I had broken it to her early on that I was gay, I was uncomfortably aware that she still, as they used to say, *entertained hopes*. I did my best not to encourage her.

"Did you decide if you're spending Christmas day here?" Her expression was studiedly casual.

I'd known the question was coming, so I'm not sure why I didn't have an answer for her. I *did* have an answer; only I didn't want to deliver it. Nobody should have to be alone at Christmas.

And Darcy knew I didn't have anyone to spend it with, so to refuse was just...personal.

Thinking that love has left them dry...

She was lonely and God knew I was lonely. What did it matter if she was a little dull, a little desperate? The same could be said about me.

Darcy swallowed, met my eyes, and found a cheerful smile with which to meet my impending rejection.

"Yes," I heard myself say. "Christmas. Christmas would be... Thank you. Yes."

Darcy's face lit up. "*Really?*"

I nodded. "What do I—? Should I bring something?"

"Just yourself."

"I can do that. That I can do." I was nodding encouragingly—encouraging myself—like one of those bobble-headed dogs.

She was still beaming at me and I was still nodding as I let

153

myself in my apartment. I waved, she waved, and I shut the door, leaning against it.

"Is that supposed to be your idea of a good deed?" I asked aloud. It was rhetorical. I had no answer and there was no one else to answer—and hadn't been since Corey kicked me out of our Laurel Canyon home nearly three years ago to the day.

I really didn't want to start thinking about Corey Navona. It was only the time of year, and Stephanopoulos's crack about the Louis Strauss debacle—but that was all ancient history. I had a job. A real job instead of the usual slinging books at "barnsonovels". Things were looking good.

I shoved off the door and opened the mini fridge that served as an end table to the room's only comfortable chair. I scanned its contents. That took approximately one and one half seconds. I had the choice of two eggs, a jar of raspberry preserves, a jar of possibly moldy Hoisin sauce and a bottle of white grape juice.

I finished the white grape juice and sat down to phone Professor Crisparkle at his hotel. I was astonished to find that my palms were perspiring. Was I afraid the mysterious professor wasn't going to agree to see me? No. Because I wouldn't accept his refusal. I was more resourceful than that. If he turned me down, I'd go to the hotel and find his room and camp outside it until he let me have a peek at that manuscript.

Or was I afraid he *would* let me see the manuscript? That once I saw it I'd know it wasn't genuine?

Wouldn't it be worse to know that it was genuine and I was purchasing it for Stephanopoulos?

I couldn't afford to start thinking like that.

I asked for Professor Crisparkle's room feeling like an idiot. That *couldn't* be his real name. Was this some elaborate hoax? Yes, I could believe that more easily than I could believe in this lost Christmas manuscript.

I was placed briefly on hold. Doris Day whispered fuzzily in my ear about the joys of Toyland, Toyland, Little Girl and Boy Land.

Then Doris vanished and a male voice, deep and definitely English, inquired, "Yes?"

"Professor Crisparkle?"

"Yes?" A trace of impatience.

"My name is James Winter. I'm an antiquarian book appraiser representing a collector who wishes at this time to remain anonymous. He's requested that I be allowed to examine the Dickens manuscript you'll be putting up for auction on Saturday at the LAABF."

"The book has already been authenticated by Angela Nixon and Ford Standish. I believe their credentials are impeccable." He wasn't haughty so much as...unequivocal.

"Yes. My client is aware of that fact. If it's all right, he'd like me to take a look as well."

He drawled, "And just who might you be when you're at home, Mr. Winter?"

"Sorry?"

"Why exactly should I permit you to examine this book?"

I said patiently, "Because if it's what you believe it to be, my client will make you an offer for it immediately."

"The book is already going to auction on Saturday."

"This would be in the nature of a preemptive bid."

Silence.

"Surely that defeats the purpose of going to auction," Professor Crisparkle said at last.

I said carefully, because he seemed irascible enough to cut me off and hang up, "If you're choosing to auction the manuscript, you're hoping to get the highest possible price for it. My client is in a position to pay above and beyond what you could get at auction."

"Then why doesn't he simply come to auction and bid on the book?"

Because he's an arrogant, unprincipled asshole.

I said pleasantly, "For security reasons and others, my client is very careful about his privacy. He rarely makes public appearances." Not when he can outflank his rivals with an end run.

Silence.

I coaxed, "If the manuscript is genuine, you've nothing to lose by letting me take a look. You can always decline my client's offer if you ultimately believe you can get more at auction."

"Very well," he said curtly. "When did you wish to examine the book?"

"What about this afternoon? I could be there in, say, an hour?"

Crisparkle didn't exactly sigh, but I could feel his irritation. "Very well. I'm in room number 103. One hour." He hung up.

It was clear to me that if I was late, I was out of luck. I pulled off my shirt—I tended to perspire a lot around Mr. S.— shrugged into a fresh one, doing up the buttons hurriedly.

I didn't expect the manuscript to be the genuine thing, of course. I knew it couldn't be. All the same as I changed clothes I had that funny tingle in my chest. I mentally reviewed what I knew about the Christmas books. From a literary standpoint, with the exception of *A Christmas Carol*, they're not considered Dickens' best work, but I had an illogical affection for them. Granted, I had an illogical affection for Christmas itself. Used to anyway. Now days I hated this time of year.

All told, Dickens wrote five Christmas books starting in 1843 with *A Christmas Carol in Prose, Being a Ghost Story of Christmas.* That's the holiday classic commonly known as *A Christmas Carol. CC* was followed by *The Chimes* in 1844, *The Cricket on the Hearth* in 1845, *The Battle of Life* in 1846, and *The Haunted Man and the Ghost's Bargain* in 1848.

There had been no Christmas story in 1847. Dickens was losing interest in the books, and *The Battle of Life* had not been very well-received by critics or his public. But the mysterious Professor Crisparkle claimed that there *had* been a Christmas story—and that he possessed the missing manuscript.

Even knowing better it was hard to rein my imagination in, daydreaming about what might be contained in such a manuscript.

Why wouldn't Dickens have released it? Was the manuscript unfinished?

I frowned at my reflection in the white and gold framed mirror over the waist-high bookshelves lining the west wall. My eyes were shining, my cheeks were flushed. For all my vaunted cynicism, I had the collector's bug as bad as anyone. I *wanted* to believe this manuscript was the real thing.

This is the first and most important step toward getting ripped off.

If anyone should have learned that lesson, it was me. I shook my head at my reflection, and the glint of the tiny black star in my earlobe caught my eye. I stared at it. Stared at my reflection as though running into an old acquaintance after many years. It seemed odd to me that I didn't look any different. True, three years wasn't exactly a lifetime, but I'd traveled metaphysical leagues in that time. The marks of that journey should have been on my face and threaded through my hair, but I looked the same as always. A tall and slender man with green eyes and chestnut hair. Granted, I needed a hair cut. The rain was making my hair curl. Three years ago I'd been getting my hair trimmed at The Green Room. Three years ago I would not have been heading out on an appraisal job in jeans. I'd have been wearing Kenneth Cole—right down to a tie. But then three years ago I wouldn't have considered taking a job from Mr. Stephanopoulos.

Not that there was anything wrong with this job. Very straightforward from the sound of it. Nor was there anything wrong with jeans—or the way I looked. I was clean, shaven, and presentable enough. Maybe the real change was on the inside.

Safe to say, it wasn't a change for the better.

Chapter Two

The Hotel Del Monte sat on twelve lushly wooded acres in the middle of some of the most expensive real estate in Southern California. The hotel's secluded location and small size, the rambling, pink stucco Spanish style ninety-two-room complex and its tranquil and luxuriant gardens full of trees, ornamental ponds and fragrant flowers made it one of the most romantic settings in Los Angeles. No long, anonymous corridors lined with room numbers. Most guest rooms and suites had private entrances and opened directly onto the hotel's gardens. If I was a guy in the market for a honeymoon, Hotel Del Monte would be my first choice.

I asked at the front desk for Room 103 and then headed out through the ancient sycamores and tree ferns. I crossed a small arched red and gold bridge from where I could see the graceful bell tower on the other side of the small lake where the swans were taking shelter. The rain pattered on the leaves of the lemon and orange trees lining the cobbled path, glittered on the petals of the rose bushes. It smelled good, like walking in the woods. The city seemed very far away.

I found Room 103 without too much trouble, ducking into the stone alcove and knocking on the door. Rain dripped musically from the eaves and ran down the back of my neck.

I shivered. I needed a raincoat, but with only about fifteen to twenty days of rain a year, there were better things to spend one's pennies on. Like books. There was a 1924 edition of Gertrude Chandler Warner's *The Box-Car Children* I had my eye on for this year's Christmas present to myself.

The hotel room door swung abruptly open. An unsmiling, dark-haired man stood framed against an elegant background of pale cabbage roses and ivy. He was about forty. Tall, rawboned, lean. He wore faded jeans, a cream-colored sweater over a white tee shirt, and horn-rimmed glasses that made him look like a bookish angel.

"James Winter?" he inquired, looking me over like he'd caught me cheating on my chemistry quiz.

"Professor Crisparkle?"

My surprise must have been obvious. "Is there a problem?" he returned sternly.

"No. Not at all."

The problem was he was gorgeous. It was a no-nonsense brand of gorgeousness, though. Far from detracting from his dark, grave good looks, the glasses accentuated them.

I smiled my very best smile—despite the rain trickling down the back of my neck—and offered my hand. After a hesitation, he shook it.

His grip was firm, his palm and fingers smooth but not clammy or soft. An academic, but not one of the ones who never left his ivory tower.

No wedding ring.

"It's a pleasure to meet you." I meant it. I was sort of nonplussed at how much I meant it.

"Come in," Crisparkle replied, moving aside.

I stepped inside the room which was cozily warm and smelled indefinably expensive, a combination of fine linens, fresh coffee and cut flowers. A fire burned cheerily in the fireplace. The remains of the professor's lunch were on a tray on the low table before the sage velvet sofa. Soothing classical piano played off the laptop next to his lunch tray.

Corey and I had stayed at the Hotel Del Monte on our one year anniversary. The rooms were all furnished in romantic country-French décor—each unique but with the famous signature touches of Alicante marble, vintage silk or chenille upholstery, and original artwork. It was the best weekend of my life—or maybe it seemed that way in contrast to the following week, which was when my entire world had shattered.

"You must have brought the rainy weather with you." I smiled again, not bothering to analyze why I was displaying such uncharacteristic cordiality. "Have you seen much of the city since you've been here?"

"The book is on the desk." Crisparkle nodded at the writing desk near the white French doors leading out to a private patio.

Not one for chitchat, was he? Maybe it was an English thing. In any case, I lost all interest in rude Professor Crisparkle. The only thing in that room for me now was the faded red leather book lying on the polished desktop. As I approached the writing table my heart was banging so hard I thought I might be having my first ever panic attack.

A book. Not a manuscript. I'd been thinking that Crisparkle and Mr. S. were playing fast and loose with their terminology, but no. It was a bound book. All the more unlikely, then, that this could be the real thing. Hard enough to believe a manuscript had been lost, let alone an entire print run. Impossible, in fact. And yet, as I reached for the thin volume, finely bound in red Morocco leather, I noted that my hand was shaking. Well, scratch a cynic and you'll find a disappointed idealist.

I drew back as I realized that I was in danger of dripping on the desk.

"Could I borrow a towel?" I asked.

Crisparkle gave me a funny look, and then disappeared into the bathroom.

I took a moment to remind myself of all the possibilities of any such appraisal. The novel might be the real thing, but it was more likely to be a forgery. It might be a modern forgery or it might be a contemporary forgery. Knowing which would depend partially on discovering the book's provenance—the documented or authenticated history of its ownership—of which I so far knew nothing.

The professor reappeared with a peach-colored plush towel and I scrubbed my face and hair, tossed the towel to the fireplace hearth and sat down at the desk. I still didn't touch the book, simply gazing at the gold lettering on the front cover. *Miss Anjaley Coutts* surrounded in gold-stamped holly and ivy.

That wouldn't be the title. So the book was a gift and Miss Coutts was the recipient. Why was that name familiar? Who was Miss Anjaley Coutts? Not Mrs. Dickens or a sister-in-law. Not a daughter. Not an alias of Dickens' mistress, the actress Ellen Ternan, because he didn't meet her until 1857. Who then?

"It doesn't bite," Professor Crisparkle said sardonically, and I realized that I'd been sitting there for more than a minute, unmoving, staring at the cover.

I threw him a quick, distracted look, and then delicately edged the book around to examine its spine. Gold lettering read *The Christmas Cake / Dickens / MDCCCXLVII.*

The Christmas Cake?

I carefully opened the book and turned the flyleaf. On the frontispiece was a hand-colored etching of a truly sumptuous cake—topped by a sly, smiling mouse with crumbs on her whiskers. I looked at the title page: another smaller illustration of an elderly man and woman who appeared, to my wondering eye, to be getting sloshed on the Christmas punch. And the words *The Christmas Cake* in a familiar, faded hand that most people only viewed through glass.

I turned the page and stared, feeling decidedly light-headed, at the first sentence. *Our story begins with a fallen star. But the star is not the story.*

I was vaguely aware that Professor Crisparkle spoke to me, but I didn't hear what he said, and I didn't care. I was absorbing—devouring—the words with my eyes.

Roofed with the ragged ermine of a newly-fallen snow glittering by starlight, the Doctor's old-fashioned house loomed grey-white through the snow-fringed branches of the trees, a quaint iron lantern, which was picturesque by day and luminous and cheerful by night, hanging within the square, white-pillared portico to one side. That the many-paned window on the right framed the snow-white head of Mrs. Dimpledolly, the Doctor's wife, the old Doctor himself was comfortably aware—for his kindly eyes missed nothing, so it was that he spied the falling...

I read for some time before I finally raised my head. I no longer saw the hotel room. I don't think I even saw the book or the handwritten pages anymore. I was seeing benevolent old Doctor Dimpledolly and his amiable missus as they opened their home to a coachload of strangers stranded on Christmas Eve.

"Satisfied?" Professor Crisparkle asked dryly.

I snapped back to awareness, blinking up at him, dimly taking in the details of elegant nose, long eyelashes, soft dark hair...I couldn't tell what color his eyes were behind the horn-rims. That mercurial shade of light brown that looked green in certain light and gold in other. He seemed so awfully stern, so awfully strict, reminding me of an uptight schoolmaster. But that was right, wasn't it? He taught chemistry like Mr. Redlaw, the professor of chemistry in *The Haunted Man.*

As I stared at him, it occurred to me that Professor Crisparkle didn't like me much.

Didn't like me at all.

Why? Not that I was universally beloved—hardly—but what had I done to earn such instant dislike from an out-of-towner?

I said slowly. "It looks...very promising." My voice nearly gave out. *Promising?* Who was I kidding? I knew, knew in my bones, this was the real thing. I said more solidly, "I'd have to examine it more closely, of course. To be absolutely sure."

He gazed at me with an expression of utter contempt.

No, I wasn't misreading him. I repeated uncertainly, "I'd like to spend a little more time—"

"I'm sure you would."

Color heated my face at that dry, ironic tone—and I wasn't quite sure why. I said evenly, "It certainly looks authentic, but you never know."

"You don't, do you?"

Again: barely concealed scorn. Too obvious by now to politely ignore.

"Is there a problem?" I asked.

"There is no mysterious client, is there?"

"I didn't say he was mysterious, but of course there's a client."

"What is the name of your client?"

"I've already told you he wishes to remain anonymous."

Crisparkle said, looking me straight in the eyes, "After we

spoke on the phone, Mr. Winter, I did a bit of checking up on you with your colleagues in the ABAA. You have quite an interesting—and not entirely admirable—past."

I'm not sure why that struck home the way it did. I'd certainly heard worse, but hearing it from Crisparkle—knowing the stories he would have heard about me—was, quite simply, humiliating. I managed to say, "There are two sides to every story, Mr. Crisparkle."

He didn't answer.

After a painfully long pause, I said, "I take it you've decided not to permit me further access to the book?"

He said, as though it gave him great satisfaction, "You take it correctly, Mr. Winter."

So why the hell had he permitted me up here to look at it at all? Curiosity? Or had I blown my one and only chance when I pretended not to know for sure that the book was genuine?

I wanted to shout out, *it's not fair*. But when was life ever fair? Instead, I expelled a long, shaky breath and managed to keep from saying all the furious, foolish things that wouldn't help my cause anyway. I could hardly bear to take a final glance at the book. Leaving it lying there in the shadows of reflected rain and firelight, knowing I would never see or hold it again, was like physical pain. I felt it in my core of my body like a physiological reaction to grief. I felt ill. I felt like crying.

Rising, I began gathering my things. Surprisingly, my hands were quite steady now.

I dragged on my coat, still damp with the earlier walk in the rain. All the while Crisparkle stood there watching me in an icy silence like a head butler waiting to expel a grubby tradesman.

I went to the door of his suite and he followed me, still unspeaking. I had my hand on the knob when my anger overtook me, and I turned to face him.

"Not that it's any of your goddamned business, but I had nothing to do with Louis Strauss's forgeries, let alone murder. I was never accused or even implicated in any wrongdoing. I merely had the misfortune of working for Strauss. So did several other book hunters. The difference is, they didn't stay in the business. I stayed because this is my passion and my life."

"Ah, I *see*," he said mockingly. "Why, then, do you suppose so many people say the unflattering things they do about you?"

"Because I was *too* good at my job. And I was...arrogant. Nearly as arrogant as you."

His expression altered infinitesimally right before I quietly, carefully, shut his hotel room door.

It was raining harder than ever as I started back down the cobbled path, making my way through the playful statuary and miniature waterfalls, back over the pretty bridge and the lake where the rain sent ripples spreading across the green-gray surface. I strode right across the wet lawns, marched down the steps leading to the long patio with its rustic terra-cotta pavers and urns of massive flower arrangements, pushed open the French doors and went inside the comfortably dark hotel bar to order a drink while I tried to think what to do next.

I'd been to the so-called Champagne Bar many times—back when I was the hot-shot number one book hunter for the leading antiquarian bookseller in Los Angeles. At times it was hard to remember those days. Mostly I didn't want to. But however much my fortunes had changed, the Champagne Bar was still a gorgeous, welcoming room with gilt-framed paintings, classic dark wood and rich, luxuriously comfortable chairs and sofas, and a large fireplace that was cheerfully ablaze on this cold, wet afternoon. It looked more like the handsome library of a manor house than a trendy Los Angeles bar. From the tapestry cushions, wooden ducks on the mantelpiece and live orchids, every elegant detail was perfect.

I settled into a stool at the bar and ordered a brandy. In a spirit of defiance, an Asbach Uralt.

No use pretending I wasn't badly shaken by Crisparkle's censure. Not that I ever forgot my inglorious past, but three years later I no longer brooded on it twenty-four seven. Sometimes I even managed to convince myself that one day people would forget and I'd be respectable again. Never mind respectable. I'd be happy to be regarded as employable again by people besides the Stephanopouloses of the world.

I wasn't sure what bothered me more: being reminded I was still persona non grata among my former colleagues or knowing I wasn't going to be able to finish reading *The Christmas Cake*. Book collecting had never only been about money for me. First and foremost I was a reader, and beneath what probably seemed like a knowledgeable and somewhat jaded exterior was the kid who stayed up late at night reading *Mystery of the Witches' Bridge* by flashlight beneath the blankets.

I wanted to know what Doctor and Mrs. Dimpledolly were going to do with the little schoolmaster still grieving for his dead wife, two mischievous schoolboys on their way home for the holidays, and the mysterious pregnant lady who appeared to be on the run from her rich papa, I wanted to know where the Christmas cake came in. Hell, I wanted to know about the mouse.

I sipped my brandy and tried to come up with reasons for postponing calling Mr. S. I could only put it off for so long, of course. My gut feeling was that the book was authentic, but I couldn't be sure without further examination. After Strauss, I was never going to recommend anything solely based on instinct. Not even my own once-renowned instinct.

But someone else would have to do the appraisal—someone

else was going to get that nice fat commission. Someone else would have the privilege of reading that wonderful, magical book.

Three fucking years. They felt like forever. Apparently they were no time at all.

I fought the burning desire to get blind drunk. Not only was it no solution, I couldn't afford it. Bad enough losing the commission and the chance to further examine the book without having the disgrace and scandal of the Strauss thing dug up again. For the first time I wondered what would have happened had I just kept my mouth shut three years earlier? Suppose I'd just minded my own business and quietly taken another job with another antiquarian book dealer? God knows I'd had plenty of offers back then.

If I'd known then what I knew now?

I finished my brandy and ordered another.

How the hell was I supposed to pay my rent after this? How was I supposed to *eat*? I could *not* go on working at Barnes and Noble selling textbooks to college students and romance novels to housewives. I *couldn't.*

I realized that I was traveling swiftly from depressed to self-pitying. Maudlin was the next stop, but it didn't seem to matter. I felt like I'd hit rock bottom.

An orchestral version of "God Rest Ye Merry Gentlemen" came on the piped-in music, and I was fleetingly distracted. Or perhaps the brandy was kicking in, muting my misery. Weird to think we were listening to carols Dickens would have heard. He even mentioned "God Rest Ye Merry Gentlemen" in *A Christmas Carol.*

Why the fuck couldn't people ever forgive and forget? Why didn't they have the imagination or honesty to see that…there but for the grace of God goes…any of us.

I squinted thoughtfully into the distance. *Anjaley Coutts.* Why was that name so familiar? Why had Dickens dedicated that Christmas book to her?

Dedicated it? Apparently he'd written it for her. The only copy in existence, or at least that anyone knew of, was the one he'd penned for her. Literally penned. Eighty pages of penning. A novella. A Christmas novella for Anjaley Coutts.

A few more people wandered into the bar and then wandered out again. I checked my watch. Five thirty. It should have been more crowded given that it was happy hour. Maybe the rain was keeping people away. Or holiday shopping.

I considered ordering a third brandy but not only did I not need a DUI for Christmas, I was going to regret drinking the week's food budget in one afternoon.

Undecided, restless, I turned my glass on the counter. I got that feeling between my shoulder blades—the feeling you get when you're being watched.

I glanced around. Nobody was watching me, but Sedgwick Crisparkle was seated in one of the comfortable leather chairs, reading the newspaper.

I stared down at my empty glass, my heart pounding as hard as if I'd had a narrow escape.

Why? Whatever Professor Fizzwizzle believed, I had every right to sit in that bar and drink myself stupid if I chose. I considered going over to his table to straighten him out on a few points—and was unnerved at myself. I didn't want another confrontation with him. I had no doubt Crisparkle would unhesitatingly rip me a new one in public if I annoyed him for even an instant. That kind of press I could do without.

But the inexplicable desire to explain myself to him persisted. Annoyingly. What did I care if he had the wrong idea about me? Especially since it really wasn't that wrong an idea. I might have been innocent of any wrongdoing in the Strauss affair, but the difficulty of finding work afterwards had led me into more than one, let us say...delicately nuanced transaction. Nothing illegal, but rather close for comfort—and getting closer all the time.

There's nothing like being treated like a crook to make you start thinking and behaving like one.

I wasn't a crook. But I wasn't a choirboy either.

I nursed my drink and thought firmly about getting home. Home to my cold, lonely studio apartment and the never-ending concert by America. Right after I called Mr. S. so he could give my job away to another book hunter.

Right on cue the piped-in music chimed in. "I'll have a blue Christmas without you..."

There was a ripple of alarm through the bar tables. I put it down to the idea of the restrained strings and harps giving way to Elvis Presley, but I caught puzzling movement out of the corner of my eye.

I turned on my stool.

An ocelot stood about a foot away, staring at me as though he'd just scented prey.

Chapter Three

An ocelot.

A living, breathing ocelot. Not a stuffed toy. A fanged, clawed jungle predator.

Wearing a rhinestone collar.

How much had I had to drink? I closed my eyes, opened them, but the ocelot was still there, whiskers twitching.

"Oh. My. God," a girl said at a nearby table as she slowly, slowly rose and backed away toward the door.

The ocelot never looked away from me. Statue-still, it stared me down as though waiting for me to break and run. Where had it come from? More to the point, what the hell had I done to attract its attention?

Nice kitty, I thought, sending positive, friendly vibes skipping across the universe.

Or not. The cat made a sound like it was growling through clenched teeth.

"Uh...okay," I said. "What'll you have?"

"Jesus fucking Christ." The bartender leaned over the bar to get a better look. "Is that a leopard?"

"It's too small to be a leopard," objected the female bartender, joining him. They obviously felt safe behind that barrier. I could have clarified that point for them, but I was otherwise occupied. Meanwhile they continued to debate, as though watching an episode of *Animal Planet.*

"It's a baby leopard."

"No way. Maybe a miniature leopard."

I said, trying to keep my voice calm and soothing—not that I had any idea whether ocelots liked calm, soothing voices, "It's an ocelot. It's wearing a collar. It must belong to one of the guests."

"How would an ocelot get in here?"

I didn't know and neither did I care. "I think you should call someone. Now."

"I think we should call the police."

"I think we should call security."

The ocelot's paw flashed out as he struck at my jean-clad legs. His claws snagged in the denim and we both yanked speedily free, me nearly toppling off the stool in my fright. The ocelot clearly thought this was all my fault and let me know in no uncertain terms. I got behind the stool, gripping it like a lion tamer, no longer caring if I looked foolish or cowardly. Ridiculous though it was, it was also roughly the equivalent of being cornered by a rottweiler.

The female bartender retreated, squeaking maidenly alarm, to the other side of the bar. The remaining bar patrons retreated to the other side of the room. It was only me and the cat in the center ring.

I said weakly, "This is odd. Usually cats like me."

The problem with a life spent reading is you know too much. I knew for example that an ocelot was extremely fast, strong and agile. That they could be very aggressive on occasion—and this seemed to be An Occasion. I knew that they were spectacular climbers. Able to leap to impressive heights, like the top of a bookshelf—or some unfortunate person's head. I knew their bite could be vicious, that they liked to eviscerate their prey with their back legs, and that they had the uncanny ability to sense pressure points and seek them out during an attack.

Attacked by an ocelot in the Champagne Bar of the Hotel Del Monte? Try topping that for freak-show value. I'd have to hope he killed me outright because I'd never live it down.

Safely across the elegant room, Professor Crisparkle slipped out of his tweed blazer and started toward us, holding the jacket out with the clear intent of using it as a kind of net. A couple of people, lined against the wall as though for a firing squad, offered their suggestions and advice. They were ignored.

"Don't move," Crisparkle instructed quietly.

"Who are you talking to? Me or it?" I flicked a nervous gaze from Crisparkle to the cat, which was apparently trying to calculate the best way to get around the flimsy barrier I'd placed between us. "Are you sure you want to do that?"

"I don't think there's much of an option. I believe it's going to attack you." He sounded perfectly calm. That was probably the whole British sang-froid thing. Or perhaps the University of London was a rougher school than it sounded.

Crisparkle sidestepped a fallen chair, and sensing his approach, the ocelot turned with a sneeze-type snarl. Maybe he was in a bad mood because he had the flu.

The side entrance door flew open and a chubby woman in a pink and black checked suit rushed into the bar crying, "Oscar! Oscar! Oh you bad, *bad* kitty."

The ocelot cringed like a guilty dog and the next minute she had scooped it up in her arms and was scurrying away. The rest of us gaped and gawked after her and then the remaining customers burst into conversation.

I dropped the tall stool and slumped against the bar. Crisparkle walked up to me. "Well." It took me a few seconds to collect myself enough to say, "Thank you."

Crisparkle nodded, serious as ever. Not that I was ready to laugh about it myself quite yet. "That was most peculiar," he said, which had to be the understatement of the century. "Even for this city."

"You can say that again." Belatedly it occurred to me that I should probably make more of an effort. I asked, fully expecting rejection, "May I buy you a drink?"

I was surprised when he assented.

He gave the bartender his order and we moved to his table near the fireplace. I sat down, met his gaze, and looked away feeling weirdly self-conscious. Well, maybe not so weird given the circumstances.

As conversation seemed required and he wasn't making an effort, I said, "I've read that they typically go for your groin or armpit. Ocelots, I mean. It was very hard not to visualize that."

"You seemed remarkably calm. I wondered if you knew what you were dealing with."

Oh, I knew. I'd read a lot of boys' adventure novels growing up. All small cats have certain target areas. The ocelot tends to target the armpit, inside of elbows, groin and neck. That makes even a simple bite from an ocelot a big deal. They also tend to repeat strike when deflected. Try blocking an ocelot leaping for your throat, and he'll hit the ground and rebound straight back at you.

I reached for the bar menu as Crisparkle added disapprovingly, "Someone was remarkably, criminally careless in allowing that animal to roam free."

I agreed, but then the whole day had an unreal, almost fantasy quality to it. Sort of like that Steve Martin movie, *L.A.*

Story. I wouldn't have been at all surprised if the selections on the bar menu had suddenly wavered and morphed into secret messages meant only for my eyes. "This is how the other half lives." I shrugged. "I suppose it's how you live too, since you're staying in the hotel."

He frowned—his normal expression with me—but was distracted by the female bartender delivering his drink.

It was the loveliest cocktail I'd ever seen. Real flecks of apparently edible gold sparkled and floated in the sleek martini glass.

"What is that?" I could hardly look away from the glittering concoction.

"A Stardust." He said it rather repressively, and I felt a flicker of amusement.

"I'll have one of those," I told the bartender.

"Did you want to run a tab?"

I shook my head. While Crisparkle sipped his martini, I watched the bartender combine four parts vodka with one part of crème de cacao. I watched with all the attention of a man having to pass his bartender's exam. It was easier than trying to make conversation with my companion. I wasn't even sure why I'd thought sitting down with him was a good idea.

Crisparkle seemed to have equal disinterest in conversing with me. He drank his cocktail and stared at the painting on the far wall, and I watched the bartender slowly empty the cocktail shaker into a martini glass. She slowly, ever so gently, added the sparkling Goldschlager, a cinnamon-flavored liqueur, so that gold flakes drifted slowly through the drink.

She brought the magical-looking brew over to the table along with a small plate of gougères.

"Compliments of the house," she said. At my surprise, she

joked, "The ocelot is paying."

"Oh. Right. Thank you." I put my wallet away.

Crisparkle observed me silently throughout this transaction. The bartender retreated and I took a sip of my drink. A bit sweeter than I liked, but interesting.

He said abruptly, "It's only fair to tell you that no one suggested you were involved in murder. In fact, no one actually said you were even suspected of knowingly participating in forgery."

"You didn't have time to talk to many people."

"Enough. You're not liked, but you're respected. At least..."

I grinned a crooked grin and selected one of the cheese savories. "I know what you mean," I assured him. "It's generally accepted that I have an instinct for the real thing."

"Why did you pretend, then, that you didn't know my book is the genuine article?"

"Because I don't go by instinct anymore."

He waited for me to continue, but I had no intention of spilling my guts to the disapproving Professor Crisparkle. I raised my glass in a mock toast and finished off my drink.

The frown grew more pronounced.

"Are you driving?"

"Eventually."

He was silent, then said shortly, "I probably owe you an apology."

"Don't bother if it hurts that much." His face tightened. I said, "Anyway, saving me from being mauled was apology enough."

Some internal struggle seemed to take place. "Evan Amherst of Amherst Rare Books said that you voluntarily cooperated with the police. That had you not helped them, Strauss would probably have got away with murder."

I curled my lip. "Yes? Well, the fact of the matter is that nobody likes a snitch."

He studied me for a long moment and then said slowly, quite gently, "You were hurt very badly, weren't you?"

I felt myself turn scarlet. Men do not say that kind of thing to each other. They just…don't. I returned harshly, "I was very stupid. I deserved everything that happened to me."

"You're very cynical."

"I have good reason to be." This was my cue to exit. I pushed my empty glass away, shoved my chair back, opened my mouth to say goodnight.

Crisparkle astonished me by getting up first. "My round, I think." He went to the bar leaving me blinking after him.

I relaxed in my chair and listened to the Christmas carols and the quiet murmur of voices from other tables. It occurred to me that I was already over the legal limit. That meant calling a taxi or sleeping in my car. Neither idea appealed—especially as I might be sleeping in my car full-time soon enough.

Crisparkle was back in a very short while with two more of those sparkling chocolate-cinnamon cocktails.

"What are you planning to spend all that money on?" I inquired, taking my glass and trying hard not to spill a precious drop.

He raised his eyebrows.

"When the Dickens sells," I clarified.

"So you admit that the book is genuine?"

"Off the record? Yes. I believe it's genuine. I'm not putting my name to an appraisal without fully examining the book, though."

"The appraisal destined for this mysterious client of yours?"

Instead of responding to that, I tilted my head, studied him, asked, "Is Crisparkle your real name?"

"Yes."

"You do know Crisparkle is the name of a Dickens character?"

"Mm. Canon Crisparkle. My great-great-great-grandfather."

"Your..."

He smiled. It was breathtaking. Literally. He had dimples.

"Who *are* you?" I couldn't help asking.

"Quite right. We should do this over again." He reached across the table and offered his hand. "Sedgwick Crisparkle."

And I had thought the ocelot incident was odd. I shook hands automatically. "James Winter."

He released my hand, I picked up my glass, and he inquired smoothly, "Would you like to come up to my hotel room and look at my etchings, James?"

Chapter Four

On the glossy surface of the table, tiny gold flecks, like microscopic gold fish, floated in the pool of my spilled drink. I tore my fascinated gaze away from the puddle and stared at Professor Crisparkle's serious expression.

"Sorry?"

"Would you like to come back to my hotel room?"

I tried very hard to read his face. "To take another look at the book?" I asked cautiously. Very cautiously, because I couldn't believe that he was suggesting what he apparently—possibly—was.

"The book has been returned to the hotel safe."

"Oh."

"I thought you might like to come to my room anyway."

"This is...sudden."

"Yes, it is. But I had the impression when we met that you would not be adverse to the idea." He sounded so precise, almost...mathematical.

"I had the impression when we met that you disliked me. A lot."

"I should know better than to form preconceived notions." It was the serious, half-smile again. "Shall I tell you what two things convinced me I was wrong about you?"

I wondered if I'd gotten in a car accident on my way to the Hotel Del Monte and was, in fact, happily hallucinating in a coma somewhere. "Sure." I sipped what was left of my drink, waiting to hear this revelation.

"Your hands were shaking when you saw *The Christmas Cake.*"

I had absolutely no answer to that.

"And you were brave when you thought you were going to be mauled by that cat."

"Brave? I wasn't brave at all. I was scared shitless."

"Yes, but you made yourself stay calm. Bravery isn't the absence of fear, it's how you deal with being afraid. When you asked the ocelot what it wanted to drink, I realized I had probably been wrong about you."

"You are a very weird guy and this is a very weird night."

"Also," Crisparkle said, as though needing to keep the record absolutely straight, "you blush. I find that very endearing in a man of your age."

I opened my mouth and then closed it.

"Would you like to come back to my hotel room?"

"Uh...yes," I replied.

The night smelled of rain and lemon and wood smoke as we made our way back across the arched bridge. The moon's red reflection in the still water of the lake was absurdly magnified, the tall reeds appeared gilded, the face in the clock tower shone benignly.

As we walked through the dripping trees I was trying to

remember the last time I'd got laid. After Corey and I split up I'd pretty much slept with everything that would lie down with me—or merely hold still—but I'd tired of that before long. Now that I thought about it, I really couldn't remember the last time I'd had sex with something besides my right hand—maybe because none of it had been worth remembering. Not that sex for its own sake wasn't a good and useful thing, but it was a pleasant novelty to be preparing for sex with someone I was actually interested in.

Because whatever else Sedgwick Crisparkle was, he was certainly interesting.

We reached his room and he let us inside the warm darkness. Moonlight shone through the French doors and made a butterfly net of pale squares and cross-hatching across the plush carpet. The embers in the fireplace glowed orange, throwing the furniture in shadow. Except for the bed. The king-sized bed was perfectly illuminated like a stage prop in the footlights, which for reasons unknown I found funny. But then I'd had enough to drink that I found pretty much everything funny.

Amused and horny: not a bad state in which to find yourself when you're about to fuck with a handsome stranger.

The whisper of buttons popping and zippers sliding—and our rather heavy breathing—were the only sounds as we shed our clothes, heeled out of our shoes. Crisparkle—no, I couldn't go to bed with a guy named Crisparkle—*Sedgwick* caught my hand, drawing me to the bed. I could see the gleam of his eyes in the darkness. He'd taken his glasses off. His face looked much younger and almost mischievous in the moonlight as he grabbed me around the waist and tumbled us both to the duvet-covered mattress. It was like landing in a cloud—with an angel on top of me. An angel that tasted like cinnamon and chocolate and stardust.

I'd sort of forgotten how nice kissing was. How...personal. I tried to take a more active role but Sedgwick seemed to have his heart set on taste-testing me. He kissed and licked and nibbled his way along my jawline, down my throat. His mouth latched onto one of my nipples and I arched up, gulping for air.

He half-lifted off me. "Did I hurt you?"

"I wasn't expecting teeth."

"Sorry. I got rather carried away."

"It's okay. Only..." I forgot what I was trying to say as his mouth closed on me again, only this time softly, sweetly. I relaxed back into the rose-embossed cloud, squirming pleasurably as he continued with that distracting wet pressure of expert tongue and lips. He moved to the other nipple.

Jeeeeeeesus. It had been longer than I thought because—

"Wait," I gasped.

Sedgwick raised his head. "I couldn't have hurt you that time." He sounded mildly indignant.

"N-no. You've got to slow down or you're going to make me come."

"*Oh.*" He considered this. "But you'd like that, wouldn't you?"

"Not in the first four minutes."

"Ah. Right." He was smiling—rather a wicked smile. Then he bent again and proceeded to graze and nuzzle his way down my midsection and abdomen. By the time his mouth got to my groin I was about ready to hyperventilate—except that I wouldn't have willingly missed one instant of that incredible sensation of hot wet mouth on my shivering nakedness.

I ran my hands over the hard, smooth contours of his broad shoulders and surprisingly muscular back. He obviously didn't simply sit around watching test tubes all day. He had a nice taut ass too, but that was well out of my reach by then.

I waited, literally quivering in anticipation. His breath gusted warmly over the head of my cock as he sighed. "As much as I want to do this, we probably should take precautions."

Manfully, I bit back my groan of disappointment. I felt a totally uncharacteristic desire to urge him on, to assure him I was clean as the driven snow and remind him that even if I wasn't, the chances of contracting anything from fellatio were a slim .04 percent. Except with my luck...

"Yeah," I said huskily. "Do you—?" The days when I carried a condom in my wallet were long behind me. I barely carried money anymore.

"Hang about," he said with unseemly cheerfulness. The mattress springs pinged as he jumped up. He was back in a flash. And, in fact, something *was* flashing in his hand. Something palely green and mildly glowing.

"What on earth?" I sat up. My cock sat down. "What the hell is *that?*"

"A friend's idea of a joke, but I think it'll serve our purpose." He held his hand up, apparently dangling a pale green tongue from his fist.

"Is that supposed to be a condom?"

"Mm. They come in red and green. Christmas colors. And they're flavored. Peppermint or piña colada." He tossed a couple of shining unopened packets on the duvet.

Now it all made sense. A nutty professor on a business vacation. Crisparkle was here to sell his book and get laid. It wasn't my luck that had changed, it was *his*. Still comfortably inebriated, I didn't begrudge him. It wasn't as though I'd imagined this was anything real. As though we were falling in love like the stars of a sappy here! channel holiday romance.

"What flavor did you choose?" I asked curiously, as he tore into a packet.

"Peppermint. You strike me as the peppermint type."

As opposed to piña colada? Probably. I reached for the rubber beacon, but Sedgwick held it out of reach. "Relax. I'll take care of this."

"Be my guest." I crooked my arm behind my head, watching with almost detached interest as he settled himself beside me again. By then I'd lost my erection, but I was more than happy to let him try to recapture my interest.

He managed that by putting the condom on me using his mouth. His whole face seemed to be getting into the act—quite literally—and within moist, warm seconds I was stiff and straight as a flagpole flying the regimental colors. The fact that my regimental colors were apparently peppermint-flavored evergreen was beside the point. The graze of teeth and razor stubble and tongue...it was very difficult to hold still long enough to allow him to pull the rubber down the shaft of my penis with his lips.

"I wish I'd been there while you were practicing this parlor trick," I managed.

He huffed a laugh, his breath warm against my balls. "Mmm hmm..."

I threw my head back gulping for air. If this was the preliminary—

His hot knowing mouth closed on the faintly tingling head of my cock, and I made a sound probably similar to that the mouse had made when it first beheld the Christmas cake. I could feel my nutty professor smiling as he wrapped one long-fingered hand around the base of my penis as though I were a peppermint stick and he was about to snack.

Oh my God it was delicious—even through the rubber—

that hard suction and slathery warmth. And it went on and *on.* Or as long as I could take, which actually wasn't that long because it had been way too long...long...*long...*

My balls drew up tight to my body, taut and aching. He cupped them with a gentle hand, and that combination of strength and gentleness was my undoing. I reached out to trace the line of his jaw and felt his cheeks hollowing as he sucked harder. My entire focus narrowed to one glimmering point like a shining star that grew hotter and whiter and hotter and then suddenly exploded through me. I could no more have smothered the scream that tore out of me than I could have stopped the starfire pulsing out of my cock—only to be lapped up by that shining peppermint tongue.

Sedgwick continued to gently mouth me as I softened.

I drifted, vaguely aware that he was dealing with the practicalities and not particularly interested. But after a time he was lying beside me again and I became aware of his growing impatience. It was nudging me in the belly.

I opened my eyes. What I really wanted was to curl up in this wonderful bed and fall asleep listening to the rain which had started again. I was on the downside of the alcohol, relaxed and satisfied with sexual release. I could feel the tension practically humming through his long, lean frame.

"Would you like the same?" I made myself ask.

"Well..."

There was a certain awkwardness in his tone. I considered it, blinking drowsily. It dawned on me what he wanted but wasn't comfortable asking for.

"You want to fuck me?" I guessed.

"I do. Yes." He reached out and stroked my chest. "Very much."

I considered it. Frankly, it was probably less effort than giving him a return blowjob, and...it wasn't like I didn't like it. If he was half as skilful and inventive at fucking as he was sucking I was probably in for a treat.

I glanced to the side of the bed. "Well, I know you have another condom."

"Oh yes." I could see the gleam of his teeth in the gloom. "One for every day of my visit, and I've already been here three days."

"Good God."

"He is tonight." Sedgwick was already rising—in every sense. What was he going to get now? I heard the slide of drawers; he had actually unpacked and put his clothes away in the dressers. Then he vanished briefly into the bathroom. He returned to the bed and dropped down beside me with a bounce.

I rolled onto my side, the better to see him. "What flavor did you pick this time?"

"Red. For sake of variety."

"Red isn't a flavor."

"You'd be surprised. How would you like to do this?"

I shrugged. "I'm reasonably versatile."

"I thought you might be."

"What's that supposed to mean?"

I heard the edge in my voice and knew he did too because he said immediately, "You have a sort of...sexual confidence. It's in the way you stand, even the way you sit, the way you looked into my eyes when we met. You have your insecurities, but they don't extend to your sexuality. You're very comfortable in your skin." He added—not as a compliment but as a matter of fact, "It's a very beautiful skin."

It took me an instant to recover enough to say, "You have a very appealing surface yourself."

"Thank you." I thought he might be laughing at me but it was impossible to tell in the darkness. Then again, perhaps he thought I was laughing at him.

I sat up the rest of the way and said briskly, "You've done this before, I assume?"

"Yes. I'm no virgin. You won't hurt me and I won't hurt you."

Not a virgin but his friends had sent him off on vacation with a fistful of condoms. On the rebound then? Probably better not to concern myself. Sedgwick had already made it clear that this was not the beginning of a beautiful relationship—not that I was looking for that either. At this point I was hoping that he'd let me spend the night once we finished up.

I was still turning this over in my mind when he leaned forward and covered my mouth in a kiss that was both delicate and deliberate, a reclaiming of attention—and unexpectedly, expertly arousing. We went into each other's arms and it felt like the most natural thing in the world. I could feel myself turning on again, that electric awareness, bright and twinkling, as if someone had plugged in the Christmas tree lights.

We kissed a little more, light and easy, Sedgwick whispered words I didn't catch, but the tone was sufficiently admiring and the hand stroking me was certainly pleasurable. He seemed to know what he was doing, and I was surprised to find my cock raising its hopeful head, apparently not completely tired out after all.

Sedgwick's fingers traced a delicate brushing stroke against the entrance of my body and pushed inside. There was something soft and silky on his fingers, a sweet scent. I lifted my head.

"What is that?"

"Whipped chocolate crème brûlée."

"What?"

"It's a body cream soufflé."

"Did you pack for an orgy or what?"

He chuckled, his fingers still slip-sliding deliciously and intimately inside the channel of my body. I moaned as he managed to hit the sensitive nub of my prostate, sending shivers of sensation through me. I shifted to give him better access, and he whispered, "You're so wonderfully uninhibited."

He withdrew his fingers, and the large blunt head of his cock rubbed against the tight hole of my body. He bent his head, his mouth nuzzled me behind the ear and he gave me another of those ghostly nips.

A small shock, like a spark or a short, rippled through me. I jumped, and as I did, his cock shoved past the ring of tight quivering muscle, sheathing itself in my body. The silky hair of his groin dusted my sensitized skin.

"Oh, that's brilliant," he groaned. "So hot, so blood hot."

Or maybe he said "bloody hot", but either way it was exciting to hear him saying those things in that dark, guttural voice. "Like a suede glove grabbing me, stroking me…"

It was disconcerting too, to get this blow-by-blow commentary, when all I wanted to do was focus on that fullness pulsing inside me. We were so close, hearts banging away against each other, damp and feverish bodies smelling of clean sweat and musk and…well, cocoa and peppermint, breath stirring each other's heated faces—although his breath was doing more stirring than mine.

"Like a hot, black fist…"

"My *God* you talk a lot," I gasped, arching up in an attempt to get him going. I pushed back on that long, thick shaft, and he pushed back, and we fell into a steady rhythm. The earthy sounds we made fucking, the faint smack and suck, the grunts and gasps, were disturbingly intimate.

That pump and pull was like a hammer striking the golden frames of angel wings, pounding them into shining, glinting pennons. Perspiration sheened our bodies and our breath grew harsher as we bent our backs and worked this forge, and then the wings began to beat, trying to take flight, moving faster and faster, and we seemed to lift right off the ground, right off the pillows and bedding, and hang there transfixed as warm, white Halle-fricking-lujah surged through.

And then we dropped back to earth, wet, winded and weak. Human again.

I was very drowsy. I knew I should get up and start dressing, but it had been a tiring day and an exhausting evening, I'd had too much to drink, and had been attacked by wild beasts...

I was vaguely aware that Sedgwick was muttering as he fussed with the bedclothes. I wished he'd knock it off and go to sleep. I'd be out of his hair the minute the sun came up.

The duvet slid out from under me and I was tumbled with considerate efficiency between the sheets. A long, lithe body landed next to me. I opened bleary eyes as a friendly hand shoved a pillow beneath my head. The covers floated down over us, warm and downy soft.

"Pleasant dreams," Sedgwick whispered and gave my forehead a peppermint-scented kiss.

Chapter Five

I dreamed that an ocelot was chewing on a first edition of *A Christmas Carol*. When I tried to snatch the book away, it sank its fangs into my hand.

Head throbbing, I opened my eyes to watery green daylight. I was in a hotel room. A very comfortable hotel room that smelled of orange furniture polish and sex. The fluffy duvet and long draperies were in matching old-fashioned pink and gray cabbage rose print. Rain trickled down the windowpanes of a pair of French doors and sent sperm-shaped shadows twitching and jerking across the sage green walls.

My head hurt. That was because I'd had too much to drink. My hand hurt. That was because a strange man was lying on it.

I wriggled my hand out from under my naked companion and studied him. Sedgwick Crisparkle looked less angelic and more rakishly debauched that morning. He had quite a heavy beard and the longest eyelashes I'd ever seen on a guy. He did not snore, but he made a gentle puffing sound. He looked deeply asleep and unreasonably content.

I flexed my fingers a couple of times, then sat up carefully, wincing, and looked around for my clothes. They were on the floor near the door where I'd apparently dropped them. I inched over, trying not to wake my host, and got slowly, cautiously out of bed.

I had to stop halfway to the door to give my spinning head a rest. How the hell much had I had to drink the night before? Not that much really, but I hadn't eaten. Those shooting stars, or whatever they were called, packed an unexpected wallop. I tried to make out the numbers on my watch. They seemed very tiny. I peered harder.

Six thirty. Plenty of time. I didn't need to be at work until four. I could go home, sleep more, shower, and...call Mr. S.

"Not feeling well?"

I jumped, whimpered and clutched my head. "Must you shout?"

"Sorry." Part of what he said was lost in a gigantic yawn. "Didn't mean to startle you."

I heard the rustle of bedclothes being thrown back and the pad of bare feet on carpet. The drapes were jerked shut and the room returned to a soothing darkness. I heard him pad past me on his way back to bed, so when a warm hand was laid on my naked shoulder I did another of those starts and yelps.

"You have a very nervous disposition," Sedgwick said disapprovingly. "You ought to consider supplementing your diet with bee pollen."

I gazed up at him, opened my mouth. Closed it. Closed my eyes. Why not? I was clearly still dreaming. *Bee pollen?*

"I think you should come back to bed." I opened my eyes at that particular note in his voice. Sedgwick was smiling a funny sort of shy half-smile. "I think you'd feel much better in bed."

He put his arm around me and I permitted myself to be led back to bed.

When I woke the next time the sun was shining and a busboy was carefully lowering a large tray with covered dishes to the table in front of the fireplace.

"Lovely," Sedgwick was saying as he signed the busboy's chit.

I raised my head, peering owlishly over the edge of the duvet, and the busboy grinned at me before taking his bill book and departing.

When the door had safely closed, I climbed out of bed, pulled on my jeans—to Sedgwick's evident disappointment—and investigated the breakfast tray. A white teapot, two gold-rimmed china cups, a jar of honey, a small basket of muffins and nut breads, a bowl of fresh berries. One plate offered eggs Benedict with shaved honey ham and what appeared to be an herbed Hollandaise sauce. Another plate had thick round Belgian waffles, richly, sweetly scented of vanilla, cinnamon and topped with whipped cream, fresh strawberries and pecans.

"I wasn't sure what you liked," Sedgwick said at whatever he read in my expression. "We can share or I can order you something completely different." He was wearing the kind of gorgeous silk dressing gown people only wear in old movies and the horn-rimmed glasses, but even behind those severe glasses his face looked much younger and softer that morning.

I dropped down on the fat comfortable chair cattycorner to the table. "No. This is...amazing. Any of this is fine." I couldn't remember the last time I'd had a breakfast like this.

He looked smug. "We'll split everything down the middle."

"We will if we eat all this."

He laughed. "I admit I don't usually eat like this, although I do like my breakfasts. I'm on holiday, though, so...when in Rome."

"I'm very glad you're not in Rome this morning." I heard myself say that and cringed. Talk about sappy. I added quickly, "I'd be eating a bowl of Cheerios right now."

"I'm glad I'm not in Rome too." He smiled right into my eyes.

After that I couldn't think of anything to say, and I devoted myself to eating that fantastic breakfast.

As vocal as Sedgwick had been in bed, he was not terribly chatty over breakfast. It seemed to be a replete and satisfied silence, though. He appeared content, and each time our eyes met, he offered that disarming smile.

In fact, it felt so natural and comfortable between us, I was encouraged to ask, "Will you let me have another look at *The Christmas Cake?*"

Sedgwick's gaze dropped to the egg-topped muffin he was neatly cutting through. "No."

"*No?*" I felt bewildered, not least by the brusqueness of this. "Why?"

He sighed. "After last night I'd hoped you'd let this go."

What the hell did last night have to do with it? "I was hired to appraise the book. I'm being paid to do that. If I 'let this go' I also have to let go of that commission. Which I need."

He said quietly, "James, I think we're both realists."

"You've lost me."

"If you don't stop now, you're liable to spoil this, you know."

"No, I don't know. Spoil this? How is asking to see the book spoiling anything?" And now I was starting to get annoyed.

Behind the severe glasses, Sedgwick raised his green-gold eyes, gave me a long, direct stare.

"I don't know what that look is supposed to mean."

"It means we're having a very nice time together. Let's not ruin it by bringing up...unpleasant memories."

It took me a beat or two to work out what he was referring to. The rush of anger and hurt left me feeling winded. Lack of oxygen made my voice come out flat and compressed. "I thought you didn't believe the rumors about me."

He said with all the dispassionate exactitude one could ask of a science teacher, "What I said was, no one accused you of being directly involved in murder or forgery. That is *all* I said."

I'm sure my disbelief showed on my face. Hopefully nothing else showed. The laugh that escaped me took us both by surprise. "You're right. My mistake."

I got up, my knee knocking the edge of my plate and tipping it over. The waffle landed in a sticky plop face down on the plush carpet. I didn't give a fuck about that. I didn't give a fuck about anything at that point. It was all very clear, diamond-edged and razor-bright. He didn't trust me. He thought I had possibly been involved in murder and forgery, but he liked having sex with me—or possibly with anyone and I happened to be willing—and he didn't want me to spoil that by bringing up something as awkward as business.

Sedgwick rose too. "James."

I ignored him, finding my shirt and buttoning it up quickly. I got one of the buttonholes misaligned, so it hung crookedly— appropriately, it seemed—but I didn't care. Was not going to stay in that room one instant longer than I had to.

"James—?"

I was hunting with fierce attention for my other shoe. I found it under his side of the bed.

"Apparently I've offended you. I...didn't intend to."

Now that was almost funny. I slipped the shoe on. I was missing my socks, but that really seemed a small price to pay for getting out of there without committing murder for real.

"I'm not sure what I—oft times I put things more bluntly than I intend," Sedgwick was saying. He sounded a fraction impatient. "Don't you think you're overreacting?"

I found my jacket and headed for the door. He was right behind me.

"James, I really don't *see*—" He put a hand on my shoulder, and I spun around and shoved him back. The arm of the sofa caught him behind his thighs, and he half fell back over it, glasses crooked, blinking up in astonishment at me.

I said, "Enjoy the rest of your stay in L.A., arsehole."

I managed not to slam the door on my way out.

I ran into Darcy on the way up to my apartment. She was dragging—literally dragging—plastic bags of groceries up the stairs. She'd already lost a can of condensed milk and a packet of lime Jell-O on the lower steps. The frozen turkey was perched precariously about midway up the staircase. I picked it up, tucked it under my arm, adding to my collection, and overtook Darcy near the top level.

The amount of groceries, clearly destined for Christmas day, made me feel queasy. Why did she have to go to so much trouble? Why did she have to make such a big deal of it? Why had I ever agreed to spend the day with her? The last thing I wanted to do was have to try to pretend holiday civility for hours on end.

She greeted me, flushed and panting. "They're saying we may have snow for Christmas!"

"They're lying. As usual."

"James." She sounded as wounded as though I had control

of the weather and was deliberately withholding snowfall.

I got control. "Snow in Los Angeles? Come on, Dar. Besides, the sun is shining." Way too brightly.

"It might," she said stubbornly. "It could be a freak storm."

"Well, that would be right for L.A." While she fished for her keys, I deposited the bags and turkey outside her door and moved on to my own.

I let myself in to my dark apartment, closed the blinds tight so it would be even darker, and pulled down the wall bed. I stripped off my clothes and threw myself on the cool, rumpled sheets.

Sedgwick Crisparkle could go fuck himself.

Granted, he shouldn't have any trouble finding help with that, given his single-mindedness.

I lay there brooding, and eventually my mind wandered back to the Christmas book. What was the connection with Miss Anjaley Coutts, though? Why was that name familiar to me?

Suddenly restless, I rose and went over to the bookshelves. My books were about all I'd managed to salvage from the financial ruins of my previous life. Corey and I had lived well and inevitably a percentage of that living had been on extended credit. It hadn't been a problem because I earned good money, but finding myself abruptly unemployed—and homeless—had wreaked financial havoc. They say the average American family is four paychecks from the street. In my case it was four credit card cash advances. I'd paid the cards off—including the horrific interest—but I was literally living paycheck to paycheck. Needless to say I earned a lot less these days.

But I still had my books. Most of them. So far.

I stroked the green cloth cover of Chesterton's *Charles*

Dickens, opened the book, flipping through.

It was as I scanned a section on Dickens' involvement with Urania Cottage, a home for fallen women, that I remembered. One of the wealthiest women of her day, Angela Burdett-Coutts shared with her friend Charles Dickens, "a fellow campaigner and reformer", a passion for practical do-gooding. Urania Cottage had been their second joint venture.

Although he had initially resisted involvement in the asylum for fallen women, Dickens had eventually become active in every aspect of the home, even debating with Burdett-Coutts what uniforms the fallen ladies should wear. (Dickens had pleaded for color but been overruled.)

Anjaley Coutts and Angela Burdett-Coutts. Too close to be a coincidence. *Martin Chuzzlewit* was dedicated to Burdett-Coutts in 1844, and so apparently had the missing Christmas novella written in 1847, the year Urania Cottage was established.

This was absolutely...fascinating. At least to someone like me—and certainly anyone who collected Dickens.

I read a bit more about Urania Cottage and Dickens' involvement, but nothing shed insight into *The Christmas Cake*. At last my adventures of the night overtook me and I put the book aside, returned to bed and closed my eyes.

I was drifting off into exhausted sleep as the strains of America filtered softly through the wall.

"I'm disappointed, James," Mr. Stephanopoulos said when I called him later that afternoon. "You usually show more initiative."

I closed my eyes against the throb behind them—a throb that had been there ever since I left the Hotel Del Monte that morning. "The book looks genuine to me, but I need to examine

197

it more closely to be sure."

"When do you think you'll have the opportunity? We're running out of time."

I opened my mouth to tell him the truth, to tell him to find another errand boy, that even if Sedgwick Crisparkle would let me within ten miles of that book, I wouldn't go near him or it.

Through the wall of my apartment I could hear America. *Don't give up until you drink from the silver cup...*

I was going to gift this entire apartment complex and buy Darcy a Crosby, Stills, Nash and Young album for Christmas.

"James?" Mr. S. prodded.

I could always go with my gut instinct and tell Stephanopoulos that the book was the real thing. But then he would ask me to broker the deal between himself and Sedgwick, and even if I could bring myself to speak to Sedgwick again, he'd clearly never accept a deal that I was any part of. Especially since Mr. S. had made it clear I couldn't tell Sedgwick who the real buyer was.

What was that about anyway?

Not that it was any of my business now. I needed to put the whole matter out of my mind—except that wasn't easy to do when I needed the commission so urgently.

I took a deep breath and lied, "I'm supposed to talk to him later this evening."

I could feel Mr. S.'s frustration clear across the city. "I don't understand the delay."

"Crisparkle doesn't share your sense of urgency. He's happy to have the book go to auction."

"No. I must have that book," Stephanopoulos insisted.

"We're not even sure it's the real thing."

"You're sure," he said with unexpected certainty.

The fight went abruptly out of me. Perhaps it was the reflection that I would be having two eggs and Hoisin sauce for supper. "I—perhaps."

"I *must* have that book."

"I know."

"*Whatever* you have to do, James."

"I'll do whatever I can. Within the legal limits, of course."

He laughed. "Of course, of course."

My thoughts were decidedly unmerry as I replaced the phone receiver.

Ebenezer Scrooge would have learned a few things about the dark side of humanity if he'd happened to work in a national chain bookstore three days before Christmas.

The depressing fact is, no one reads anymore. Most of the people collecting books don't even read them. Book collecting is very hot, don't get me wrong. In certain circles rare books are considered sexy and exotic. But for the average person, books remind them of the bad old days of homework and report cards. For these folks, books and bookstores are the last resort, the last desperate option for befuddled holiday-makers who have run out of ideas for presents for people they don't know that well. Books rank somewhere between a tie and a box of chocolates. It's a book or go home empty-handed—and empty-handed means again facing the stores and parking lots that one frightening day closer to Christmas.

I had learned to get through the Season of Plastic with the minimum of anguish by simply playing the class card. As in, "*Mastering the Art of French Cooking* is a classy gift." People like the thought that they are giving classy gifts.

I'm looking for...

"*The Beatles Anthology* is a classy gift."

Do you have anything for...?

"*The Case for God* is a classy gift."

She's always saying...

"*Eat, Pray, Love: One Woman's Search for Everything Across Italy, India and Indonesia* is a classy gift."

Maybe you can help me...

"*A Christmas Carol* is a classy gift."

Now where had that come from? Not that it wasn't true. And, in fact, Dickens sold quite well—continued to sell quite well—around the holidays. But I didn't want to think about Dickens right then. It reminded me of the promise I had made Mr. Stephanopoulos.

Worse, it reminded me of Sedgwick Crisparkle.

No sooner had I re-resolved to think no more about Dickens, Stephanopoulos or bloody Professor Crisparkle than the fates seemed to conspire to keep the latter in my mind. Constantly. A customer asked for *The Secret Life of Bees.* Another asked for *The Backyard Beekeeper: An Absolute Beginner's Guide to Keeping Bees in Your Yard and Garden.*

Up until then I'd felt I was doing a very good job of not thinking about Sedgwick or the night before, but I couldn't help remembering his bee pollen comment that morning—it felt like a lifetime ago. I had liked him. A lot. Although he was clearly a nut.

After an hour or two of hell I was rescued from the book floor and sent to man one of the registers up front. I considered that a reprieve. The extent of required socializing amounted to asking if it was cash or credit and if the customer had a membership card.

I rang up a few hundred books on automatic pilot and the line to the bank of registers never grew any shorter. I spared a glance for my fellow sweating, flushed sales associates. We were like the last centurions, backs to the wall, facing down the barbarian hordes.

At one point I knocked a stack of bookmarks to the floor. Smothering an un-holiday-spirited curse, I knelt, scooped them up, rose from behind the desk. "May I help you?"

Sedgwick Crisparkle stood on the other side of the counter.

Chapter Six

Infuriatingly, my initial reaction was a totally illogical leap of shocked delight. This was followed by a far more understandable surge of wary hostility.

"Hello," he said when I didn't speak.

I nodded curtly.

He persisted in that polite conversational tone. "You have no idea how hard it was to track you down."

I was torn between horror that he must have spoken to my former colleagues, one of whom—at least—obviously knew what I had been reduced to, and flattered confusion that he was trying to find me. I was also aware of the line of customers shifting and grumbling restlessly behind him.

"Is there something I can help you with?" I asked frostily.

"Oh." He offered a self-conscious peep of the dimples and set an enormous stack of children's books on the counter.

I began ringing up books. *Three Cups of Tea, To Kill a Mockingbird, The Lightning Thief,* a paperback edition of *The Boxcar Children*—which I nearly dropped. It's hard to remain unmoved at the sight of a big, strong man buying cute little children's books. I did my best. "Did you want these gift wrapped?"

"Yes. Look, do you have a break soon? I need to speak with

you."

"No." I kept ringing up books. Who were all these books for? He was probably married. Married, closeted, and enjoying a short break from real life.

"No, you don't have a break?"

"No. I mean, yes. I do not have a break. I already had it. And no. I am not going to speak with you on or off my break." It occurred to me that I was passing up an opportunity I could not afford to pass up if I wanted to earn Mr. S.'s commission, but pride and anger was working me like an intrusive hand up a puppet's sleeve. In fact, I was getting angrier by the minute as I relived the various humiliations of my day. Not that they were all his fault, but a good portion were.

I finished ringing him up and delivered the total. He barely blinked as he handed over his credit card. I slid it, handed it back to him. Nodded to the gift wrap table at the end of the aisle. "They'll take care of you over there."

He didn't move. "James, I realize you're angry, but I do need to speak to you."

"*Next*," I called more vehemently than necessary.

He flushed. The next customer stepped to the counter, and after a hesitation, Sedgwick fumblingly gathered his books and receipt and moved away.

I spared him a couple of glances between customers. He stood frowning and abstracted as his books were wrapped by one of the community volunteers.

The third time I looked up, he was walking out through the glass doors, scowling.

As the doors swung shut behind him and he vanished into the night, the angry energy that had fueled me seeped away. All at once I was tired and depressed. It was going to be a very long evening.

As I automatically worked the register I decided I had been foolish and hasty in sending Sedgwick off like that. I should have heard him out. Perhaps it had belatedly occurred to the arrogant asshole that maybe I did really have a wealthy client, and brushing me and my client off was a stupid move.

Perhaps he was willing to bargain now that he'd had time to think things over. Yes, I shouldn't have let my hurt ego get the better of me without seeing whether there was a way to turn the situation to my advantage.

Dickens wrote it himself: "The first rule of business is: Do other men for they would do you."

I needed to get over my hurt pride so that I could do Sedgwick Crisparkle properly. In a matter of speaking.

Or maybe it was something else. Maybe he wanted to make some sort of lame-ass apology in order to sleep with me again. He was obviously hard up if his friends and well-wishers sent him off on vacation with that much encouragement to get laid.

Well, even if that was the case, why not use that? Why not treat him exactly as he deserved—like the person he imagined I was would treat him? Why not use him the way he'd used me?

The more I considered the idea, the better I liked it.

Yes. Since Sedgwick Crisparkle already believed I was a scheming crook capable of everything from forgery to murder, why not give him a taste of real double-dealing?

I decided that when I got home I would call him—hopefully waking him out of a sound sleep—and agree to meet. And then I would do everything in my power to get another look at that book and arrange a sale between him and Stephanopoulos. In fact, I was going to do my best to arrange that sale whether I got another look at the book or not—since according to Mr. S. he would be the last person Sedgwick would want to sell to. It delighted me to think the book would go to a man Sedgwick didn't want it to go to.

And yet, even as I made these plans, there was a small dismayed corner of my heart. Like those stupid cartoons when you're a kid: little red devil on one shoulder and the little angel in his nightie on the other. My good angel was hiding his eyes.

By the time we got out of the store it was nearly twelve thirty.

I said goodnight to my coworkers and was making my way across the now nearly empty parking lot when a car door opened and a familiar voice called, "James!"

I halted. Sedgwick walked quickly toward me. "James." He sounded out of breath though it was only a few feet from where I stood to his innocuous rental car. "Please listen to me for one minute."

I stared at him stonily. I knew I was going to have to unbend if I was really going to put my evil plans into effect, but he'd caught me off guard again and my instinctive reaction was emotional and unproductive.

"I'm very bad at this kind of conversation," Sedgwick informed me, like this was supposed to be a news bulletin.

"Fifty seconds."

"What?"

"You asked for a minute. You've got forty-five seconds left."

"I apologize for anything I might have said that offended you this morning."

"Apology accepted. Goodnight." I turned away.

"Wait a sec." He caught my arm. I stood still. I'd have liked to glare haughtily down at him, but he was—annoyingly—just that bit taller than me. So it was Sedgwick gazing down at me—

and the expression in his eyes was disconcerting. "I've been waiting two and a half hours and I *am* going to talk to you."

"You still have fifteen seconds, go ahead."

"I gave you the wrong impression this morning. I do not—categorically *do not*—believe you had anything to do with murder or forgery. But I feel that there's something not aboveboard with this anonymous client of yours. This whole preemptive bid business. I've never heard of such a thing. It doesn't seem…" I could see him think twice about finishing that sentence.

"It's not playing nice, but there's nothing unusual about it. Look it up on the goddamned internet if you think it's such an outlandish idea." I was genuinely exasperated. Of all the things to be suspicious of, he was taking exception to the piece of the equation that was actually reasonably legitimate.

"Can we find a place to discuss this in a civilized manner?"

I dearly wanted to tell him no, we couldn't. But that hardly fit with my plans. Plus…I did want to see him again. I did want the chance to justify myself to him. My injured ego and hurt feelings pretty much demanded it.

We went to an all-night coffee shop on Brand Avenue, settling in a booth near the back of the brightly lit room. I was surprised to find how nervous I was, and I tried to cover it by memorizing all the pies on the menu.

The waiter arrived and Sedgwick ordered coffee and cherry pie. I ordered coffee.

As soon as the waiter departed, Sedgwick said, with that unexpected self-consciousness, "First of all, I wanted to say that…I had a really nice time last night."

My face warmed. I unbent enough to say grudgingly, "Me too."

"Secondly, you should know that I am, per my family and friends, an insensitive clod. I tend to speak without considering other people's feelings."

I said coolly, "Sugarcoating it wouldn't have changed anything. You think I'm a crook."

"No."

"Have you changed your mind about letting me examine the book?"

He hesitated.

The injured pride and hurt feelings I'd been struggling with all day and evening came bubbling back to the surface like magma expanding toward the mouth of a volcano.

I said, "The fact is, I'm tired, I didn't really want a cup of coffee, and I don't feel like being polite to you anymore tonight." I rose. "Since you're so into the unvarnished truth, the truth is I don't want to see you again and I don't want to talk to you again."

He rose too, and now he was irritated. "I have never met *anyone* as oversensitive as you."

"You should get out more." My control, such as it was, slipped. "If you'd been through what I went through, you'd be oversensitive too."

I turned and walked out to the interest of our fellow late-night diners.

It was getting to be quite a habit with me.

The amazing thing was, chasing after me was apparently getting to be a habit with Sedgwick. He was out the door about four seconds after me, hastily tucking bills back in his wallet and shoving the wallet in his jeans' pocket as he half-ran down the cement walkway.

"You're right," he said. "I don't know. I have no concept of what the Strauss affair did to you, although it's clearly changed your life in all kinds of ways. If you don't want coffee, let me buy you a drink and you can tell me about this client of yours and this preemptive bid process."

Well, of course that settled it. I had to have a drink with him now.

We found a small dive that stayed open till two a.m. and managed to get our drink order placed before last call. Sedgwick ordered a Stardust and I ordered a brandy.

"I've got it," he said quickly, reaching for his wallet.

I nodded shortly. It was his party. Anyway, even if I'd wanted to object, I wasn't in position to. I'd spent my entertainment budget for the month at the Champagne Bar the night before.

"Who were the books for?" I asked. I felt obliged to make conversation. A holdover from the days when I'd only had sex with people I liked and wanted to know better.

He looked puzzled, then smiled. "My niece and nephew. Connor and Caitlyn. Twins. Their birthday is in January."

I realized that he would be going home to England in a few days. It gave me an odd feeling to think that I'd never see him again. One thing for sure, he wouldn't be easy to forget.

"Do you have a lot of family?"

"Two older sisters and a younger brother. Selena, Samantha and Swithin."

Swithin and Sedgwick. I nobly refrained from comment, restraining myself to a mild, "A middle child."

"Yes."

"Are you close to your family?" I was surprised at my own curiosity, but it was genuine. He seemed like a very unusual person.

"I am. Yes. My father is the vicar at Rye Harbour Church. My mother paints religious triptychs. My family has lived in East Sussex since William the Conqueror landed on the coast. What about you?"

I was still trying to synthesize the glow-in-the-dark condoms with the fact that he apparently came from a devoutly religious family. "Actually, I'm an orphan."

He looked startled. "Straight up?"

"Yep." He appeared so taken aback, I had to ask, "Did you think it only happened in books?"

"Were you—you must have been adopted, surely?"

"My parents died when I was eleven. That's an awkward age for adoption. And I was not a cooperative kid."

His curiosity was neutral: neither sympathetic nor skeptical. It made it easier to talk about a thing I very rarely spoke of. "The fact is, I was very angry. Very hostile. I didn't want to be placed. I didn't want anything or anyone but my own parents. Since I couldn't have that, I wouldn't have anything."

"Do you regret that?"

"Probably. This time of year I'm sorry I don't have family."

"Wasn't there anyone? No grandparents or aunts or uncles?"

"If there were, I didn't know about them. My mom and dad had cut themselves off from their own folks—or maybe they were orphans themselves." I said it lightly, but it wasn't funny to me. It never had been, it never would be.

"I'm sorry." He seemed to mean it, but then having grown up in what was clearly a large and affectionate family, my situation probably did strike a chord with him.

"Thanks. I'm not looking for sympathy, though. I don't ever think about it except at birthdays or this time of year. I'm giving you a little background so you understand why I'm maybe overly touchy about certain things."

"Like the Strauss affair?"

He made it sound like a 1960s Cold War novel. All we needed was a guy in a trench coat to show up and buy the next round.

I admitted, "If I'd had some sort of emotional support, I might have been better able to handle everything that happened afterwards." Granted, in theory Corey should have been my emotional support, but Corey had pulled out the minute suspicion fell on me. Looking back, I realized the cracks must have already been there—or the foundation of our relationship was built on nothing more substantial than papier-mâché.

Interestingly enough the thought of Corey didn't bother me as I sat across the table from Sedgwick.

"What did happen with Strauss?"

"Don't tell me my former colleagues weren't delighted to fill you in on all the gory details?"

He said gravely, "None of your colleagues think you were involved. If I didn't make that clear enough before, I want to do that now."

I shrugged. "Oh, I believe you. Everyone knows that if there had been anything to connect me, I'd have been arrested. The police did their best. The truth is, Louis took me in like everyone else. That's why I don't trust my instinct anymore."

It was weird thinking back to that time. Weird to think I had ever been so completely and uncomplicatedly happy. I had loved that old bookstore on West 6th Street with its bow windows and maze of narrow shelves. It had felt like home for nearly the first time in my life. I'd loved the adventure and challenge of hunting down books; loved working with people as obsessed about books as me. Granted, it had always been more about the books and less about the people for me.

"Strauss was selling forgeries from the beginning?"

I smiled bitterly. "Well, it makes sense in hindsight. No one could really be that lucky. To discover that many rare and valuable unpublished works and lost documents? It defied the odds. But Louis had built up such an impeccable reputation through the years, and a dealer's reputation is one of the primary considerations when considering the authenticity of items."

I paused as our drinks arrived, waiting till the weary cocktail waitress—in her coat and clearly on her way out the door—departed.

"It shouldn't be, but that's human nature, and so there's usually more attention paid to the dealer and his credentials than the actual attributes of the item in question. Like how many such items the dealer has handled, his record of successful and unquestioned dealings, the number of forged docs he's identified."

"And Louis Strauss was actually forging these items?"

"He was working with another man. Alphonse Kidman. Kidman was the forger. A brilliant artist in his own way. He created what was supposed to be a previously unpublished poem by Edna St. Vincent Millay, and I was instrumental in getting it consigned to Christie's."

"The auction house?"

I nodded. "It sold for...well, a substantial amount."

"That can't have been all your responsibility, surely?"

"No. But it was certainly partly my responsibility. I didn't recognize that it was a fake. I put my reputation on the line."

Sedgwick sipped his glittering drink. "How did forgery lead to murder?"

"I don't know." I balanced the rounded bottom of the snifter in my palm, letting it warm. "Nobody knows the entire truth and I don't think anyone ever will. Apparently Kidman was falling further and further in debt despite the fact that he and Louis were making a fortune on all these forgeries. He kept coming up with more and more items for Louis to 'discover'. And the items were getting more and more outlandish. Letters between Lewis and Clark supposedly proving they were gay, an unpublished story by Edgar Allen Poe, Kit Carson's will, a signed engraved portrait of Abraham Lincoln. When Louis tried to refuse handling this flood of stuff, Kidman became more and more belligerent and threatening. He tried to blackmail Louis and when that didn't work, he hired a thug to break into his house and beat him up."

"How could he think he would get away with that?"

"Well, he knew Louis couldn't go to the police. His reputation as one of the leading antiquarians in the country, his social position in Los Angeles society, his comfortable lifestyle...Louis wasn't about to give any of that up. He'd have died first, no question. But instead of dying, he decided to kill Kidman and try and make it look like suicide."

"Meanwhile you were getting suspicious?"

"No." I shook my head. "Not really. Oh, I knew something was wrong, and I was uneasy about the provenance of a few of the items we were selling to collectors, but it never occurred to me what was really going on." I said with difficulty, "You have to understand. Louis was good to me. He took me on when I was right out of college. When I had nothing more going for me than ambition and eagerness. He taught me everything I know—and, believe it or not, that's quite a bit. With his help I became one of the best known and best respected book hunters in the city. I made a lot of money thanks to Louis."

I sipped my brandy and added, "Mostly legitimately. I think. It's hard to be sure because Kidman was very good at what he did."

Sedgwick had that grave angelic look again. "What finally tipped the scales?"

"Louis asked me to alibi him for the night Kidman supposedly shot himself. Oh, he didn't tell me why he needed an alibi, but the minute I read about Kidman's suicide, I knew. He'd been to the bookstore several times to see Louis. I read the newspaper article and...I knew. I asked Louis and he denied it all. Said he needed the alibi because he feared that people were liable to jump to the same conclusion I had, but I knew he was lying." I sighed. "And I couldn't do it. I owed him everything, but I couldn't do it."

In the silence between us I could faintly hear music. I recognized the melody first, and then I realized it was America singing "It's Beginning to Look a Lot like Christmas."

As the poets say: *yeesh.*

Sedgwick observed, "You sound like you feel guilty because you refused to alibi a murderer. He lied, stole, cheated, killed and ultimately tried to make you part of it. You have nothing to feel guilty about."

"And yet, I do feel guilty. And I guarantee you that all those people who assured you they didn't think I had anything to do with the forgeries or murder, think I have something to feel guilty about. No one in this town would hire me after it was all over. No one will hire me now."

"Someone's hired you," he pointed out. "This mysterious collector of yours."

I blinked at him. "A few private collectors still deal with me, yes. I mean no bookstore, no dealer, no auction house."

"Which is why you're working at a chain bookstore?"

For twenty hours a week at barely over minimum wage. How art the mighty fallen. That's what my book hunter rivals thought—if they thought of me at all, which was doubtful.

"Books are what I know. Books are *all* I know."

"If you know books, you know a great deal else, surely?"

The truth of that surprised me.

The overhead lights flashed, jarring the intimate mood between us.

"Last call," the bartender announced.

I glanced around and realized the place was nearly empty, only the hardcore drunks left brooding over their glasses. Sedgwick gave me an inquiring look. I shook my head. "I need to get home."

His disappointment was almost funny. "Perhaps we could get another drink at my hotel?"

"Your hotel is not exactly on the way to my place."

"No. Well." He gathered his nerve. "All the same, why don't you come back to my hotel?"

I laughed, though not unkindly. "You have a one-track mind. You know, there are other guys in this city who would probably enjoy the...er...peppermint."

"I don't want *other guys*. I want you."

His stubbornness was unexpected and flattering. I considered him. He met my gaze straight on.

"A bloke in the hand is worth two in the bush?" I was still teasing, but I had decided to go back with him—strictly because it was in my best interests to do so. I wanted a look at that book and I would do what I needed to make that happen. Still, I figured it wouldn't hurt to play hard to get.

"You're selling yourself short."

"Am I? Well, at least you know my price."

His eyes narrowed as he worked that out. He said softly, disbelievingly, "Are you saying you'll let me fuck you again if I let you look at the book? You're putting a price on having sex with me?"

My heart began to pound very hard. I had conducted certain borderline transactions over the past three years, but this was different. Very different. I had effectively taken this from playful and flirtatious to something else. Something not too pretty.

I felt a little numb. But I nodded.

Sedgwick stared at me for a very long time as the bar lights dimmed and then flashed bright again. I refused to let anything show on my face, but I felt...shaken. Worried. Why? What did it matter if I put a price tag on it? I wanted to sleep with him again, so this was simply killing two birds with one stone. Did it matter that the birds were a pair of Christmas turtledoves?

He said at last, smoothly, "In that case, come back to my hotel. I'd like to share a bedtime story with you."

Chapter Seven

I followed Sedgwick's rental car down Sunset, my eyes on the red taillights ahead of me flying like embers through the night. We turned left on Stone Canyon Road and I could see the trees and the clock tower ahead, like a fairytale kingdom in an enchanted forest.

We parked and handed our keys over to the valets. We didn't talk as we crossed the little bridge and walked through the starlight. The woods smelled damp and mysterious. I wondered if Sedgwick was having second thoughts. I was—though not enough of them to change my mind.

We reached the private alcove of his hotel room entrance, and he let us inside the room. To my surprise he turned on the light, which seemed very prosaic.

He said, "I won't be able to get into the hotel safe until tomorrow morning. Will that be all right?"

His gaze was curious as the heat rushed into my face and then drained out again.

"Of course."

"All right?" he asked quite gently.

"Why wouldn't I be?" I asked belligerently.

His dark eyebrows rose. "I don't know. You seem...tense. You're quite pale."

"It's been a long day."

"I suppose so."

"Are we going to spend the whole night talking?"

"I hope not." He was smiling. The sweetness of that grin—those dimples—took my breath away. "Do you mind if I order us nosh from room service? I didn't have time for dinner."

Because he'd been too busy tracking me down across the mean streets of Los Angeles.

I stopped unbuttoning my shirt. "Of course not."

He went to the phone, asking over his shoulder, "What would you like?"

"Nothing. I'm fine." I sat on the sage green sofa. I felt off-stride. It had been easier the last time; the darkness and the frantic rush we'd been in had made it so.

"A nightcap?"

Now that I thought about it, a nightcap sounded like a good idea. If I was any more tightly wound, he'd need a fishing reel to get any satisfaction out of me.

"A brandy, thank you."

He came over to join me on the couch, sitting next to me. That was a first and I felt inexplicably self-conscious. We'd lain together in the same bed, but sitting next to each other on the sofa fully clothed seemed more intimate. Odd.

He rested a casual arm along the back of the sofa. The brush of his arm against my shoulders unsettled me as did the light press of his muscular thigh against my own.

His lifted his arm and his fingertips lightly tickled the back of my neck. I shivered. He chuckled. "How old are you?"

"Why?"

"Is it a secret?" He offered, "I'm forty-two."

"You look older."

Sedgwick chuckled. "You have a sharp tongue when you're agitated. I'm not imagining it. What's wrong?"

"Nothing." I said irritably, "I'm thirty-five."

"Swithin is thirty-five. My brother," he said in answer to my look of mystification. "He's the baby of the family."

This brought up a point I was actually curious about. "If your father's a vicar, what does your family make of you being gay?"

"Oh." He did a kind of droll eye roll. "They're attempting to come to terms with it."

"What does that mean?"

"I've only just come out. Officially." At my look of inquiry, he said, "I was fully determined to go to my grave as kindly, reliable, stodgy Uncle Sedge, the perennial bachelor."

My jaw must have dropped. But it was ridiculous. He was young, gorgeous and gainfully employed, and he had planned to spend his entire life alone? Sedge smiled wryly at my expression.

"I know. But you have to understand how very conservative my family is—and how close we all are. I didn't think I could ever contemplate...shattering their understanding of me." He clarified, "Certainly not while my parents were still alive."

"Are your parents in ill health?"

"No. Thankfully, no. Healthy as horses, both of them."

"So what was your plan? You've obviously had sex before. No amateur is that gifted."

"Well, it wasn't all me, you know," he pointed out gallantly. "You're right, though, I've had more than a few...illicit encounters, but never, well, an actual relationship. By which I mean, a romantic relationship. With a man."

218

"Have you had one with a woman?"

"Er...yes. Before I realized that that was not going to be fair to either of us."

"Jesus."

"And that, in fact, was what decided me that I should live celibate."

"Celibate?"

He nodded gravely.

"Celibacy is your default button?"

"It seemed safer for everyone that way."

I really had no idea what to say to him. No wonder he was determined to spend every night getting laid. "So...this is merely a kind of sexual holiday for you and when you go back home you'll be resuming the Depo-Provera?"

"The what?"

"It's a drug used in chemical castration."

"Oh. No. No, not at all. You see everything changed a month and a half ago. You probably didn't hear about a train crash just outside London? Six people died."

I shook my head.

"It was a train that I frequently traveled on. In fact, I was supposed to be traveling on it that afternoon. I was held up in traffic and missed it."

A cold fist seemed to grab my heart at the idea Sedgwick might have died before I ever met him. Why? People had close calls all the time and I didn't generally suffer a panic attack over them.

"So?" I made myself say indifferently.

"So it made me see that I could have died without ever having really lived. That I had been living a half-life. That I was denying myself everything that made life worth living: companionship, love—"

"Sex."

"Definitely sex. But also...my true identity." He took a deep breath, and I saw by his expression what it had cost him to reveal the truth to the people he loved best. "When I went down to Rye that weekend, I told my family the truth."

"That was brave."

He looked at me as though he thought I was mocking him, but I wasn't. Not at all.

"I told them that I wanted certain things from my life and that I had to be honest about who I was in order to get them. And as much as I didn't want to hurt them...I had to be true to myself."

"How did they take it?"

"Er...it could have been worse."

Clearly it could have been better too.

"So you came out of the closet and decided to sell the family heirloom Dickens?"

"The book is all part of that, yes."

There was a knock on the door as room service arrived. Sedge rose from the sofa and went to answer the door. I stared down at the carpet where I had dropped the plate of waffles that morning. Was it only that morning? I could barely make out the faintest discoloration in the carpet.

I felt like I was a million miles away while the bell captain deposited the tray and Sedgwick signed his ticket. Sedgwick Crisparkle had turned out to be such a different person from whatever I had imagined.

Did that really make a difference to my plans? Could I afford to let it make a difference?

Sedgwick returned to the sofa and lifted one of the lids off the nearest plate. The nutty lemon aroma of almond-crusted halibut wafted up. I don't even care for seafood, but it made me realize how hungry I was.

My stomach growled, and Sedge glanced at me and laughed. "Luckily there's plenty here. I even ordered dessert." He handed me the snifter of brandy.

I gently swirled the brandy, sipped it. I watched the fire and ignored offers to share Sedgwick's dinner. However, I was pretty hungry and when he offered a forkful of profiteroles with hazelnut gelato drizzled in hot fudge sauce, I accepted.

He smiled into my eyes as my lips closed around the sweet, nutty chocolate.

I warned myself not to get carried away. Part of this was Sedgwick acting out a romantic fantasy after forty-two years of emotional and sexual deprivation.

And part of it was me feeling a bit sentimental and lonely around the holidays.

And part of this—most of this—was we happened to be two healthy, horny guys.

Taking any of this seriously would be a mistake. I needed to relax and enjoy the moment.

So when the moment came—not many minutes later—I was in a relaxed and receptive state of mind. Sedgwick decided he wanted the pleasure of undressing me, so I sat still and let him unbutton my shirt.

"You're smirking," he remarked.

I opened my mouth, but he kissed my bared collarbone, and the words dried in my throat. He shoved the shirt back and kissed my shoulder, and the warm softness of his generally stern mouth sent tingles through my nerves.

"What would you like?" he murmured.

"What would *I* like?"

He was quite serious.

"I like it all," I admitted. "Feel free to...er..."

He smiled, lighting up. It reminded me of something I hadn't thought of in years: Christmas when I was a kid. Before. Our tree-topper was a kitschy plastic angel, and when the tree lights were turned on, the angel's face glowed happily. That's what Sedgwick's smile reminded me of.

He was still alight as he tumbled me back on the sofa. I caught fire from him. In a couple of kicks I was free of my painfully constricted trousers and helping him peel out of his own clothes. He landed on me, but lightly, lithely, and he kissed me more hungrily. I'd never known anyone who seemed to enjoy kissing more than Sedgwick. But then he was very good at it, and the expert, tantalizing pressure moved from my mouth to my chin, to beneath my jaw, down my gulping throat, trailing over my sternum on the way to my belly.

His hand cupped my balls, and I let my knees fall wide, making it easy for him to do whatever he liked. I knew I would enjoy it. Raising my head, I fastened my mouth onto one of his rose-brown nipples, and he groaned from down in his belly, his fingers delicately squeezing me, massaging that fragile sack.

His head dipped lower and he nipped the thin skin over my hip. I bucked.

"What is with you?" I gasped, letting go of his nipple.

"Can't help it, you're good enough to eat."

"You're orally fixated. *Not* that that's a bad thing."

We fooled around a little more, most agreeably, but it was sort of like Twister, and the near misses were starting to get frustrating.

"Can we—?"

"Shall we—?"

We started laughing, and we carefully disentangled, picking ourselves up from the carpet and moving toward the bed— though still hanging onto each other, kissing, stroking.

In the downy snowdrift of the bed there was more of the playful business of preparation: the colored condoms, the chocolate soufflé body cream.

"We could try the real thing?" Sedgwick suggested hopefully at one point. "There's still a bit of dessert left on the dish."

"I'll forgo the charms of hazelnut up my ass."

He seemed to find that breath-robbingly funny, and when he could speak again, he said solemnly, "Your arse is delicious in its own right, true enough."

This time we tried it with Sedgwick on his back. His cock sprang straight up, straight and shining. I took my turn at putting the condom on him, and it was sadly like a hood over the head of an angel, but better safe than sorry.

The angel continued to blindly feel its way to the hot, candy-slick center hovering tentatively above.

"That's it," Sedgwick encouraged, hands on my hips, positioning me as I lowered myself onto that silk-textured thrust. The angel spread his wings as Sedgwick's thick shaft pushed in past muscle and self-consciousness. I ground down. And so it began again: the rush to glory.

The world spun and spun, faster and faster, a glittering blue green top, and then flew away into the darkness.

"You're wonderful." He kissed my ear, drew me closer.

It was nice being held. I'd always liked cuddling in bed with a lover. I'd have been happy to sleep wrapped in Corey's arms all night, but he disliked sleeping close to anyone. Too warm, he said. Sedge seemed to like the closeness and warmth. Seemed to require it.

I could feel him smiling against my hair as he said, "I've never felt anything like this. Do you suppose—" He broke off.

"What?"

He shook his head. A tiny movement. "You'd think I was mad. I probably am."

Neither of us said anything. Into the silence that grew slowly but not uncomfortably between us came a faint, faraway cry...like a squall.

"What was that?" I asked, raising my head.

"A baby?"

"An ocelot?"

We started laughing, that quiet intimate laughter of lovers. I dropped my head back on the pillow, and he rested his face in my hair.

"Sedge?"

I felt his smile. "That's the first time you've called me that," he murmured.

I realized that in the illusory emotional aftermath of really good sex I was in danger of spilling my guts. Not only telling him about who had hired me to look at his book, but telling him how much this night had meant, how much I felt for him— ridiculous because how could I even know what I felt for him? I'd only known him a couple of days.

"Good night," I whispered at last, retreating to a safe distance.

"The best," he whispered back.

Chapter Eight

"Bless my soul! Such a dreadful waste of candles!" scolded Miss Hayhem. *"People are growing terribly extravagant."*

"Are you having any of this?" Sedgwick asked muffledly.

I looked up vaguely. True to his word, Sedgwick had gone to get *The Christmas Cake* out of the hotel safe first thing that morning, and I had curled up on the sofa, reading while he ordered room service and had breakfast. I shuddered to think what his hotel bill would be like, but he had said he had been saving for this trip for most of his adult life.

He sounded muffled because he was speaking around a mouthful of French toast that had been stuffed with ricotta, cream cheese and honey, sautéed then baked to plump and moist perfection.

"I've never seen anyone with a sweet tooth like yours. Your teeth are going to fall out. Not that that wouldn't be a good thing."

He looked abashed. "Sorry. I know I get a tad carried away now and then. It's only...something about you makes me want to eat you up."

I pretended that didn't send a shiver of delighted anticipation down my spine. "You did a fair job last night."

He smiled at me beatifically. I couldn't help smiling back.

"What do you plan on spending the money from the auction on?" I asked. "You never said."

"You're satisfied with the book?"

"The book is wonderful."

I heard that and inwardly shook my head. Gushing was so not my style, but he looked pleased. "As a matter of fact, I plan to open a school."

"A...school?"

"For gifted but economically and socially disadvantaged kids." He looked very serious, very earnest. "It's something I've been thinking about for a long time. I have a number of ideas about education."

"*You?* You're kidding," I deadpanned.

"Yes," he said missing the teasing entirely. "I have the perfect property picked out in Rye, and I have commitments from several friends who've pledged to come in on the venture with me. My mother and my sister Selena have volunteered to run the art classes. I have it all planned out."

Clearly. So much so that I felt strangely disappointed. What had I imagined? He might decide to move to the States? That this week might be the first week in the rest of his new life? I said, "I thought you had a job. I thought you taught chemistry at the University of London?"

"I do. And I enjoy my job. I love teaching. But I've always wanted to run my own school, and I thought rather than waiting forever I would take the book and sell it and out my dream into reality while I'm still young enough to make it happen."

"Your dream is to teach disadvantaged children?" I must have looked as appalled as I felt because he laughed.

"It's not as bad as it sounds."

"How could it not be?"

He was amused as I shook my head and went back to reading.

The London street was white with snow which had fallen a few hours earlier, piled in white drifts along the curb of the little-traveled terrace. But the pavements were neatly shoveled and swept clean, as became the eminently respectable part of the city where Miss Hayhem lived.

A long flight of steps, with iron railing at the side, led down from the front door, upon which a silver plate had for generations in decorous flourishes announced the name of Hayhem.

"Maybe you should explain to me how this preemptive bidding works."

"Hmm?" I said without looking up.

"Come and eat breakfast, James," Sedgwick ordered firmly. "And you can explain why it's to my advantage to sell my book to your mysterious buyer."

I saw that perhaps he did have the makings of a good headmaster, after all. I carefully set the book aside and scooted over to the breakfast tray.

"Would you stop calling him my 'mysterious buyer'?" I muttered.

"Well," he asked reasonably, "who is he then?"

I avoided meeting his eyes by paying strict attention to a breakfast burrito stuffed with eggs, cheese, smoked chicken sausage, roasted peppers and chilies.

If I knew what Sedgwick's objection to Mr. S. was—other than the obvious one that Stephanopoulos was rather a loathsome specimen—I'd know better how to proceed.

Perhaps Mr. S. had it wrong and Sedgwick could care less who bought the book; he had already revealed his quixotic plans for how he wanted to spend the money, and I would do my best to guarantee that he was paid top dollar if he sold to Mr. S.

If Mr. S. was right and Sedgwick did have some objection to selling him the Dickens, then I would lose my commission. We would all lose out, in fact. So it was in the best interests of all of us that I conceal the fact that Mr. Stephanopoulos was the prospective buyer.

"You don't know him," I said.

"You'd be surprised," Sedgwick returned. "I've met a great many book buyers and dealers since I arrived this week." He held up a forkful of French toast. "Try this."

I obediently opened my mouth. The tang of the ricotta cheese and the sweetness of the honey were amazing. The whole breakfast was amazing. Not simply the cuisine, although I'd practically forgotten how wonderful it was to eat well-prepared good food. I'd never been with anyone who wanted to feed me or cuddle with me or show such open and unabashed affection. It was disconcerting, not least because I was very much afraid I was going to develop a taste for it, and then what would happen once Sedgwick returned home and I was left with the usual run of predatory horndogs for romance and sex?

"Good," I conceded, wiping at the sticky sweetness on my lips.

His eyes were focused on my mouth. "What time do you have to go into work today?"

"Eleven."

"Damn." He considered. "What time do you get off? Could I see you later?"

I swallowed hard. That smile of his felt like a punch in the chest. He was so beautiful and so...nice.

It was horrible. The bastard was going to make me fall in love with him if I wasn't very careful.

"I get off at six."

He was thinking. "I'm having dinner with some people tonight. But what about later this evening?"

I hedged—fooling myself more than him, "You could call me when you're free and we could go from there."

"You have to give me your mobile number."

I wrote it down.

He took it and said, "How does this preemptive bid business work?"

"How much are you expecting to get at auction for the Dickens?"

Sedgwick suddenly looked uncomfortable. "Evan Amherst seems to think that the bidding might go as high as...er...several hundred thousand dollars."

"It'll almost certainly go over a million. Didn't he tell you that?"

He gave me an odd look. "It seems hard to believe."

I used to know Evan Amherst quite well. He was old school—and very convincing. I couldn't imagine Sedgwick seriously doubting any professional opinion Evan delivered. "Are you testing me?" I asked bluntly.

"No."

"In 1998 the Archimedes Palimpsest sold for two million. In 2004 Christie's auctioned off Sir Arthur Conan Doyle's papers for 1.69 million." I said very precisely, "Dickens remains one of the most popular and bestselling writers of all time. First editions of *A Christmas Carol* go for between 30 and 50K. I think the discovery of a lost work by him will fetch top dollar. I'm sure Evan told you that."

"Something like," he admitted.

"I guess my question is, why are you not going through Christie's or Sotheby's for this auction? They would jump at this."

"I'm hoping to avoid the publicity that would ensue from such a public auction."

"Why?"

He looked down at the breakfast tray; the first time I'd ever known him to avoid my gaze. "Because of the way the book came into my family's possession. It would prove embarrassing to my father, in particular. But also to Sam who's married to an MP."

"Who's Sam?"

"My sister. Samantha. She's married to a Member of Parliament. Rather a stuffed shirt, actually. But it's different in England. There's still quite a strong class system."

"Okay. But I have no idea what you're talking about."

"The...you called it 'provenance' of this book would be embarrassing to several members of my family if it were made public."

I digested this slowly, skeptically. "Is this book yours to sell?"

He looked genuinely shocked. "Yes, it's mine to sell. Do you think I stole it?"

"No." No, that was pretty much impossible to believe. But there was certainly something hinky about this deal. Not that I was in a position to object to hinkyness.

I looked at my watch. "Hell. I've got to go or I'll be late. I'll talk to my buyer and assure him the book is genuine and worth...well, at the least 1.5." I was going to do my best to get two million for Sedgwick, but I didn't want to promise more than I could deliver. I didn't want to disappoint him.

Ever.

Which was a good reason for finding an excuse to be too busy that evening, assuming he did end up calling me after his dinner. Not that I had that kind of willpower, but I tried to tell myself I did. I tried to tell myself that my interest in Sedgwick was strictly business. Well, and sex.

I went in the shower, half-hoping that Sedgwick might join me. Even so I was startled—and delighted—when the door to the granite stall opened and he crowded inside.

He was beautiful. I'd already noticed that, yes, but his skin was like warm, supple alabaster. None of the freckles or suntan lines of my own. The water beaded on his marble perfection and rivulets trickled through his silky dark body hair. His face, minus the specs, was young and happy.

"I thought you might be lonely."

I laughed.

He reached for the complimentary shower gel, green tea and ginseng, lathering his hands with insane amounts of cool-scented foam. He held his bubble-coated hands up. "Did you wash behind your ears?"

"I repeat. You're a nut."

"Did you wash behind your...*balls*?" We were laughing as he grabbed for me, and we wrangled a little—not much because the floor was slippery with glops of white spume. I let him win and he turned me to the wall. His soapy fingers rubbed and kneaded my shoulders. Nice. Very nice. I loved to be massaged. I let my head fall back, let the light shower spray mist on my face. He took his time poking and prodding my muscles with those hard but cherishing hands. He slapped my thigh lightly.

"Spread 'em."

Shaking my head, I straddled my legs, and his finger rubbed over the clenched ring of my asshole and pushed into me, pushed the soft clouds right into me. I protested feebly, "What are you doing? We don't have time for this."

His answer was to nip the nape of my neck and swirl his finger inside the flight path of my body. I pushed back moaning and shivering as he covered my body with love bites and licks, while his finger—two fingers now—played havoc with my control panel. Pleasure took wing once more. It felt so good it made me weak in the knees. I leaned heavily against the wall, groaning his name.

"Do that again. Say my name like that." His breath was hot against my ear.

"*Sedge...*"

Our bodies were snug together. One. "I like that, like how...you sound as though you..."

He didn't finish the thought and my concentration was sent spiraling a few heartbeats later.

"Oh, *God.*"

Well, they said cleanliness was next to godliness. I could vouch for that. It started me thinking though. When we were languidly rinsing off, smoothing away the seed and silky lather, I asked, "Do you believe in that? God, I mean."

"Yes." He looked sincere, even surprised that I would ask. "Don't you?"

I shrugged.

"There has to be more than this, don't you think?"

"More than sex? No. This will do me fine."

He smiled, but his eyes were serious. "Oh, but there has to be more. More to life and this world. Some purpose. Some point. When you see a beautiful piece of art or listen to music.

Well, or read Dickens—"

"Or turn on the news and see who killed whom."

He was frowning. "Do you truly not believe in God?"

"I truly don't know. I'd like to think there is a God. That some entity was looking out for us, cared what happened to us, that there was some point to all this. All I can tell you is, God has never answered any of my prayers."

Did I know how to kill the afterglow or what? Sedgwick stood, absently drying himself, his face troubled. He said at last, having clearly thought about it for a bit, "James, sometimes the answer is no."

"What?"

"God hears all our prayers, but sometimes the answer is no."

I stared at him. How had this lovely encounter moved into such dark territory? My fault. I said lightly, "Well, I'm probably asking for the wrong things. From now on I'll ask for the stuff He keeps on the shelf in front."

Sedge chuckled, but he seemed preoccupied as we dressed.

"I'll call you as soon as my dinner is over."

We kissed quickly—and then not so quickly. It was increasingly hard to turn away, and when I did, he pulled me back and kissed me again. His mouth was warm and honey sweet.

I had to tear myself away.

"Safe home," he said.

At my look of inquiry, he looked self-conscious. "Only...be safe today."

I knew then that it wasn't just me. He felt it too, the thing happening between us. The fragile, magical thing growing, connecting us. So fragile, so magical, so utterly unexpected.

I was late by then and had to run down the cobbled path, feet pounding across the small bridge, and then cut across the lawn to the parking lot where the bored valets were listening to a boom box.

In the distance I could see a chubby woman in fuchsia trotting along behind a dog pulling vigorously at its leash. As I drew closer, I realized that the dog was actually my friend the ocelot. I gave them wide berth as I headed for the valet parking.

"I knew you would manage it, James." Mr. Stephanopoulos was jubilant when I called him on my break later that afternoon.

"The book is authentic," I said. "I've never seen anything quite like it."

"Coming from you that is truly praise."

That was true. But then I'd never been so staunchly on the side of the seller versus buyer before.

"He knows what he's got, though," I warned Mr. S. "There's no way he'll consider less than two million."

"T-t-two million?" Mr. S. repeated faintly.

"He's been talking to Evan Amherst among others. I think Evan may have his own buyer in mind."

That worked exactly as I'd thought it would. Mr. S. was nothing if not competitive. He began speculating on his possible rivals for the book, while disparaging each man and woman's brains, taste and lineage. He finished up with, "But you're sure the book is everything you say it is?"

"And more. If I had a reputation left, I'd stake it on this one."

He laughed. Then he said anxiously, "And you were careful not to let Professor Crisparkle know you were acting on my behalf?"

"I was careful. What exactly is the situation there?"

"English pigheadedness."

"It sounded more serious than that."

"You don't know the English." He added silkily, "In any case, I don't pay you to stick your nose into things that don't concern you. It's enough that I tell you what I need done."

I opened my mouth. The words trembled on the tip of my tongue. I swallowed them. Beggars can't be choosers. And the fact was that I was taking Stephanopoulos for an extra half million. Taking it for Sedgwick, true, but that made it all the sweeter. And my commission on two million would go a long way to soothing my injured feelings.

"Very true," I said coolly. "Then shall I go ahead and broker the deal?"

"I would like you to get it for less than two million if possible."

"It's not possible. I've already told you."

Silence.

"Whose side are you on in this transaction, James?" Mr. S. sounded mildly amused. I wasn't deceived.

"I've already told you Crisparkle knows what he's got. He's open to the idea of a preemptive bid, which means Amherst may get in there first. Or another dealer. I'm not going to waste time haggling with this guy. If you want to try your hand at horse trading, feel free."

"This is the old James talking," he said slowly. "Something has happened."

"Nothing has happened—beyond the discovery of this quite

unique book."

"Yes, but I think something *has* happened." Mr. S. was thoughtful. "I don't quite trust you, James. There is a certain note in your voice. It's most annoying."

"I'm sorry. I'm not sure what you—"

"But that's it. You're not sorry. You're...confident. You haven't been confident in a long time. I wonder why you're so confident now?"

I was starting to hate Stephanopoulos with an intensity that surprised even me. Still, it would be a very bad idea to give into that dislike.

I said as calmly as I could, "I'm confident because this book is the real deal, the find of the decade. And, frankly, I believe you're paying me top dollar for more than my diplomacy skills. Which, I'll be the first to admit, are not strong."

His silence grew more unpleasant in quality.

He said at last, very mildly, "You are the expert, James. I'll be guided by you. I know you are well aware how unwise it would be to cross me."

That did give me pause. I said, "I'll call you with Crisparkle's answer."

The day flew by.

Employees talked about the possibility of a white Christmas and whether we could legitimately have a snow day in Los Angeles. "It's not even raining," I pointed out irritably to the third person who gleefully asked if I thought it would snow. "Has anyone noticed the sun is shining?"

Customers asked for books on England, on the Victorians, and on Christmas baking. Three people bought the newest illustrated edition of *A Christmas Carol*. If I believed in signs and omens, I'd have thought someone was trying to tell me something.

In the afternoon, the floor manager asked if I could stay late. Since Sedgwick would be at his dinner, I decided I might as well work a few extra hours.

I ate my raspberry jam sandwich in the break room using Louis Bayard's *Mr. Timothy* as a barrier from employees who wanted to talk about what they hoped they were getting for Christmas and how they were going to spend their snow day.

But against my best effort the conversation around me infiltrated my force field and I found, to my dismay, that I was wondering if Sedgwick would want to spend Christmas together. Then I remembered Darcy. But that was all right. Maybe Sedgwick would be open to spending a few hours at her place. If not, I could spend the afternoon with Darcy and meet Sedgwick later in the evening.

I wanted to spend Christmas with him. More than I had wanted anything in a long time.

I glanced at the break room clock. He would be at his dinner by now.

I finished my break and returned once more to the fray.

I was too busy to worry about not hearing from Sedgwick. When he didn't call at eight or nine, I assumed his dinner ran late. I was finally freed from bondage at nine thirty and I tried calling from the parking lot. No point driving back to Glendale if I was then going to have to turn around and head out to Stone Canyon.

The hotel room phone rang and rang.

I waited fifteen minutes and tried again. By now it was ten o'clock. Surely he would have tried to get free and back to his hotel knowing we were supposed to meet?

It was cold in the car and I was getting chilled and stiff

waiting. I headed home, telling myself the chances of anything happening to him were nil.

I got back to my apartment. In Darcy's apartment, America was weirdly mute. I tried calling the Hotel Del Monte at ten thirty, ten forty-five, ten fifty, and eleven.

Nothing.

I tried again at eleven thirty and then at twelve. By then I was worried. Scared to death. What the hell could have happened to him? Anything. It was Los Angeles. Anything could happen to him. A gang shooting. A car accident. I remembered my parents' deaths on such a night. Remembered waiting for them to come home from their date night. Remembered the mounting irritation and impatience of the college student babysitter as it grew later and later—until the police showed up at our front door.

When I tried his hotel room again at fifteen minutes after twelve o'clock my throat was so tight, I wasn't sure I'd be able to speak even if he was there.

He wasn't. I let the phone ring ten times. I was dangerously close to crying as I let it ring a hopeless eleventh time.

The phone rattled off the hook.

"Yes?" Cold and crisp. I almost didn't recognize the voice as Sedgwick's.

In fact, I was so shocked, I could hardly manage a thick, "Sedge?"

"Yes?"

We seemed to have come full circle. He sounded as frosty and distant as he had the first time we'd spoken on the phone.

"It's me. I thought...did you try to call me?"

"No."

I absorbed that with a sick churning in my belly.

Something was very wrong. I swallowed hard, made myself say in as calm a voice as I could manage, "I thought we were getting together tonight."

"No. We're not getting together tonight. Or any other night."

I opened my mouth but nothing came out. That was probably a good thing because anything that came out would have been humiliating. I'd forgotten how painful and pointless it was to care about another person.

Into my thoughts, he said in that same clipped, cold voice, "Who is your buyer for *The Christmas Cake*. What's his name?"

"I told you, he wishes to—"

"Remain anonymous? Yes. I imagine he does. Your buyer is Grigori Stephanopoulos, correct?"

I sucked in a sharp breath. Safe to say, I'd have never made it as a spy. "I can't—"

"You don't have to. Stephanopoulos told you that if I knew he was the buyer, I would not entertain his bid. You knew that. Even if you don't know the full story, you knew by his own account that this was a man that I would not wish to deal with. You deliberately withheld that information from me. That's correct, isn't it?"

I couldn't seem to find the oxygen to answer him.

Into my stricken silence Sedgwick said, "I already know that it's correct."

Words came to me. The wrong words, but I said them anyway. "He's offering you two million for the book."

"I don't care if he's offering ten million. I don't care if he's the last buyer on the planet. I won't deal with him—or you. You lied to me from the start."

"If you would just—"

"You're a liar and a cheat and a whore. It's been very

instructional getting to know you, Mr. Winter, but our acquaintance is now at an end. Don't call me again."

He replaced the receiver with a quiet click.

I listened numbly to the dial tone for long seconds before it occurred to me to hang up.

Chapter Nine

Happy, happy Christmas, that can win us back to the delusions of our childhood days, recall to the old man the pleasures of his youth, and transport the traveler back to his own fireside and quiet home!

Happy, happy Dickens who never spent Christmas Eve in a department store or mall. Personally, I doubt if anything was more likely to drive man to want to kill his fellow man than Christmas shopping. Simply trying to find a place to park is grounds for homicide.

I was scheduled to work early Christmas Eve, and the morning and early afternoon passed in a numb blur of increasingly frantic customers. By four o'clock I was off with a day and a half of holiday ahead of me. It stretched like a wasteland.

Staying busy helped. Or as busy as one can stay who has virtually no personal obligations. I ordered America concert tickets for Darcy and that concluded my Christmas shopping. That's one of the bright sides of not having anyone in your life around the holidays. No time wasted writing Christmas cards, a fortune saved in stamps and presents. It's really a positive thing if you look at it right.

I went to Aldine Books on West Sunset and paid for the 1924 edition of Gertrude Chandler Warner's *The Box-Car*

Children which I'd had the legendary "Old Guy" who owned the place put on hold for me. On the drive home I decided a numb Christmas would be better than a blue one, and I stopped at a liquor store and bought a bottle of E&J VSOP.

I reached home, poured myself a brandy and did my best not to listen to America's *Holiday Harmony* through the wall. I couldn't help trying to identify the familiar melody, and then it came to me: "A Christmas to Remember."

As the snow is gently falling, hang the mistletoe you said, A Christmas to remember lay ahead.

I opened the window to the street and let in the sounds of traffic to drown the music.

It struck me how silly this was. Before I'd heard of that damned *Christmas Cake* book or met Sedgwick Crisparkle, I'd been looking forward to nearly two days of nothing to do but read and rest. Nothing had changed, really. What was I getting so worked up over?

Other than the fact that I had been foolish enough to commit to spending what was sure to be a very long and tedious Christmas day with Darcy, everything could still be exactly as I had originally planned. I needed to buck up and start enjoying my restful solitude. To despair at the way things had ended between me and Sedgwick was stupid. Regardless of how, it was always going to end this way. Perhaps not in Sedgwick believing that I had betrayed him, but with the same result ultimately. In fact, it was probably better this way because I had been getting way too...well, fond of him.

I merely needed to show self-discipline and stop thinking about it.

And I tried. I did.

But apparently it required more discipline than I possessed. Instead, I found myself going over and over the last three days in my mind, trying to pinpoint the exact moment when I should have told Sedgwick the truth, the moment when I had passed the point of no return, the moment I had lost him.

Stupidly, embarrassingly, I kept hoping the phone would ring. That Sedgwick would relent like he had the other time he'd judged me unfairly. Except, he hadn't judged me unfairly, had he? I was exactly was he thought I was. A liar, a cheat, and a whore.

At four o'clock Mr. S. called to find out how Professor Crisparkle had responded to his offer. I didn't have the guts to take his call. Instead I let it go to message and then listened to it.

I considered delivering the bad news by phone. If I was lucky I might be able to get away with leaving a message. Then I considered ignoring his call. But if I ever wanted to work for him again I would need to do damage control. This was presupposing that the damage could be controlled, which was highly doubtful, but I had to try.

I ran into Darcy in the stairwell as I was on my way out to Stephanopoulos's. She was dressed up for a party and looked almost pretty. In fact, she did look pretty. Her eyes were shining, she wore frosted lip gloss, and her plastic animal barrettes had been replaced by rhinestone clips.

"Look at you," I admired. "Where are you going?"

"Office party. I don't know why I ever agreed. I hate these things." She made a moue, but I thought she looked sort of excited too.

"How bad can it be? Free booze, free snacks. And you look great."

"No I don't." But she seemed willing to be convinced, eyeing me with a sort of hopefulness.

But Oz never did give nuthin' to the Tin Man that he didn't already have...

I said firmly, "Okay, well, here's your mission for tonight. Your mission, should you choose to accept it, is to say something to every single person there."

She looked astonished, but then she seemed to consider it. "Okay. I will."

I nodded, turned away, and she said quickly, "James, you won't forget about tomorrow, right?"

I faced her. "No. What time?"

I could see in her eyes that she was braced for me to bail on her at the last minute. And if I hadn't seen that turkey and all the groceries she'd bought, I would have been tempted. And yet the idea hurt. Did I really seem like the kind of guy who would break my word? Disappoint my friends? Friend. I probably did, but I had done my best never to do either of those things. Granted, weighed against the things I *had* done, they weren't much in my favor.

"One o'clock?"

"Sure. I'll be there."

"Have a great evening."

"Oh yeah," I said, heading off in the opposite direction.

The glass-walled elevator rose slowly to Mr. S.'s penthouse, offering an aerial view of lush green tropical plants and fountains in the courtyard below. Tiny white Christmas lights were threaded through the foliage like fallen stars.

Muzak played fuzzily over my head. A troublingly familiar

melody. Dear God. There it was again. "A Christmas to Remember."

Please remember (please remember)

Please remember (please remember)

Were those guys following me or what? What had I ever done to them that they needed to haunt me like the Ghosts of Christmas past?

Maybe the elevator cable would break and send me plummeting to a blessed escape.

But no such luck. I arrived safely at the penthouse and Mr. S. himself let me in, which alerted me belatedly to the fact that he was having a cocktail party.

A lot of people in the glittering city were having parties. It was Christmas Eve. I wanted nothing more than to duck out and come back later to deliver my bad news while he was alone, but he didn't give me the opportunity.

"James. Just in time!" he exclaimed, drawing me in. "What will you have to drink?"

"Nothing. Thank you."

I looked around the room, but while the faces were probably familiar to anyone who read the society pages, I didn't recognize anyone there—and that was a relief. I was only too aware that this was probably going to end unpleasantly. The Mr. S.'s of the world don't deal well with disappointment. But then, they don't have much practice.

Mr. Stephanopoulos snagged caviar smeared on a cracker, popped it in his mouth and asked thickly, "Well? What did he say?"

Even if things had gone well with *The Christmas Cake*, this was not a transaction that should be discussed in public. I asked, "Is there someplace we can talk?"

The excitement and pleasure died out of Mr. S.'s face. He looked suspicious, leading me through the elegant, half-crocked partygoers to his study.

Once upon a time I'd had a study like this. Dark wood and red leather, a couple of lithographs on the wall, a drinks cart and an illuminated globe in a wooden stand. A gentleman's study, though I don't know that either Stephanopoulos or I qualified.

He closed the door behind us with a slight bang. "Well?" he demanded again, and his voice was impatient, petulant. I wondered how much he'd had to drink. His face was flushed and his eyes had the unpleasant glitter of the mean drunk.

Drunk or angry, there was no way to delay or soften it. I spoke the truth. "He refused your offer."

He stared at me. "You offered him two million dollars?"

"Yes."

"He refused?"

"Yes. I'm sorry."

His brows drew together. "Up the offer then," he said arrogantly.

Up it?

To what dollar amount would he have been willing to go? It almost gave me a feeling of vertigo. I said, "I'm sorry. It really is no use."

"Don't be stupid. Of course we must up the bid. He's received another offer exactly as you suspected he might."

"No. It's nothing to do with the money. Crisparkle knows that you're the buyer."

He slammed his whisky glass down so hard I expected to see the crystal shatter. "You told him? I told you he could not find out!"

I said quickly, "I didn't tell him."

"Of course you told him. How else would he find out?"

I didn't like the way Stephanopoulos lunged forward or the way he was breathing heavily as he advanced on me. He sounded like the Minotaur finding something young and comely waiting in the Cretan Labyrinth.

"I don't know how he found out, but I didn't tell him. It wasn't any more in my interests for him to find out than it was in yours. He had a dinner engagement last night, so maybe he talked to—"

"Who?"

"I don't know. I'm guessing. I don't know what happened. He was fine earlier."

"What do you mean 'earlier'?"

"He was fine in the morning."

"The morning?"

I was aghast at what I'd nearly admitted. I disassembled quickly, "When I made my final examination of the book yesterday morning, he was fine. I told him I would talk to my buyer. He was perfectly agreeable. When I tried to reach him last night—"

The memory of Sedgwick's words was still too painful.

Whatever Mr. S. read on my face, he entirely misinterpreted. Maybe that was just as well, but he said in a hoarse whisper, "You're lying to me."

Withholding facts, certainly, but not lying. I stuck to the basics. "I didn't tell him. I don't know how he learned you were the buyer."

"You arrogant shit," he said, and he was across the room in two steps. "I should never have trusted you. I knew you couldn't be trusted. You thought you would be clever and play both sides against each other and so you told him who your buyer was."

I protested, "Why would I?"

Stephanopoulos had stopped listening. He grabbed my jacket collar and punched me in the face. I went down like a house of cards. I didn't see it coming. You'd think growing up in a place like Hollygrove I'd be quicker on the ball. But no. His meaty fist connected painfully with my left cheekbone and the next thing I knew I was scrambling out of the wreckage of a broken vintage lighted globe and its wooden stand.

"I didn't tell him a goddamned thing," I cried. "He found out on his own." I wondered if he'd broken my cheekbone. The left half of my face felt numb. I touched my nose to see if it was bleeding.

"*Leave my home,*" Stephanopoulos roared. "I personally guarantee you will never work in this town again."

I was already going, yanking open the door to his study. I saw the astonished wall of faces in the living room as I went out the front door.

In lieu of the traditional lump of coal, Santa left me a black eye on Christmas morning. I examined it bleakly in the mirror over the sink in my bathroom. It was a beaut.

I was grateful Stephanopoulos hadn't punched me in the nose. Not so much because it would mar my good looks as I couldn't afford the medical costs of a broken nose.

Colliding with the giant globe and its large wooden stand hadn't done a lot for my back and ribs. Examining the black and blue marks over my flanks and back, I reminded myself that I was lucky I hadn't broken anything—besides the world.

I didn't feel lucky.

I made myself a raspberry jam sandwich and had a brandy.

I hated Christmas. The truth was, I had hated it for years. Only I hadn't wanted to admit it to myself. But of course I hated it. The traffic, the noise, the bustle and bother for what? For fifteen minutes of hysteria and flying papers on Christmas morning?

Any sane person would hate Christmas.

And if you weren't into Christmas what was there to do? No bookstores were open. No libraries. Nothing useful was open.

Church was open.

Sedgwick probably went to church on Christmas. Had he gone today? A stranger in a strange land?

I hadn't been to church in years, and it was pretty late to start now. If I'd had someone to go with...

I heard these thoughts echoing in my mind with something like shock. What was going on with me? *Church?*

Seriously?

Clearly Stephanopoulos had hit me harder than I realized.

I decided to read *The Box-Car Children* and have another brandy. And for an extra special Christmas treat maybe I could splurge on a movie at the Americana that evening. One thing I was not going to do was spend the day brooding over the way things had ended with Sedgwick. I was quite determined to put all thought of him and that book—that wonderful, magical book—out of my mind. Forever.

But it was like having a loose tooth. Once you knew it was there, you couldn't stop pushing and prodding it with your tongue.

I did not want to think about anyone's tongue.

How could a vicar's son have a tongue like Sedgwick's?

I wondered what Sedgwick was doing. Who he was sleeping with, waking up with, spending Christmas with?

I wondered how *The Christmas Cake* had come into his family. What was the connection between Angela Burdett-Coutts and the Crisparkle family? Sedgwick had actually said Canon Crisparkle was his great-great-great-grandfather. What did that mean?

I wondered what Stephanopoulos had done to piss Sedgwick off.

He almost had my sympathy because one thing for sure, Sedgwick was not the forgiving type. Better to know that up front, right?

Not that it had ever been anything but a holiday romance for Sedgwick. I knew that. Only I'd wanted the holiday to last longer.

Next door Darcy had turned the music on and the smells of cooking and America were wafting through the wall.

I wondered how *The Christmas Cake* ended. I'd had to stop reading at the point where poor little Miss Dorinda Love had gone to stay with her batty Auntie Hayhem in London. I'd been hoping she might eventually get together with the shy schoolmaster, Mr. Jasper Pennyworth. I wondered whether the schoolboys, Benjamin or Alfred, would ever fess up to stealing the Christmas cake and what terrible consequences would result from such a simple transgression if they didn't, because Dickens was never simple.

Then again, neither was life.

Chapter Ten

At one o'clock sharp I went next door with my America concert tickets cunningly concealed in a foil-wrapped CD case.

Darcy opened the door. "It's hailing," she caroled.

"Hail is not snow," I reminded her.

Her expression had already changed to one of shock. "What happened to your face? Were you beat up?"

"Oh." Instinctively, I put a hand to my eye. "No. I...ran into a door."

"No way. That's the lamest lie I ever heard. Did someone try to bash you?"

"Yes, but not the way you mean. This was strictly personal. Anyway, don't worry about it. I'm fine. And on the positive side it's even in Christmas colors."

"Oh, James." She spluttered an appalled laugh as she led the way into the apartment still burbling about turkey and the snow.

"It's going to snow. I *know* it. Everyone is saying so on the news."

I shook my head at this insane optimism—and the idea that anyone could believe the weathermen.

Darcy fetched me a brandy and insisted I sit while she finished preparing the meal. I was surprised at how pretty and happy she looked. Her de rigueur plaid shirt was silk today and her overalls were a forest green that actually suited her very well.

I sipped my brandy and looked around the cozy apartment. Her apartment was no larger than mine but it smelled wonderful. It looked festive and comfy too. There were dozens of greeting cards lined on the countertops and shelves. A diminutive Christmas tree was braced in a stand on a table in front of the window looking over the street. Its tiny lights flashed on and off at regular intervals.

Best of all, a Carpenters Christmas album was playing. I could have wept my relief—and I don't even like the Carpenters.

Darcy finished doing whatever it was she was doing in the kitchen, and came to join me.

"I have a few things for you too," she said gaily, as she handed over several parcels. My heart sank. I was afraid she had bought something expensive and personal, and I flat out couldn't deal with another emotional complication right now. I desperately hoped all this prettiness and homemaking was not on my behalf. I'd tried again and again to make it clear I only wanted to be friends.

I opened the CD-shaped parcel first. America's *Holiday Harmony*. "You shouldn't have," I murmured.

"My turn!" She ripped apart the foil-wrapping of her parcel and gave a scream of delight. "*James.* Oh, James, you shouldn't have."

That was probably true, especially if she was going to drag me along with her to see them in concert. But maybe that wasn't such a danger as I thought, looking around this room with the litter of Christmas cards and parcels under the miniature tree. The fact was, Darcy had more people in her life than I did. A lot more people by the look of things.

She danced across to me, hugged me tightly, and then looked stricken. "My gosh. I didn't... I mean, the things I got you were... I didn't think you'd buy me anything *nice.*"

I laughed. I was actually sort of relieved though I felt silly for spending all that money on tickets.

No. Actually, I didn't. She was inviting me to share her Christmas and had made us a wonderful dinner. She was kind and generous and good-hearted. She was a much better friend to me than I had ever been to her. I was glad I'd bought those tickets.

"It was my pleasure. What should I open next?"

She indicated the small square parcel wrapped in leering snowmen.

I unwrapped it. Asbach Uralt brandy-filled chocolate tree ornaments.

"Of course you don't have a Christmas tree," she said regretfully.

"You didn't really think I could have left these hanging on a tree for more than three minutes, did you?" I smiled. "Thank you." I picked up the last parcel, about the size of a Christmas ornament, which is what I deduced it was.

She said hurriedly, "That's sort of a...well, not a gag gift exactly, but you have such a terrible diet—when you remember to eat—and you're always so stressed."

I was? The box rattled as I gently shook it. "What is it, Viagra?"

She sputtered. "*James.*"

I tore off the paper. A small jar was emblazoned with the label *New Zealand Bee Pollen.*

I swallowed hard. "Oh."

Maybe I looked a little dazed, she rushed into worried

speech. "Was it a bad idea? Are you allergic to bees? It was just a...a thought. It just came to me."

"It's really sweet of you," I said.

She sat on the footstool in front of me. "James, what's wrong? I could tell the minute you walked in something was really wrong."

For one very bizarre and confusing moment I wondered if I was going to have a total breakdown and cry in front of Darcy. But then I pulled myself together. "Nothing is wrong. Well, nothing serious."

"Someone beat you up. Something's wrong."

I stared at her worried face and realized I couldn't even begin to explain what was wrong. Wrong with me, wrong with my life.

"Basically, I had too much to drink last night and didn't get enough sleep."

She was shaking her head stubbornly.

I reached across and squeezed her hand. "Let it go, okay?"

She frowned, hesitated, and then to my relief, she let it go.

It was a nice day. The food was good and the company was surprisingly pleasant, and I wondered why I always worked so hard to avoid this. What was I so afraid of? That if I let anyone get close...

Actually, I knew what I was afraid of, and I was right to be afraid. But maybe I didn't have to cut myself off so entirely from everyone. Hopefully I'd learned something since I was eleven years old.

Since I couldn't have my old life back, it was time to concentrate on building a new one.

After I helped Darcy do the dishes, I looked at the clock. "I was thinking about catching a movie at the Americana this evening. Would you like to come along?"

To my surprise, her cheeks turned pink. "Well..." She gave me a funny look and then burst out, "The thing is, I've got a date."

"*You* do?" I hastily corrected for that. "You *do*. That's great."

"It's really due to you," she said.

"It is?"

"I took your advice last night, and I made a point of talking to every single person at that party, and, well, one of the people I talked to was Jeff Jablonski. He's the manager of our warehouse department. It turned out that he's always sort of..."

"That's great," I said again, and this time I really meant it.

I said thank you and goodbye to Darcy and went back next door. I ate a brandy chocolate, took two bee pollen tablets and looked up the show times at the Americana. I had the choice of a film about Nelson Mandela, a murdered girl whose spirit was watching over her family and her killer, the new Sherlock Holmes or a James Cameron fantasy.

These days I didn't find murder mysteries very amusing, so I opted for Mandela and the Rugby team.

When the film was over, I decided I did not want to go back to my apartment and I went around the corner to a dive bar where I occasionally went for a drink when I wanted company— or at least the presence of living, breathing beings without having to talk to anyone.

"What's the other guy look like?" the bartender inquired.

I'd forgotten that I was beginning to look a lot like Halloween. Now that I was reminded of it, my face hurt, my back hurt, my ribs hurt. My brain hurt. It had been a long day. A long week.

"He was ugly to start with," I said.

The bartender laughed.

"What's your name, by the way?" I asked. I'd been going to that bar for three years and never thought to ask his name. Never paid any attention at all.

"Fred."

I ordered a Stardust from Fred.

"A what?" he asked.

"A Stardust. I think it has four parts vodka, one part crème de cacao. Goldschlager liqueur fits in there somewhere."

He stared at me, perplexed, and then retreated to the backroom. I listened to the music piped in from wherever. Still Christmas music, even here, but that would all be over by tomorrow. A lot of things would be over tomorrow. Sedgwick would auction *The Christmas Cake* and I would probably never see the book or him again.

I wasn't sure why that seemed so hard to believe. So difficult to accept. I'd only known him a couple of days. How could he have become so important?

I listened to the overhead music. Jackson Browne singing "The Rebel Jesus". I felt cheered. If I had to pick a favorite Christmas song, it would have to be that one. Perhaps this was a positive nudge from the cosmos. I had done some hard thinking that day and maybe this was my atta boy. At least "A Christmas to Remember" no longer seemed to be stalking me.

As I listened to the song, I thought that maybe when I got back to my apartment I could try calling Sedgwick. Simply to wish him a merry Christmas. Simply to apologize. If there was ever a day on which he might be open to forgiveness, it was probably today.

Peace and love for one's fellow man, right? And I was a

fellow man.

I had nothing to lose, that was for sure.

Fred came out of the backroom, filled a shaker cup with ice, and started pouring in Blue Curacao, citrus vodka, peach schnapps, pineapple juice, grenadine, and sweet and sour mix.

"Wait, that's not right," I said. "It's supposed to be made with crème de cacao."

"This is what the recipe book says."

"Yeah, but when I had it before it was this kind of silver gold with glitters floating through it. It was beautiful."

"How much had you had to drink at that stage?"

"I'm serious."

Fred shook his head. "It's this or nothing, my friend."

Ah. Another of those celestial nudge in the ribs, right? I was getting better at picking them up.

"I'll try that."

He nodded approvingly.

I was sipping the blue Stardust—it was okay, nothing to die for—when a tall figure slid into the barstool next to me.

A curt, familiar voice inquired, "Don't you ever go home? This is the second time I've been to your local this evening."

My heart jumped. I turned and got a glimpse of the full-on headmaster. Stern mouth, forbidding glasses. I was too shocked and happy to speak. As we gazed at each other, Sedgwick's disapproving expression changed to consternation.

"What the hell happened to you?" He reached out to touch my cheek with gentle fingers.

"I walked into a reindeer."

He wasn't smiling. Nothing new there. I felt that brush of fingertips in every skin cell.

"Did that bloody man hit you?" He sounded very angry. Serious anger. The kind of anger that was not for show and not mere venting. Archangel anger. And on my behalf. It wasn't exactly in keeping with the spirit of the season, but I was touched.

"It doesn't matter. Really." I realized that was true. I was glad the lies and deception were over. I had tried to make the right thing happen by doing the wrong things, and it had destroyed everything I'd hoped to achieve. I wanted it behind me. I wanted to believe I had learned something at last.

He didn't say anything, but his thumb traced the corner of my mouth. My bottom lip quivered. I turned my head. I could see my face reflected in the mirror behind the glittering array of jewel-colored bottles and stemware. I could see Fred the bartender's face too, and I said, "Let's get out of here."

Sedgwick was already rising, one hand resting on the small of my back as we wove our way through the chairs and tables. I felt that light, guiding touch all the way to my groin.

"How did you find me?" I asked as we stepped outside into the brisk and cold and smog-scented night. There was a fine mist falling on our hair and faces.

"I went to your flat. Your neighbor told me you had gone to a movie. So I waited. Then it occurred to me that you might have come here. I checked, but no joy. I went back to your flat and waited more. Then I checked back here again."

The usual precise accounting.

"Why are you here, Sedge?" I asked quietly. "You were pretty definite Wednesday night that you didn't want to see me again."

A muscle in his jaw moved. "I was very angry on Wednesday. Angry and hurt."

I nodded. It wasn't an explanation, though.

He said grimly, "I woke up this morning and realized that the only person I wanted to spend this day with was you. The only Christmas present I wanted was to magically undo everything that happened Wednesday from the minute you walked out of my hotel room."

I went to him, his arms folded tightly around me. We held each other, held on tight, as though we had narrowly missed some terrible disaster, as though a train had rushed by without hitting us or a tornado had landed a few feet from us and bounced away again.

I was distantly aware that the rain was coming down harder, but I didn't want to move from the shelter of Sedgwick's arms. I sensed he felt the same.

At last he loosened his grip on me and said, "I'm parked down the street."

"Where are we going?"

"A place we can talk." He hesitated. "You decide."

"What are we talking about?"

"You. Me. The Dickens." He paused and then said, "Love."

"The Dickens with love. There's a mix."

His smile was perfunctory. He still looked very grave. Unsmiling in the pallid lamplight.

I admitted, "I'm suddenly afraid of what you're going to tell me."

He shook his head. "You don't have to be. I owe you an explanation. We can start there. If you still want to continue the conversation after that, it will be your choice."

That sounded pretty cold-blooded, but when I thought of that bone-crushing hug I felt a fraction more confident. He had used the "L" word, and I had felt it in the way he held me.

"We can talk at my place."

He nodded. I had the impression he wanted to say more. If so, he restrained himself. We walked across the street to my apartment. The building felt deserted. The silence next door was blessed.

Sedgwick looked around my room curiously. I don't know what he made of it. He didn't comment, but I could see through his eyes how barren it was, how unwelcoming. Except that he *was* welcome. And always would be.

"Before you say anything," I said. "I know I was in the wrong. I did deliberately avoid telling you who the buyer was. I did know from Stephanopoulos that if you discovered I was acting as his go-between, you wouldn't consider his offer. I wanted the commission. I won't deny that. But once I...started to care for you, I wanted to take Stephanopoulos for every penny I could get *for you*. I swear that's the truth."

He sighed.

I persisted, "I know it sounds self-serving, but I did think it would be the best thing for all of us if the deal went through."

"But you were wrong. Do you see that?"

"Yes."

He said almost sadly, "I couldn't believe you had done that. I couldn't believe you would betray my trust like that."

"Please don't say anything more," I pleaded. "I'm truly sorry. I can't tell you how sorry I am. My only excuse is I haven't thought clearly about these things for a long time. You've made me see...so many things. Made me see myself."

I could see him weighing his words before he said at last, "I needed to hear you say that. But to be perfectly honest, if you'd told the truth from the first, I wouldn't have got to know you. That's what I kept thinking today. God works in mysterious ways. You *were* wrong, but...if you hadn't done it, I wouldn't have fallen in love with you." He added steadily, "Or you with me."

"I do love you."

"I know."

At my expression, he gave that wry look. "Oh, I knew long before you did. You fell almost at once."

"You're pretty sure of yourself, Professor."

He said in that gentle way, "I've had a lot of experience with love. You haven't. But I'm going to see that that changes. If you'll let me."

He'd had a lot of experience with love? Why, I'd been with ten ti—and then I understood what he was actually saying. What he was offering. The sound that came out of me was supposed to be a laugh, but it was frighteningly close to the other thing. I got up and went to pour a brandy.

"Would you like a drink?" I asked him over my shoulder.

"Yes. But it can wait."

That was better. I could turn that into a joke. I glanced around and he was right behind me, and the expression on his face dried the laughter in my throat.

"I love you so much," he said. "I've waited my entire life for you."

We were holding each other again, and I whispered, "I'll make it up to you, Sedge. I swear it. I'll never let you down again."

He kissed me. "I want to give you your Christmas present. It's at the hotel."

I tried for lightness because any more emotion and I was going to embarrass myself completely. "You don't think I could unwrap it here?"

He smiled faintly but shook his head.

"Did you really get me a present?"

He nodded.

I felt indescribably touched at the idea of Sedgwick choosing a gift especially for me. I hoped it wasn't a tie. Or another jar of chocolate soufflé. "Before or after we fell out?"

"After."

"After?" That seemed significant—unlikely too. I did very much want to see this present.

It was bitterly cold and still raining as we went down to his rental car.

The streets were largely empty of traffic as we drove down Sunset. Christmas lights still shone brightly despite the bedraggled and dripping decorations.

Watching the wet splatter against the windshield, I said, "Does that look like snow to you?"

Sedgwick was amused. "Haven't you ever seen snow?"

"Of course I've seen snow."

"It's not snow. It's slushy, I'll give you that."

It was warm and sort of steamy in the car as our wet clothes dried in the blast from the heater. Christmas music played softly on the radio as we talked. Not about anything important. Now and then he reached over and gave my hand a squeeze.

We were heading up Stone Canyon when I asked, "How *did* your family come into possession of *The Christmas Cake*?"

"Ah. Well, it was a gift, you see."

"A *gift*? That would have been an awfully nice gift even in Dickens' day."

"Yes, it would have. Do you know who Angela Burdett-Coutts was?"

"Yes."

"Do you know about Urania Cottage?"

"The asylum for fallen women? Yes. I know that Dickens and Burdett-Coutts were involved in the endeavor together."

"Yes. Originally Dickens wanted no part of it and even tried to convince Burdett-Coutts to withdraw from the project. But she persisted and eventually he was won over. He became actively involved in the asylum and considered it one of his greatest achievements—as did Burdett-Coutts."

I wondered where this was headed. "So he wrote her *The Christmas Cake* as a gift? A token of affection? An apology?"

"All of those, perhaps. As you know from what you read, *The Christmas Cake* is a story about redemption and the power of love."

"And a fallen woman. Dorinda Love," I said. That was a connection I hadn't thought much about.

"Yes. Anyway, Burdett-Coutts was very proud of her success with Urania Cottage. There was one young woman in particular she was very proud of, a young woman who dragged herself from the most base circumstances but worked to reshape her life into something worthwhile. That young woman became a sort of protégé and in time Burdett-Coutts helped her find work as a governess."

I guessed, "She gave her the book as a gift."

"Yes." Sedgwick threw me a quick glance. "Can you guess the rest of it?"

"Where did the young woman work as a governess?"

"She worked for a widowed canon by the name of Crisparkle. In time she married him. They had three children. The book went to their daughter, and then to her daughter, and then finally to my great-aunt who bequeathed it to me."

"Where did Stephanopoulos come into it? Why do you hate him so much?"

"I don't hate him, but I would never knowingly allow him to take possession of that book. Years ago when my great-aunt was financially strapped, she—very discreetly—had the book appraised. Even so, word of it got out to a handful of collectors. Stephanopoulos was one of them. My aunt had already decided not to sell when he tried to force her hand by threatening to publicly reveal what you call the provenance of the book. That provenance is not a legend as the handful of people who know about the book believe. That provenance is my family history."

"But how would he be able to do that? Reveal your family history."

"He couldn't without the actual book as proof. But the fact that he attempted to use coercion to force my aunt to sell is a matter I can't forget or forgive—as I told him at the time I inherited the book."

We reached the hotel at last, handed the keys over to the valet and started across the wet and sparkling grass.

The clock-tower face seemed to be smiling benignly. The lake appeared to be empty of swans. We were crossing the bridge when Sedgwick said suddenly, "Good God." He stopped stock-still.

"What?"

"Look." He pointed upwards.

I tipped my head back and tiny white feathers seemed to be swirling down over our heads.

"It's snowing," I said in disbelief.

He was laughing. "It is."

"It's *snowing* in L.A."

"Yes."

We were laughing as we ran the rest of the way to his hotel room. Sedgwick slammed the door shut and I went across to pull back the drapes and stare at the white flakes tumbling down, landing lightly on the patio, the wall, the flower urns.

"I don't believe it," I murmured.

"But it's there all the same. Whether you believe in it or not."

I turned to face him. He was smiling, but it was an odd sort of smile. He nodded to the table between us.

There was a flat parcel: gold and white paper, tolerantly amused angels blowing long horns and playing harps. The ribbon was red and there was a wilted sprig of mistletoe.

I sat on the sofa and picked up the package, tucking the mistletoe behind my ear. "That will come in useful later."

Sedgwick smiled, but he seemed grave—perhaps even anxious.

Gazing down at the parcel, I was inexplicably touched. "Did you really go Christmas shopping for me?"

He smiled, but his eyes were serious.

"I feel bad I didn't get you anything."

He said solemnly, "If you'll accept this, that will be my gift."

That sounded portentous. Was this a Bible perhaps? I considered it as my fingers absently stroked the ribbon. Did I have a problem with that? Truthfully, I didn't know a lot about God or Christianity. Oh, I knew intellectual things, but I was pretty sure my understanding of religion was not the same as a man like Sedgwick's. What was he offering Faith? Hope? Love?

All of them?

I nerved myself and opened the parcel. Disbelieving, I stared at the red Morocco leather and the gold embossed words.

It took me a bit to get the words out. "You're giving me *The*

Christmas Cake?"

"If you'll have it."

I stared at him. I didn't know what to say. It had to have occurred to him that if I took the book but didn't accept *him*, he was giving up his own dream. Or if I chose not to sell the book...

I said, and my voice was almost steady, "Do you know what you're doing?"

"Oh yes."

"What if I—?" I must have looked as stunned as I felt. He came and sat next to me, put his arm around me.

"There are no conditions. It's yours to do whatever you like with. I want you to have it. I wanted you to have something you didn't believe you could ever have." His smile seemed to squeeze my heart. "Two things."

I had to put my hands up to my eyes. "I can't...I don't..."

"Oh yes you can. And you do."

I opened my eyes and he was still smiling. "Merry Christmas." His mouth covered mine, sweet and hungry.

Sometime later, I turned my head on the pillow. "Have you read *The Christmas Cake*? The whole thing, I mean?"

"Of course."

"Does it have a happy ending?"

"Yes." He pulled me still closer, smiling and sleepy. "It's a Christmas story."

Author's Note

Alas, I'm sorry to say there is no Dickens story called *The Christmas Cake*. I strung bits of Victorian stories together, cadging in particular from "When the Yule-Log Burns" by Leona Dalrymple, in order to come up with the excerpts for *The Dickens With Love*. Between 1843 and 1848 Charles Dickens wrote five Christmas books. So far as we know there was no Christmas novel in 1847. We don't know why. Dickens did go on to write other Christmas stories. Though the stories and the lesser-known Christmas books were popular in their time, none have endured in the minds and hearts of readers like *A Christmas Carol*. In fact, *A Christmas Carol* is credited with influencing how we celebrate Christmas to this very day.

About the Author

A distinct voice in GLBT fiction, multi-award winning author Josh Lanyon has written numerous novels, novellas and short stories. He is the author of the critically praised Adrien English mystery series as well as the new Holmes and Moriarity series. Josh is an Eppie Award winner and a three-time Lambda Literary Award finalist. To learn more about Josh, please visit www.joshlanyon.com or join his mailing list at groups.yahoo.com/group/JoshLanyon.

Look for these titles by
Josh Lanyon

Now Available:

Crimes & Cocktails
Mexican Heat
(Writing with Laura Baumbach)

Holmes & Moriarity
Somebody Killed His Editor

The Dark Farewell
Strange Fortune

A temporary arrangement? Don't bet the ranch on it...

His Convenient Husband
© 2009 J.L. Langley

At the tender age of seven, newly orphaned Micah Jiminez lost everything—and got lucky. The Delaney family opened their hearts and their home, treated him like one of their own. One Delaney in particular, though, became more than a brother to Micah. The handsome and protective Tucker is the man to whom he wants to give his love.

But after a single passionate night together, Tucker rebuffs him and hightails it to Dallas to pursue his dreams. Leaving Micah to pick up the pieces of his broken heart—and feeling like a fool.

The impending death of the Delaney patriarch brings an unsavory relative out of the woodwork, threatening Micah's beloved adopted family. They're going to need all hands in the fight to keep The Bar D from being pulled out from under them all—including Tucker. Micah steels himself to convince the man he can't forget to come home.

To his everlasting surprise, it's Tucker who comes up with the perfect solution: a marriage of convenience—to Micah. His gut tells him Tucker's motivation involves nothing more than saving the ranch. Now he just has to convince his fragile heart.

Warning: This book contains threatening emails, imaginary sex, excessive use of antacids, non-homophobic cowboys, a bed being misused as a trampoline, male bonding during a gynecological examination of a pregnant mare, steamy manlove and a very hot-tempered Latino.

Available now in ebook from Samhain Publishing.

In this world, love can put you on the wrong end of a stake...

Blood and Roses
© *2009 Aislinn Kerry*

The last thing Arjen wants is a vampire in his bed. The rest of the world may be enamored of the creatures, but he doesn't share the obsession. When local vampire Maikel van Triet pays a visit to the brothel, Arjen tries to slip away—drawing the one thing he doesn't want: Maikel's attention. Arjen's too pragmatic to refuse a paying customer, but Maikel doesn't want his services. All he asks for is a bed, shelter, and a meal before bedtime.

Arjen's reticence and open dislike intrigue Maikel, who's delighted by the jaded young prostitute's attitude, so different from the adoration he's accustomed to. He's never been a regular patron at any brothel, but now he can't keep himself away. He still refuses Arjen's services though, instead demanding Arjen tuck him in with tales of the daytime Amsterdam he hasn't known for nearly two centuries. But when Arjen tries to seduce him into leaving, he realizes they're forging something completely unfamiliar to him: emotional bonds.

It's equally obvious to Arjen that their arrangement is becoming more than either of them expected, and the thought terrifies him. Vampires are shallow, fickle creatures, and Maikel could never truly love another—could he?

Warning: Contains blood, vampire bites, unapologetic prostitution, and lots of gay vampire lovin'.

Available now in ebook from Samhain Publishing.

GREAT
cheap
FUN

Discover eBooks!
THE FASTEST WAY TO GET THE HOTTEST NAMES

Get your favorite authors on your favorite reader, long before they're
out in print! Ebooks from Samhain go wherever you go, and work with
whatever you carry—Palm, PDF, Mobi, and more.

CPSIA information can be obtained at www.ICGtesting.com
Printed in the USA
BVOW040348280513

321778BV00001B/53/P